Lynda La Plante was born in Liverpool. She trained for the stage at RADA and worked with the National Theatre and RSC before becoming a television actress. She then turned to writing – and made her breakthrough with the phenomenally successful TV series *Widows*.

Her novels have all been international best-sellers. Her original script for the much-acclaimed *Prime Suspect* won awards from the BAFTA, British Broadcasting and the Royal Television Society as well as the 1993 Edgar Allan Poe Writer's Award.

Lynda La Plante has been made an honorary fellow of the British Film Institute and was given the BAFTA Dennis Potter Writer's Award 2000. She was awarded a CBE in the Queen's Birthday Honours list in 2008 and inaugurated into the Crime Thriller Writer's Hall of Fame in 2009.

Visit Lynda at her website: www.laplanteproductions.com

Also by Lynda La Plante

Backlash
Blood Line
Blind Fury
Silent Scream
Deadly Intent
Clean Cut
The Red Dahlia
Above Suspicion
The Legacy
The Talisman
Bella Mafia
Entwined
Cold Shoulder
Cold Blood
Cold Heart
Sleeping Cruelty
Royal Flush

The Little One: Quick Read 2012

Seekers
She's Out
The Governor
The Governor II
Trial and Retribution
Trial and Retribution II
Trial and Retribution III
Trial and Retribution IV
Trial and Retribution V

Lynda
La Plante
PRIME
SUSPECT

**SIMON &
SCHUSTER**

London · New York · Sydney · Toronto · New Delhi

A CBS COMPANY

First published in Great Britain by Pan Books, 1991
This edition first published by Simon & Schuster UK Ltd, 2012
A CBS COMPANY

This paperback edition first published, 2012

Copyright © Lynda La Plante, 1991

3 5 7 9 10 8 6 4 2

Simon & Schuster UK Ltd
1st Floor
222 Gray's Inn Road
London WC1X 8HB

Simon & Schuster Australia, Sydney
Simon & Schuster India, New Delhi

www.simonandschuster.co.uk

A CIP catalogue record for this book is available
from the British Library

Paperback ISBN 978-1-47114-230-7
Ebook ISBN 978-1-47110-023-9

This book is a work of fiction. Names, characters, places and
incidents are either a product of the author's imagination or are used
fictitiously. Any resemblance to actual people, living or dead, events
or locales, is entirely coincidental.

Typeset in Bembo by M Rules
Printed and bound by CPI Group (UK) Ltd, Croydon, CR0 4YY

For Jackie,
a guiding light

Acknowledgements

My thanks to Elaine Causon, my researcher and assistant who deserves so much credit for *Prime Suspect*. To Jenny (Mealy Mouth) Sheridan who paid for the lunch at which *Prime Suspect* was conceived. My thanks to Sally Head, Don Leaver, Ken Morgan, Roy Stonehouse, Sheelagh Killeen, and to all the cast of *Prime Suspect*, and my admiration and sincere thanks to its director, Chris Menaul.

Chapter One

Mrs Corrina Salbanna was woken from a deep sleep by the sound of the front door banging in the wind. She squinted at her bedside clock; it was almost two. Swearing in her native Spanish, she threw off the bedclothes and stuffed her plump feet into her slippers.

She shuffled up the steps into the hall and towards the still-open front door, wrapping her dressing-gown around her against the chill. The naked light bulb gave the seedy hallway a yellowish hue that did nothing to enhance the peeling wallpaper and brown, flaking paint. Pursing her lips, Mrs Salbanna slammed the door hard. There was no reason why anyone else in the house should be allowed to sleep if she couldn't.

As she turned again towards her warm bed, she noticed a light beneath Della Mornay's door on the first-floor landing. She put two and two together; it must be that little tart who had left the door open. Della owed three months' rent, and had been warned about bringing men back to her room. Now was the time to catch her red-handed. Moving as fast as she could, Mrs Salbanna returned to the basement and collected the master keys, then panted back up to the first floor.

'Della, I know you're in there, open the door!'

She waited, with her ear pressed to the door. Hearing nothing, she rattled the door-handle. 'Della?'

There was no response. Her face set, Mrs Salbanna inserted the key, unlocked the door and pushed it open.

The large room was as seedy as the rest of the run-down Victorian house, which had been divided into bedsits long before Mrs Salbanna and her husband had taken it over in the sixties, and many of the rooms still had the feel of the hippie years. Only the posters in this room had changed; Jimi Hendrix had given way to more modern rock and movie heroes. The first thing Mrs Salbanna saw was a large photograph of Madonna, lips pouting, which dominated the squalid, clothes-strewn room from above the head of the old-fashioned double bed. A red shawl had been draped over the bedside lamp; in its glow Mrs Salbanna could see that the pillows and red satin eiderdown had been dragged to the far side of the bed, revealing the stained ticking of the mattress.

There was no sign of Della. Shivering, Mrs Salbanna looked about her with distaste. She wouldn't put it past the little bitch to be hiding; she'd been devious enough about not paying her rent. She sniffed: stale body odour and cheap perfume. The smell was stronger when she peered into the mahogany wardrobe, but it contained only dresses and shoes.

The wardrobe door, off its hinges, was propped against the wall. Its full-length, fly-blown mirror was cracked and missing a corner, but reflected enough to show Mrs Salbanna a leg, protruding from beneath the bedclothes on the floor. She spun round.

'You little bitch! I knew you were in here!'

For all her weight, the landlady moved swiftly across the room and crouched down to grip Della's exposed ankle. With her other hand she threw the bedclothes aside. Her mouth opened to scream, but no sound came; she lost her balance and fell, landing on her backside. In a panic she crawled to the door, dragging herself up by the open drawer of a tallboy. Bottles and pots of make-up crashed to the floor as her scream finally surfaced. Mrs Salbanna screamed and screamed . . .

By the time Detective Chief Inspector John Shefford arrived the house in Milner Road, Gray's Inn, had been cordoned off. He was the last on the scene; two patrol cars were parked outside the house and uniformed officers were fending off the sightseers. An ambulance stood close by, its doors open, its crew sitting inside, drinking tea. The mortuary van was just drawing up and had to swerve out of the way as Shefford's car screeched to a halt just where its driver had intended to park. Shefford's door crashed open as he yanked on the handbrake. He was on the move, delving into his pocket for his ID as he stepped over the cordon. A young PC, recognizing him, ushered him up the steps to the house.

Even at two-thirty on a wintry Sunday morning, word had got round that a murder had been committed. There were lights in many windows; people in dressing-gowns huddled on their front steps. A couple of kids had appeared and were vying with each other to see how close they could get to the police cordon without breaking through it. Five Rastafarians with a ghetto-blaster were laughing together on a nearby wall, calling out remarks and jokes, as if it was a street party.

Shefford, a bear of a man at six foot two, dwarfed those around him. He had been notorious on the rugby field in the late seventies, when he played for England. With his curly hair standing on end, his crumpled shirt and tie hanging loose he didn't look or feel in a fit state to start an investigation. He had been hauled out of the celebration bash at the end of a long and tedious murder case, and he was knackered. Now he was about to lead the investigation of another murder, but this one was different.

Many of the officers in the dark, crowded hallway he had worked with before. He scanned the faces as his eyes grew accustomed to the darkness. He never forgot a face, and he greeted each man he knew by name.

At the foot of the stairs he hesitated a moment, straightening his tie. It wasn't like him to shrink from an unpleasant duty, but he had to force himself to mount each step. He was sweating. Above the confusion of voices a high-pitched wailing could be heard. It seemed to be coming from the direction of the basement.

Hearing Shefford's voice, Detective Sergeant Bill Otley stopped pacing the landing and leaned over the banister. He gestured for his guv'nor to join him in the darkness at the far end of the landing. He kept his voice low and his eye on the men coming and going from the victim's room.

'It's Della Mornay, guv. I got the tip-off from Al Franks.'

He could smell the booze on Shefford's breath. Unwrapping a peppermint, he handed it over. The boss wasn't drunk; he probably had been, but he was straightening out fast. Then Otley shook out a pair of white overalls for each of them. While they struggled to put them on, their dark recess was lit at intervals by the powerful flash of a camera from the bedsit.

As Shefford dragged on a cigarette he became aware of a familiar low, gruff voice that had been droning on all the time he had been in the house. He moved towards the door and listened.

'. . . She's lying next to the double bed, on the side nearest the window and away from the door. She's half-hidden beneath a red silk eiderdown. The window is open, a chest of drawers in front of it. We have a sheet, a blanket, a copy of the *Sunday Times* dated December 1990 . . . Looks like it's been used to wrap something in. She's lying face down, hands tied behind her back. Wearing some kind of skinny-rib top, mini-skirt, no stockings. The right shoe is on the foot, the left one lying nearby . . .'

'She been raped?' Shefford asked Otley as he fastened his overall.

'I dunno, but it's a mess in there.'

Mrs Salbanna's hysterical screaming and sobbing was getting on Shefford's nerves. He leaned over the banister and had a clear view of DC Dave Jones on the basement stairs trying to calm the landlady. An ambulance attendant tried to help move her, but she turned on him with such a torrent of mingled Spanish and English with violent gestures that he retreated, fearing for his safety.

The pathologist was ready to talk, so Shefford and Otley were given the nod to enter the room. Shefford took a last pull at his cigarette, inhaled deeply and pinched it out, putting the stub in his pocket. Then he eased past the mess of broken bottles of make-up and perfume, careful where he put his size eleven feet, to stand a little distance from the bed. All he could see of Della was her left foot.

The brightly lit room was full of white-overalled men, all going about their business quickly and quietly. Flashlights still popped, but already items were being bagged and tagged for removal. The bulky figure of Felix Norman, the pathologist, crouched over the corpse, carefully slipping plastic bags over Della's hands. He was a rotund man, oddly pear-shaped with most of his weight in his backside, topped off with a shock of thick, grey hair and an unruly grey beard. Rumour had it that his half-moon spectacles had been held together by the same piece of sticking plaster since 1983, when a corpse he was dissecting suddenly reared up and thumped him. But it was just a rumour, started by Norman himself. It was his voice Shefford had heard muttering into a tape recorder.

He looked up and gave Shefford a small wave, but continued dictating. 'Obvious head injuries ... possible penetrating wounds, through her clothes, her neck, upper shoulders ... Lot of blood-staining, blood covering the left side of her head and face. Room's damned cold, about five degrees ...' Norman broke into a coughing fit, but he didn't bother turning the tape off. He bent over the lower end of the corpse, but Shefford could not see what he was doing. Then he glanced at his watch and continued, 'Say two to three degrees when she was found, the lights and everybody tramping around must have warmed the place.' He winked at Shefford, still talking. 'Window half-open, curtains part-drawn, no source of heat ... Door to landing giving a strong draught, front door had been left open . . .' He felt the corpse's arms and legs, examined the scalp, then began checking for a weapon or anything lodged in the clothing that might fall when the body was removed, without pausing for breath. 'Complete absence of rigor, no hypostasis visible . . .' Again he bent over the body, then sat back, waving a thermometer. He squinted at it. 'Deep rectal temperature . . . Can't bloody read it for the life of me . . . Ah, time is two thirty-eight am, thirty-five point eight degrees, so assuming she started at thirty-seven that puts it back to . . .'

Shefford shifted his weight from foot to foot and swallowed hard. As Norman gently rolled the body over he could see the blood matted in the blonde hair, and he had to turn away. It wasn't the sight of the blood, he had seen enough of that in his time, but how small she seemed, small and broken.

Two white-clad men moved in to examine the carpet where the dead girl had been lying. Norman had another coughing fit and Shefford took the opportunity to ask how long she had been dead.

'Well, my old son, she would have cooled off pretty quickly in here, with that window open an' no heating on . . . Any time between midnight, maybe a little later, and . . . at a rough guess, twelve-thirty.'

'Was she raped, Felix?' Shefford asked, although he knew Norman wouldn't answer.

Norman just gave Shefford a foul look; he no longer bothered answering questions that presumed he was telepathic or had X-ray vision. He looked around the room and called to an assistant, 'Right, body-bag!'

Two men lifted the body into the black plastic bag. Shefford winced and averted his head, shocked at the disfiguration of her face. He had seen only her profile, which was hardly recognizable as human; her nose and cheek were a mass of clotted blood and the eye was completely gone.

'Not a pretty sight,' said Norman, without emotion.

Shefford nodded, but his voice was muffled as he replied, 'She was, though — pretty. Her name's Della Mornay. Booked her myself when I was on Vice.'

Norman sniffed. 'Yeah, well, let's get her out of here an' down to the mortuary. Quicker I get at her, faster you'll get results.'

Even though he had asked once, Shefford could not stop himself repeating the question, 'Was she raped?'

Norman pulled a face. 'Fuck off, I'll tell you everything you wanna know after the post-mortem.' He stared around the bedsit while the bag was closed and the body lifted onto a stretcher. 'They'll need a bloody pantechnicon to take this lot down to Forensic. You had breakfast? You'd better grab some before you schlepp over to me. Gimme a couple of hours.'

With a wave, Shefford shouldered his way to the landing. He paused and turned his back to the uniformed PC as he swiftly transferred a small object into Otley's hand. No one had seen him slip it from under the mattress. Otley quickly pocketed the little book.

It was not yet dawn, but the street was just as lively when Shefford left the house. The spectators watched avidly as the stretcher was carried to the waiting mortuary van and the police brought bag after bag of evidence from the house. Mrs Salbanna and Shefford himself had both identified the corpse.

The Scenes of Crime officers, or SOCOs, had started fingerprinting every possible surface, covering most of the room in a film of grey, shining dust. They were none too happy; many of the best spots had been carefully wiped.

After snatching a quick breakfast in the canteen and detailing Otley to make sure the Incident Room was being organized, Shefford was at the mortuary by nine o'clock. DI Frank Burkin and DC Dave Jones joined him there to discuss the day's itinerary. They sat in the ante-room of the main laboratory, all but Jones blatantly disregarding the large NO SMOKING notices.

While they waited, John Shefford used the payphone to call his home. It was his son's birthday the next day and Otley, the boy's godfather, wanted to know what to buy him. His wife, however, had more on her mind.

'Have you booked the clown for Tommy's party, John?' Sheila asked. 'I gave you the number last week, remember?'

Shefford was about to confess that he had forgotten all about it when he was saved by the bell; Felix Norman's assistant came to fetch him.

'I've got to go, love, they're ready for me. See you later!'

Gowned up, masked and wearing the regulation Wellington boots, Shefford joined Norman.

Two bare, pale feet protruded from the end of the green sheet, a label bearing Della Mornay's name and a number tied to one ankle. Norman started talking before Shefford had even reached the trolley.

'Death, old mate, was around twelve-fifteen – it's a classic, her watch got broken and stopped. The gold winder, by the way, is missing, so they'll have to comb the carpet. The watch face is intact, but the rope that was used to tie her wrists must have twisted the winding pin off the watch. Now, you asked if she was raped; could be. Recent deposits of semen in the vagina and rectum, and in the mouth, extensive bruising to the genital area. I sent the swabs over to Willy at the lab . . .' he checked his watch, 'five hours ago. Might get a blood type this afternoon. OK, the wounds . . .'

Norman threw the green sheet over the head to expose the torso, and pointed to the puncture marks. The body had been cleaned, and they showed up clearly.

'Upper right shoulder, right breast, lung punctured here, and here. Another laceration to the throat, sixth deep wound just above the navel. The wounds are neat, made with a small, rounded object, the point narrow, flat and sharp, like a sharpened screwdriver, perhaps. Not all the same depth – one three inches, one six inches, the one in the right breast is even deeper.'

Shefford examined the wounds and listened intently, nodding his head. Felix Norman was one of the best in his field, and Shefford had learned from experience to let him have his say before asking any questions.

Norman continued, 'OK, she also has a deep puncture to her left eye, probably what finished her off. A real mess, wanna see?'

'No, just carry on,' replied Shefford with distaste, running his hands through his hair.

Norman referred to his notes. 'Oh, yeah, this is interesting. Look at her hands. They seem to have been scrubbed, with a wire brush, by the look of them. But there's a nasty little nick here, and there's a smell of chlorine, some kind of household bleach. No doubt I'll find out the exact brand when I've been given the time a man of my calibre likes to have in order to do his job thoroughly! Anyway, it looks as if the scrubbing job on her hands has eliminated any possibility of blood or tissue fragments under the nails. She probably didn't put up much of a struggle, but then, her hands were tied ...'

Shefford avoided looking at the naked torso as much as possible. 'Anything else?'

Norman sniffed. 'Yeah, something strange . . .' Laying his clipboard aside, he picked up one of the corpse's arms. 'See, same on both sides? Deep welts and bruising to the upper arms. At this stage I can't say what caused it, but she might have been strung up. I'll have to do some more tests, but it looks like she was put in some kind of clamp. Interesting, huh?'

Shefford nodded. Somewhere at the back of his mind a bell rang, but he couldn't capture the memory . . . Norman covered the body again and continued, peering over his glasses, 'Right-handed killer, height difficult to estimate at this stage, especially if she was strung up, but four of the wounds entered the body on an upward slant and two are straight, so I reckon he's around five-ten. But don't quote me until I've . . .'

Shefford pulled a face. Norman, for all his bravado, went strictly by the rules and hated being pressed for results before he was one hundred per cent sure.

'Thanks mate. Get back to me as soon as you've got anything. When the report's ready, Bill can collect it personally. And, Felix – I really appreciate it!'

Norman snorted. He had worked fast, but then he and John Shefford were old friends. He watched as Shefford removed his surgical mask and began to untie his gown.

'You got anything, John?'

Shefford shook his head. 'Looks like one of her Johns was into bondage and things got out of hand. See you . . .'

At the station, Della Mornay's effects were being sorted and examined. Her handbag had been found, but it contained no keys. They were able to dismiss robbery as a motive as her purse, containing fifteen pounds, was in the bag and a jewel box on her dressing-table, containing a few silver chains and a gold bangle or two, was undisturbed.

In King's Cross, Della Mornay's territory, fifteen of Shefford's men were interviewing every known prostitute and call girl. They were getting little assistance, but the feedback was that Della had not been seen for weeks. There was a suggestion that she might have gone to Leeds to visit a friend dying of Aids, but no name was mentioned.

The painstaking task of checking every forensic sample, the tapes of fibres, the fingerprints, was barely begun, and had brought no results so far. The entire area was combed for a murder weapon without success. In that neighbourhood no one ever volunteered information, especially to the police.

Shefford and Otley met up again at Milner Road and spent an hour or so interviewing and looking over the bedsit again, but they discovered nothing new. Mrs Salbanna, recovered from her shock, was already asking when she could let the room.

Shefford was hungry and very tired. He had a few pints and a pork pie in the local, then kipped down in his office while Otley went home to his flat to fetch his guv'nor a clean shirt. Shefford often stayed over at his place and left a few items of clothing there for emergencies.

Although he could have done with putting his head down for a few hours himself, Otley sprayed the shirt with starch and ironed it, paying special attention to the collar. Pleased with his handiwork, he slipped it onto a hanger and sat down for a cup of tea. He had a system for avoiding washing up; he simply used the same cup, plate and cutlery all the time. He ate all his main meals in the station canteen, and had even given up his morning corn-flakes because they were a bugger to get off the bowl if you left them overnight.

The silver-framed photographs of his wife, his beloved Ellen, needed a good polish, but he'd have to leave them until his next weekend off. They were the only personal items in the flat that he bothered with. Ellen had been the love of his life, his only love, since he was a teenager. Her death seven years ago, from cancer of the stomach, had left him bereft, and he mourned her now as deeply as the moment she had died. He had watched helplessly as she disintegrated before his eyes. She had become so weak, so skeletal, that he had prayed, anguished and alone, for her to die.

It had been obvious to everyone at work that Skipper Bill Otley had personal problems, but he confided in no one. His solitary drinking and his angry bitterness had caused many arguments, and his boys, as he called them, had at last left him to himself. In the end, John Shefford had taken him aside and demanded to know what was going on, earning his abusive response, 'Mind yer own fuckin' business, my personal life's me own affair.'

Shefford had snapped back angrily that when it affected his work it became the boss's business, and Otley would be out on his ear if he didn't come clean about what was tormenting him. He pushed Otley to the point where he finally cracked.

Once he understood, Shefford had been like a rock. He was at the hospital, waiting outside the ward, when Ellen died. He had organized the funeral, done everything he possibly could to help. He was always there, always available, like the sweet, beloved friend Otley had buried. When Shefford's son was born he asked Otley to be godfather; the bereaved man became part of the family, his presence demanded for lunch on Sundays, for outings and parties. He and Ellen had longed for children, in vain; now his off-duty time was filled with little Tom's laughter and nonsense. So Otley wouldn't just iron his guv'nor's shirt; he would wash it, and his socks for good measure.

John Shefford meant more to him than he could ever put into words; he loved the man, admired him, and backed him to the hilt, convinced that he would make Commander one of these days. No one would be more proud of him then than Bill Otley.

With the clean shirt over his arm, Otley whistled on his way back to the station.

At eleven, Detective Chief Inspector Jane Tennison parked her Ford Fiesta and entered Southampton Row police station. It was a crisp, frosty day, and she was wrapped up well against the cold.

She was officially off-duty, but had come in to prepare some final papers for a session in court the next day.

None of the blood samples taken from the bedsitter had yielded a clue to the identity of Della Mornay's killer. Hers was a very common group and the only one found at the scene. But the DNA tests on the semen taken from her body was a different matter.

The new computerized DNA system was still at the experimental stage, but already the results of thousands of tests taken in the past two years had been entered on it. As a matter of routine, Willy Chang's forensic team ran the result from Della Mornay against the existing records and were astonished to find a match; a visual check on the negatives, using a light-box, confirmed it. The man Della

Mornay had had sex with shortly before her murder had been convicted of attempted rape and aggravated robbery in 1988.

Willy Chang was jubilant; here was the lever they needed to press the government into releasing funds for a national DNA profiling system. He picked up the phone.

The message caught Shefford on Lambeth Bridge, on his way home for lunch and only a stone's throw from the Home Office labs. He hung up the handset, turned the car around immediately and punched Otley's arm.

'You're not gonna believe this, we got a friggin' suspect! He's got a rare blood group and it's on the ruddy computer!'

For the past three months DCI Tennison had been working on a tedious fraud case involving a tobacconist who was being sued for non-payment of VAT. The man's ferret of an accountant had more tricks up his sleeve than a conjuror, and a long series of medical certificates exempting him from court appearances. But tomorrow, at last, Judge George Philpott would complete his summing-up. Known as the legal equivalent of Cary Grant for his good looks and slow delivery, Philpott had already taken two days; Tennison hoped he would finish quickly for once so she would have time to check her desk before the end of the day.

Not that there would be anything of interest; in all her time on the special Area Major Incident Team, known as AMIT, there had been little but desk work. She had often wondered why she had bothered switching from the Flying Squad, where at least she had been busy. The setup of five DCIs and their teams had appealed to her, and she had believed she would be able to use her skills to the full.

Sitting at her desk, Tennison heard a screech of brakes from the car park. She glanced out of the window in time to see Shefford racing into the building.

'What's DCI Shefford doing in today, Maureen?' she asked her assistant, WPC Havers. 'He's supposed to be on leave.'

'I think he's heading the investigation.'

'What investigation?'

'Prostitute found dead in her room in Milner Road.'

'They got a suspect?' Tennison snapped.

'Not yet, but they're getting all the Vice files on the victim's pals.'

Tennison bristled. 'How did Shefford get it? I was here until after ten last night!'

Maureen shrugged. 'I dunno, guv, I think it was a middle-of-the-night job. Probably hauled him out of the afters session in the pub.'

'But he's only just finished with that shooting in Kilburn – and there were the Iranian diplomats before that.'

Tennison clenched her fists and stormed out. Maureen winced at the banging of the door.

DCI Tennison paced up and down the corridor, trying to talk herself down. Eighteen months she'd been waiting for a decent case, dealing with more paperwork than in her entire time at the rape centre in Reading, and now the boss had gone out of his way to give DCI Shefford the case that should have been hers. She'd known when she applied for the transfer that she would be in for a tough time; had she stayed where she was she'd have been promoted to a desk job by now.

But five years with the Flying Squad had toughened her up. She went back to her room and put a call through to the Chief's office, determined to have it out with him, but he was in a meeting. She tried to work on her statements for the court hearing but her frustration wouldn't let her concentrate.

At midday Tennison was again disturbed by the racing of engines from the car park. Shefford was off again, and in a hell of a hurry. She gave up trying to work and packed her things; it was nearly lunch-time anyway.

Tennison missed the 'heat' as Shefford gathered his team together, his booming voice hurling insults as he fired orders at them. He was moving fast on the unbelievable stroke of luck that had given him his suspect on a plate.

George Arthur Marlow had been sentenced to three years for attempted rape and assault, but had served only eighteen months. He had still been protesting his innocence when he was led away from the dock.

The case had been a long-drawn-out affair as Marlow insisted he was innocent. At first he had denied even knowing the victim, referred to only as 'Miss X', but when faced with the evidence he told the police that he and 'Miss X' had been drinking together in a wine bar. He stated that she had blatantly encouraged his advances, but when it came to the crunch she refused him.

Marlow's blood tests at the time had shown him to have an exceptionally rare blood group; he belonged to a small percentage of AB secreters, of whom there is only one in 2,500 head of population. He had been one of the first to be entered on the new computer, and when a lab assistant ran his details through the system she hit the jackpot.

The warrant was ready. Shefford, high on adrenalin, called his men together. Already he had dribbled coffee down his clean shirt, and he followed it now with cigarette ash. Otley brushed him down as he bellowed, 'DCI Donald Paxman holds the record in the Met, lads, for bringing in a suspect and charging him within twenty-four hours. Gimme me raincoat . . . Fags, who's got me fags?'

He shrugged into his coat with the effortless ability of the permanently crumpled man, lighting a cigarette at the same time and switching it from hand to hand as his big fists thrust down the sleeves. 'We smash that record, lads, and it's drinks all round, so let's go! Go, go!'

Jane Tennison let herself into her small service flat which she had shared for the last three months with her boyfriend, Peter Rawlins. Six feet tall, broad-chested, his sandy hair invariably flecked with paint, he was the first man she had lived with on a permanent basis.

Peter came out of the kitchen when he heard her key in the door and beamed at her. 'OK, we've got Chicken Kiev with brown rice, how does that suit?'

'Suits me fine!'

She dumped her briefcase on the hall table and he gave her a hug, then held her at arm's length and looked into her face. 'Bad day?'

She nodded and walked into the bedroom, tossing her coat on the bed. He lolled in the doorway. 'Want to talk about it?'

'When I've had a shower.'

They had spent a lot of time talking since they had met; Peter had been in the throes of divorce and Jane had provided a sympathetic ear. Marianne had left him for another man; it had hit him hard because it was not just any other man, but Peter's best friend and partner in his building firm, And she had taken with her the little son he adored, Joey.

Jane and Peter's relationship had begun casually enough; they had been teamed together in the squash club tournament and had since met on several occasions for the odd drink or cup of coffee after a game. Eventually he had asked her to see a film with him, and on that first real date she had listened to the details of his divorce. It was only after several films that he had even made an attempt to kiss her.

Jane had helped Peter to move into a temporary flat while his house was sold, and gradually their relationship had become closer. When he started looking for a permanent place to live she suggested he move in with her for a while. It wasn't very romantic, but as the weeks passed she found herself growing more and more fond of him. He was easy-going, caring and thoughtful. When he told her he loved her and suggested they look for a bigger place together, she agreed. It was a pleasant surprise to her how much she wanted to be with him.

When she had showered, Jane sat at the table in her dressing-gown and Peter presented his Chicken Kiev with a flourish. She was so grateful and happy that she had someone to share her life with that she forgot her problems for a moment.

As he opened a bottle of wine she cocked her head to one side and smiled. 'You know, I'm getting so used to you, I don't know what I'd do if you weren't around. I guess what I'm trying to say in my roundabout way is—'

'Cheers!' he said, lifting his glass.

'Yeah, to you, to me, to us . . .'

Marlow seemed dazed by the arrival of the police. He stood in the narrow hallway of his flat, holding a cup of coffee, apparently unable to comprehend what they wanted.

'George Arthur Marlow, I am arresting you on suspicion of murder . . .' Otley had to repeat the caution, then remove the cup from Marlow's hand himself to put the handcuffs on him.

Moyra Henson, Marlow's girlfriend, appeared from the kitchen, followed by the smell of roasting lamb.

'What the hell's going on here? Oi, where are you taking him? He hasn't had his dinner . . .'

Ignoring her, they led Marlow out to the car as quickly as possible. In his bewilderment, he almost cracked his head on the roof of the patrol car as he was helped inside.

The uniformed officers went in to search the flat, while a WPC took Moyra into the kitchen and told her that Marlow had been arrested on suspicion of the murder of a prostitute. Moyra's eyes widened and she shook her head, disbelieving.

'There's been a terrible mistake, you can't do this to him, it's a mistake . . .' She broke away from the WPC and ran to the front door. She shrieked like a banshee when she realized the police were taking out clear plastic bags of clothing at a rate of knots. Marlow's shoes, jackets, shirts, all listed and tagged, were shown to Moyra while she protested shrilly. But she didn't attempt to stop the officers, and they remained for hours, searching and removing items. When they had finished, Moyra was taken to the police station for questioning.

She was no longer irate, but coldly angry. She hated the pigs, hated them. They had already put George inside for a crime she knew he hadn't committed, and now she was sure they were about to frame him for murder. All the whodunnits she watched on video and the moral stand-points of *Dallas* and *EastEnders* had taught her her rights, and not to trust the bastards.

Jane lay curled in Peter's arms, telling him about Shefford and his attitude to her; not quite openly antagonistic but near enough. It was pretty much the same with all the men, but Shefford was so macho that he took pleasure in sending her up, albeit behind her back.

It was still a new thing for her to have someone to listen to her problems. She had been in such a foul mood when she had arrived home, making love to him had taken all the tension away. It was good to have Peter, to feel loved and wanted. She told him how the Chief had given her the usual speech about waiting, but she had to make a decision soon. The longer she waited and accepted the cases no one else wanted, the more she knew she would be put upon. If Kernan didn't give her a break she would quit. The men gave her no respect ...

Peter laughed. 'They don't know you, do they?'

She grinned. 'No, I suppose they don't. I'll get a break one day, and by Christ they'll know what's hit them then.'

He bit her ear. 'Get them to play a game of squash with you, they'll soon take notice of that determined little face. First time I played against you I thought: Holy shit, this one's a maniac.'

She laughed her wonderful, deep, throaty laugh. When they made love it no longer mattered that her bosses had overlooked her; only Peter was important. She had said it to him that afternoon, and told him she loved him.

He cuddled her close. 'I'm glad we've got each other, because things are not going too well for me. We may have to stave off looking for a bigger place, the company's in bad shape and I'm having to spend capital until I get back on my feet.'

She murmured that it didn't matter, the place was big enough. She asked him then how it had felt, knowing his wife was having an affair with his best friend, a subject she had always steered clear of.

He sighed, stared up at the ceiling. 'Like my balls had been cut off. I couldn't believe it at first, it must have been going on for years behind my back. Then I felt like a bloody fool, you know, that I hadn't clocked it faster. He was always round the house, but we were partners and I just accepted that he was there to see me. And he was screwing my wife in my own bed!' He punched his palm, hard; it made a satisfying smack. He sighed again. 'I wanted to beat him up, have it out that way, but there was no point. I just walked away from it all. She's got half the money from the house and I bought him out of the company, that's one of the reasons why cash is so tight at the moment. I should have just told him to fuck off, but I'm not like that and there's Joey to consider. I reckoned that if I got nasty about the divorce she'd try to stop me seeing Joey. I love that kid, couldn't bear not to see him.'

Jane stroked his cheek gently. 'Any time you want him to stay he's welcome, you know that, don't you?'

He hugged her. 'Yeah, I do, and I appreciate it. You're the best thing that's happened to me in years. I know things'll work out for you, just be patient.'

She smiled, without mentioning that it was exactly what her Chief's attitude had been. But she had no intention of being patient. Peter didn't really understand how important her work was to her, but he was to find out sooner than either of them anticipated.

George Marlow was quiet and co-operative. His fingerprints were taken and he was led to the cells. He stammered a little when he asked to phone his lawyer, seeming shaken, and gave the number. Although on the point of tears, he went out of his way to be helpful, but he still kept asking why he had been arrested.

Shefford had been on the go all day. Now he was preparing himself to question Marlow. His face was flushed and he was chain-smoking, cracking jokes; it was obvious that the adrenalin was still flowing.

The men on the team were clapping him on the back, calling him a lucky bastard, what a break! Several were laying bets on the outcome.

DI Burkin suddenly rememberd something. 'Hey, it's his kid's birthday tomorrow! While we've all got our hands in our pockets, we gonna chip in an' buy him something? You know Otley, he's so tight-fisted the kid won't even get an ice-cream cornet from him. What d'you say, fifty pence each?' In great humour, they all coughed up.

Before he went down to the interview room, Shefford called his home to tell Sheila, his wife, that he would be late and she shouldn't wait up. He was too keyed up to pay much attention to what she was saying.

'You didn't answer me this morning, John. Have you booked the clown for Tom's party?'

'Yeah, yeah, I'll get it sorted . . .' He handed the phone to Bill Otley and whispered, 'Talk to the missus, mate, you're his bloody godfather, after all. I haven't got time . . .'

He lit another cigarette and turned to the files as Otley took the phone and promised faithfully that he would dress up as a clown himself if they couldn't get Biffo for the birthday party.

The lads had been wrong about their skipper; Otley had spent more time and money in Hamley's toy shop that weekend than they could credit. The train sets had cost an arm and a leg, but he was prepared to dip into his savings. He and Ellen had spent hours planning what they would spend it on when he retired; now his godson would be the one to benefit. It was making the decision that took the time, as well as wandering around enjoying himself in the store.

Otley replaced the receiver and turned to Shefford. 'OK, guv? Need anything else? Marlow's brief's on his way, be about an hour. Arnold Upcher, represented him on his last caper. Tough bastard, but he's fair. Doesn't scream a lot like some of the buggers.'

Shefford winked. 'I want a crack at 'im before Upcher gets here. Nice one for us, eh? What a stroke of fuckin' luck! See if we can't sew up Paxman's record. Get a bottle of fizz over to the Forensic lot, tell 'em I love 'em, and tell Willy to stand by for all the gear from Marlow's place. And, yeah, I'm ready, let's go for the bastard.'

George Marlow was sitting in the cell with his hands in his lap, head bowed. He was wearing a blue striped shirt with the white collar open at the neck; his tie had been taken away from him. His grey flannels were neatly pressed and his jacket hung over the back of his chair. With his Mediterranean looks it was obvious that he would have to shave twice a day, but as yet his chin was clean. He raised his head when a uniformed officer opened the door and asked him politely to accompany him to the interview room.

DCI Shefford had given instructions that Upcher was to be stalled if he arrived early. He wanted a chance to question Marlow without his lawyer present. He drew himself up to his full height, threw his massive shoulders back and strode down the corridor to Room 4C. He noticed the way Marlow actually jumped with shock when he kicked the door open.

With a gesture to Marlow to remain seated, he swung a hard wooden chair around with one hand, placing it exactly opposite the suspect, and sat down.

'George? I am Detective Chief Inspector John Shefford. This is Detective Sergeant Bill Otley, and that's DC Jones over by the door. Before we get involved with your lawyer – I mean, we might not even need him – I just want to ask you a few questions, OK?'

He drew the ashtray towards him, scraping it along the formica of the table until it squealed, then lit a cigarette. 'You smoke, George?'

'No, sir.'

'Good ... Right then, George, can you tell us where you were on the night of the thirteenth of January? Take your time.'

Marlow kept his head down. 'January the thirteenth? Saturday? Well, that's easy. I was at home with my wife. We don't usually go out, we get a video and a take-away ... Yeah, I was with my wife.'

'Your wife? You mean Moyra Henson, the girl you're living with? She said she's not your wife, she's your girl-friend. Which is it, George? Come on, son, don't mess us about.'

'Well, she's my common-law wife, we're not actually married.'

Shefford's tongue felt and tasted like an old carpet. He searched his pockets and found a wrinkled piece of Wrigley's chewing gum at the bottom. It must have been there for some time as it had lost its outer wrapper, and the silver paper was covered with fluff and ash from using the pocket as an ashtray. He picked the foil off, examined the grey gum, then popped it in his mouth and chewed furiously. Marlow watched his every move, as if trans-fixed.

Shefford folded the wrapper into a narrow strip, ran his fingernail down it, then tossed it aside and lit a cigarette. 'What were you doing, say around ten o'clock?' he asked casually.

'I'd be at home ... Oh, hang on, earlier ... I know what I did earlier.'

Shefford inhaled the last of his cigarette and let the smoke drift from his nostrils. 'Well, want to tell me?'

With a rueful smile, Marlow shrugged his shoulders slightly. 'I picked up a girl. She was on the game.'

'You knew the girl, did you?'

Marlow shook his head and glanced at Otley, who was sitting a few feet away taking notes. 'I'd never met her before, but I saw her outside the tube station, Ladbroke Grove. She was, you know, bending down, peering into cars as they went past ... Ladbroke Grove tube station. I pulled up and asked her how much.'

'But you didn't know her?'

'No, I'd never met her before. I asked her first how much, and she said it depends. You know they like to hustle as much as they can out of you ...'

'Oh, yeah? But you been done before, George. You don't like hassles. Della Mornay pisses you off, right? Right?'

Marlow frowned, then looked at Shefford. 'Della Mornay ...?'

Otley checked his watch and wondered how it was all going down in the interview room. It was past seven and Shefford had been at it since four-thirty, now with Arnold Upcher sitting in on the session. Otley strolled down to the basement corridor and peered through the glass panel; he could just see Marlow, sitting with his head in his hands.

'Has he confessed yet? Only it's drinking time!'

The PC on guard raised his eyebrows. 'Been a lot of shouting goin' on in there, and at the last count Shefford had consumed five beakers of coffee.'

'Ah, well, he would – this is pub hours, son!'

Otley turned away and went to the pub to join the others from Shefford's team. He ordered a round and sat down with his pint, telling them there was no news as yet.

'But he had his head in his hands, looked like the guv'nor's cracked him. Gonna break that bloody record . . .'

They set about betting, on how long it would take Shefford to get a confession from Marlow and whether or not he would break Paxman's record. They might not have been so confident if they had been privy to the statement that was being taken from Marlow right then.

Chapter Two

Shefford was using the regulation tape recorder. Marlow craned his head forward and directed his speech at the built-in microphone.

'I dropped her off at the tube station, and paid her.'

'OK, so then what did you do?'

'I went to Kilburn to get a video, and I was home by . . . about ten-thirty.'

Marlow rubbed his chin. He needed a shave now, the stubble made him look darker, swarthier.

'Like I said, Inspector, I remember, when I looked back, she was peering into another car, a red . . . maybe a Scirocco, I dunno, but she was looking for the next customer. I just got the video and went home, got there at ten-thirtyish. I can't remember the exact time, you'll have to ask Moyra, she'll remember.'

'And you maintain that you did not know this girl

you picked up? You had never met her or seen her before?'

'No, sir. Like I said, she just came over to my car.'

Shefford opened a file and held out a photograph of Della Mornay, taken from Vice records. 'Is this the girl you picked up?'

Marlow leaned forward, without actually touching the photo, then sat back in his chair. 'I'd never met her before, I didn't know her.'

He looked to his brief, then back to Shefford. 'I picked her up at about seven-thirty. It was dark, I don't remember her all that well . . .'

'You had sex with her, George! You tellin' me you didn't see her face? Come on, George . . .'

Marlow shifted his weight in his chair. 'It was in the back of the car!'

'Let's go again, George, an' I want all the details.'

Peter was stuffing his work clothes into the overflowing laundry basket when Jane woke up. He rammed the lid on the basket. 'We need a washing machine, you know.'

She yawned. 'Yeah, but the kitchen's too small. Besides, the launderette does it for me, they'll even do the ironing if you want, but it's fifty pence per article. I'll get Mrs Fry to take a load down in the morning.' She yawned again. 'What's the time?'

'It's nearly six. I've got some bad news.' He sat down

beside her. 'Well, not bad news for me, but for you, maybe! It must be telepathy . . . You know, after you said Joey could stay, Marianne called. She's bringing him over to stay the night. I didn't even have to ask, she suggested it.'

'That's OK! What time's he coming?'

Peter shrugged. 'Oh, about seven-thirty. Look, you don't have to do anything.'

Jane freaked. 'Is she bringing him? I mean, will she come in?'

He shrugged again. 'Look, I can take him for a hamburger, he'll be no problem.'

'Bollocks! Go down to the corner Indian, they're still open, and get some fish fingers. Kids like fish fingers, and baked beans, and Mars Bars . . . No, tell you what, Smarties. I'll make up the spare bed while you're gone.'

'It's already done, and I've put that Anglepoise lamp by the bed, he sleeps with a light on.'

'OK, I'll wash my hair and get dolled up.'

'You don't have to, he's only six, for Chrissake! He won't care what you look like.'

'Ah, but Marianne will be looking me over, and I want to make an impression. After all, I'm the Other Woman!'

'Not quite!'

'Oh, go on, get going . . .'

Jane rolled up the newspaper he had left on the bed and whacked him on the head with it, then dashed to the bathroom. Joey would be arriving soon, and she wanted to be ready.

At Southampton Row, Moyra Henson had been interviewed over and over again. She gave Marlow a perfect alibi and wouldn't be budged; he was at home, she insisted, as he had said in his own statement. He had been at home watching television with her. Marlow had not left the flat all evening, and they had gone to bed together.

When she was finally let go, DI Burkin was ordered back to her flat to impound Marlow's car, a brown, automatic three-litre Mark III Rover. He took two officers with him and gave Moyra a lift home.

She kept up a constant stream of abuse all the way back in the patrol car, sitting between the two officers. They didn't say a word. Burkin, uncomfortable in the front seat with his long legs cramped against the glove compartment, was also silent, though Moyra's voice was beginning to grate on his nerves and he would be glad when they got shot of her.

There was no sign of the Rover; it was not in the parking bay or anywhere in the vicinity of the flats. Sullen and uncooperative, Moyra accused the police of stealing it themselves.

As she shampooed her hair under the hot water, all Jane could think of was how John Shefford had done her out of a murder case. She had to make an effort to shake herself out of it, she was becoming obsessed. Before she knew it, Peter was back from the shop.

He yelled that he'd got a few extras. He opened the bathroom door.

'I got a chocolate cake, that one you like. It needs defrosting so I've left it on the draining-board, OK?'

'Yep, just give me a few minutes to get my glad-rags on and I'll set the table.'

But by the time she had dressed and dried her hair, Peter had done it all. Jane shrieked that she had wanted the best china, and started collecting the plates. Peter caught hold of her.

'Hey, this is just fine! Don't put out the best stuff, he's liable to smash something.'

'Do I look OK?'

He held her at arm's length. 'Yeah, nice blouse, looks Victorian.'

'Well, it's not, it's cheap Laura Ashley, so I bought two, but they're my best!'

She was wearing a full skirt from Next and a pair of red suede shoes she had never worn before; every time she had put them on she had felt they were a bit too flash, so they were pristine, not a scuff in sight. It tickled Peter that she was making such an effort, even down to perfume.

When the doorbell rang Jane flushed, and he grinned. 'Just relax, she'll only stay a minute.'

Jane hovered near the kitchen while Peter opened the door. Joey flew into his arms, yelling, 'Dad! Dad!' Peter swung him up and kissed him, then put him down, but Joey hugged his dad's legs.

Jane peered at the door, expecting the ex-wife. First came a huge bag, large enough for Joey to stay two months, then a box of toys. Finally Marianne's back was visible.

She spoke to someone who was invisible to Jane. 'I won't be a sec, darling!'

Peter's face was like stone. He had not even acknowledged Marianne's new husband, his old friend.

Marianne was wearing a short, frilly evening dress. Her blonde, shoulder-length hair was the type that novelists describe as silky, a real shampoo advert. To Jane's surprise she seemed much younger than her thirty-eight years.

'Hi, Pete, I've brought everything he could possibly need, and a lot he might not . . .'

Peter turned to introduce Jane. 'Jane, this is Marianne.'

'Hi, nice to meet you, it's good of you to have Joey.'

'Oh, that's OK, nice to meet you.' She bent down to the little boy, who still clung to his father's legs. 'And you must be Joey? You know what we've got? Fish fingers, do you like fish fingers?'

'What else have you got?'

'Chocolate cake, you want some? Yes? Come on, then, let me show you the kitchen.'

She held out a hand to Joey, who shied away at first, but then he edged forward and gripped her hand tightly. 'I got a new Revenge of the Joker mask!' he confided.

'Have you? Is that from Batman, then?'

Joey nodded. Anxious to get away from Marianne's critical gaze, Jane smiled and said, 'Would you like a drink, Marianne?'

'No, Steve is waiting . . .'

Duty done, Jane and Joey scuttled into the kitchen, but Jane could hear every word through the thin door. She showed Joey the cake box, opened it and reached into the top cupboard for a plate.

Marianne smiled and tossed her streaked, blonde hair back. She leaned confidentially towards Pete.

'Pete, I'm pregnant.' She gave him a long, direct look.

Peter swallowed. 'It's not . . .' He glanced nervously towards the kitchen.

'Who knows? Anyway, I really appreciate this. You know what I was like in the early stages with Joey, I'm so sick every morning, awful.'

He pulled himself together. 'You look OK!'

'Well, it's all show. Underneath this I'm white as a sheet and getting hideously fat.' She wasn't; as far as Peter could recall she hadn't even put on much weight with Joey.

Marianne went on, 'She's not at all what I expected! Is it working out?'

He nodded, and glanced again towards the kitchen door. 'You'd better go, I don't want him getting upset.'

'Oh, he's fine, and I should say goodbye to . . . what's her name?'

'Jane.' Again Peter looked towards the kitchen door. 'Jane! Marianne's leaving!'

The partly defrosted cake was half-way to the plate when it slipped off the bread knife and back into the box, showering Jane in the process. Peter opened the door to see her covered in chocolate and cream, trying in vain to wipe it off with a tea towel.

'Bit of an accident! Good to meet you, Marianne, hope you have a nice dance.'

'Oh, it's not a dance, just a small dinner party.'

Jane covered her astonishment with a smile. If she had got herself done up in a dress as glitzy as that, it would have been for a ball at the very least.

Joey kissed his mother, apparently unperturbed at her leaving, then ran back to the kitchen to stick his fingers in the blobs of chocolate and lick them.

As the door closed behind Marianne, Jane cocked her head to one side. 'So I wasn't what she expected, huh? Next time I'll borrow a WPC's hat!'

There was a crash from the kitchen as the entire

chocolate cake, box and all, fell to the floor. Joey looked crestfallen, expecting to be punished, but Jane just looked at the mess on the floor and handed Joey a spoon.

'OK, let's have tea!'

It was eleven-thirty when Shefford completed his inter-rogation of George Marlow. He discussed the results briefly with Arnold Upcher; he was sure he had enough evidence to charge Marlow. Upcher, tired himself, pursed his lips and gave a small shrug.

'Then if you feel you have the evidence, Inspector, there is little I can do. But he's been here since early after-noon, that means you've got twenty-four hours. You will, of course, inform me if you go for extra time?'

Shefford was confident that he could charge Marlow without having to present all his evidence to a magistrate and beg for the statutory three days' delay to consolidate his case, or 'three-day lay-down', as it was known. Exhausted though he was, and a little punchy, he was still going strong. His main concern was to get the statements transcribed from the tapes.

Upcher, needing time to review Marlow's situation, had said little as he took his leave of Shefford. He knew intu-itively that something was wrong, but until he had time to digest the case he wouldn't even contemplate discussing it.

None of it made sense; Marlow was a handsome,

attractive male, a man with a good, steady relationship at home. He was popular, he had a job that he thoroughly enjoyed and which brought him good money and his employers had even held it open for him when he was convicted of attempted rape. Upcher had succeeded in getting the burglary charge dropped, and in Marlow's defence at the trial he had played heavily upon the confusion about which party had made the initial approach, whether both of them had been drunk – they had been seen in the same bar, and Marlow's claim that she had led him on and subsequently refused him had rung true. In Upcher's opinion the victim was a very disturbed woman whose evidence was unreliable, and he had been shattered by the verdict. Not just from a professional point of view; his relationship with Marlow was good, he actually liked the man and believed him to be innocent.

Marlow had taken it well, although Upcher was surprised that he had requested his representation for this, a much more serious charge. He had borne Upcher no grudge about losing the case, and had even admitted that, drunk or sober, he should not have forced himself on the woman, even though he had truly believed it was what she wanted. He had said, with a rueful smile, 'I'll never drink more than my limit again, so I suppose some good'll come out of it. I didn't hurt her though, Arnold, she made that up, the cops got it wrong.'

Was Marlow a rapist and a murderer? Upcher thought

not, and could not believe he had misjudged the man to such an extent. The question occupied his thoughts all the way back to his Queen's Gate flat.

The Arnold Upchers of this world are expensive, and anyone seeing the tall, angular man in the hand-tailored suit parking his dark green Jaguar in the residents' bay could have been forgiven for mistaking him for the famous conductor who had once lived in the elegant service block a stone's throw from Hyde Park. With the remote control he locked his car and set the alarm, allowing the chill night air to clear his head. By the time he reached his door, Upcher was convinced that the police had got it wrong again. Marlow was innocent, and he would prove it.

Jane crawled to bed at midnight. She had exhausted her stock of stories before Joey finally fell asleep, from the three little pigs to a strange mixture of Batman confronting the Ninja Turtles.

Peter was sitting up waiting for her. He flipped the bedclothes back and patted the mattress. 'Come in, my beauty! And tell me a story . . .'

She snuggled into bed and gave him a blow-by-blow description of the goings-on at the police station.

'They were like kids playing at cops and robbers! I don't know what they were up to, but they stopped me working. They've got a nice juicy murder that should have been my case, and you know what I've got instead?

A dyspeptic accountant who's had his bloody case adjourned four times in a row! Last time I had to wait at court all morning like a prat until he sent in some fictitious doctor's note, and then I was told to go away. Next thing, the little sod'll up and leave the country – I would, in his position. He owes ten years' income tax and VAT. I've got to know the little pest so well over the past three months that I can tell you what he'll be eating for breakfast, and even when I suggested that another adjournment would be ... Am I boring you?'

Peter smiled. He had only been half-listening.

She closed her eyes. 'I don't think I could manage another sentence, I'm so tired ... Oh, God, am I tired!'

Peter switched the bedside light off and reached for her, wanting to draw her close, but she muttered, 'I'm afraid I'm too knackered ... anyway, haven't you had enough for one day? Book me in for tomorrow night, OK?' She was fast asleep as she finished speaking.

Peter lay awake for about ten minutes, then put the light back on to read his book. Jane started to snore and he gently eased her onto her side. She gave a little grunt and then a pathetic, 'Sorry ... I'm sorry ...'

John Shefford was dog-tired by the time he arrived home, but his brain was ticking like a bomb. The events of the day kept repeating themselves like a news reel in his head and he had to drink half a bottle of Scotch before he felt the dark clouds gathering to cushion him to sleep.

It seemed only a moment before the alarm woke him. His head throbbed and he took four aspirin before he could get out of bed, crunching them between his teeth and hoping that they'd reach the parts that screamed for numbness.

Sheila had his breakfast ready. As she dished it up she reminded him of his promise about the clown for Tom's party. She had wrapped the presents and heaped them on the breakfast table, where Tom had found them at the crack of dawn, and he was beside himself, in a fever of excitement. They had both been touched by the lads' whip-round for Tom, which they had presented in cash in a large Metropolitan Police envelope to be put into his Post Office savings account.

By seven, Shefford was none too happy. He tried to show enthusiasm, but he was getting ratty trying to eat his breakfast with one hand and fend off his son's new boxing gloves with the other. His nagging headache wouldn't shift, and he had another three aspirin with his coffee. Sheila was still going on about the clown, and he gave his solemn oath that not only would there be a clown, but that he would perform magic acts that would silence even Tom.

The little lad had started boxing his sister, and her screams cut through Shefford's head like a knife. Sheila removed his half-eaten scrambled eggs.

'I'm not expecting you to be here, that's why the clown's important. God forbid I should ask you to do anything so normal as to be home at half-past five with Tom's godfather for his party, it'd be an act of madness on my part . . .'

'Look, sweetheart, maybe I will make it, if things go well. We had a hell of a breakthrough yesterday; we've got a suspect and I think we can charge him. If we can do it this afternoon I can get home, and Bill's promised to dress up, how's that?'

Sheila screwed up her face and snorted. 'Haw, haw, promises, promises! And would you take those gloves off him, and tell him they can only be worn under supervision. I never wanted him to have them in the first place . . .'

Shefford crooked his finger at Tom, who shadowboxed up to him, ducking and diving as his father had taught him.

'OK, Tom, off with the gloves. The rule's been laid down by the boss, you only use them when I'm around, OK? So give me a quick jab-jab, and a left hook before I go.'

Tom was fast and managed to clip his father on the nose. Sheila laughed, but Shefford's eyes watered and he grabbed the gloves, pulling them off as the telephone began to ring.

'Daddy, it's for you!'

Shefford listened to Felix Norman with difficulty while his daughter wound the phone cord around her neck and Tom raced up and down the hall with his rugger ball, weaving around the defence – his father – and scoring a try in the kitchen doorway.

It was Norman's habit to get to the lab at seven each morning to escape the rush hour, though rumour had it that he was more concerned about avoiding his wife, as he was invariably found there late each night.

'What in God's name's going on there?' he yelled.

Shefford glared at his son and pointed in the direction of the kitchen. This gesture was famous in the household and was always obeyed. His daughter jabbed her lethally sharp elbow in his balls as she untangled herself from the curly cord and he grimaced, giving her a good whack on the back of the head, which had no effect at all. She hurtled after her brother, whooping at the top of her voice.

'OK, sorry about that, Felix old mate, but it's Tom's birthday. No, he got the ball last year, this year it's boxing gloves . . .' He reached automatically for his cigarettes.

'Noisy little sod's a real chip off the old block . . . Well, wish him happy birthday from me. How's your suspect measure up, by the way? Is he right-handed?'

Shefford sucked on his cigarette. 'Yep . . . How's this for size; he's five feet ten and a half, well-built, looks like he works out.'

On the other end of the line, Felix puffed at his cigar.

When the two men were together in one room they created such a dense fog that they were known as the Danger Zone. 'I'd say, John boy, you're a lucky sod. By the way, I was talking to Willy last night. Did he mention to you that he reckons there's not enough blood in that room?'

'You mean she wasn't killed there?'

'It's his department, but I'd say he's probably right.'

The press release that morning said little, just that a known prostitute had been murdered. Della had no family and no one volunteered any information about her movements. It was the same story all round; none of Della's friends and associates the police had contacted so far had seen her for weeks. Of ten residents of the house who had given statements, not one could say when they last saw her. Mrs Salbanna had been staying at her daughter's to help with the children while her newest grandchild made an appearance, and had not been home much for several weeks. Anyway, Della had been avoiding her for months because of the rent she owed. It was as if she had never existed, and, sadly, no one seemed to care.

By eight–thirty Shefford was at his desk, going over the typed–up statements from the previous day. He also had the full details he'd requested on Marlow's previous conviction. As he sifted through the information an alarm bell rang in his head, the same as on the previous day. Something was trying to break through . . .

Sergeant Otley brought coffee and doughnuts on a tray.

'Otters, there's something niggling me about this guy. Can you check something out for me, but tiptoe it? A girl was murdered in Oldham when I was there; get me the information on her, but keep schtum.'

Otley licked sugar off his top lip and replied, 'Yeah, what you think, he maybe did others?'

Shefford nodded. 'Yeah. Watch out for me on this, I knew the one in Oldham too, know what I mean?'

Otley sucked jam and sugar off his fingers and carried his beaker of coffee to his own desk. He inched a drawer open and brought out Della Mornay's diary.

'What do you want done with this?' he asked.

Shefford bit into his second sugar-coated bun. 'Hang on to it, old son, I'll check it out later. I'm goin' down to the cells, then upstairs, give the boss everythin' we've got. I reckon he'll give us the go-ahead to charge the bastard. If we finish it, you gotta hire a fuckin' clown's outfit!'

Laughing, Otley replaced the diary in his desk drawer. He called out as Shefford left, 'Eh, Big John, there's two hundred quid riding on us from DCI Tibbs' bunch, says we can't beat Paxman's record!' Otley could hear Shefford's big, bellowing laugh all the way down the corridor.

*

Shefford was still laughing while he waited for the cell door to be opened. He wanted to have a look at Marlow; he always did this just before he charged a suspect. There was something in a murderer's eyes, he had never been wrong yet.

Freshly shaved and showered, the prisoner looked somehow different this morning. Shefford was slightly taken aback; there was an eagerness to Marlow, a light in his eyes when he saw who it was at the door.

'Can I go?' Marlow asked.

Without speaking, Shefford shook his head slowly.

Jane Tennison parked her car with difficulty. DCI Shefford's dented and filthy Granada was angled across his space and hers and she had a tight squeeze to get out of the driving seat. Her pleated tartan skirt brushed against the Granada and she dusted it off in disgust, hoping that this would be the last time she would have to wear her court outfit for a while, unless the nasty little accountant engineered yet another stay of execution.

In the female locker room, she hung her smart black blazer with the brass buttons in her locker, straightened her high-necked Victorian-style blouse, ran a comb through her short fair hair and slicked some gloss on her lips, all in a matter of moments. She rinsed her hands at the row of washbasins and thumped the soap dispenser, which was empty as usual. Her irritation deepened when she caught sight of Maureen Havers, wasting time tittering with someone at the open locker-room door and fiddling with the Alice band she often wore to keep her thick, red hair off her pretty face. As she talked she whisked it off, shook her hair and replaced it, still giggling, then shut the door.

Havers started to sing as she opened her locker, then stopped short.

'Mornin', guv, didn't realize you were here.'

Tennison dried her hands and stepped back from the mirror. 'D'you think this skirt could do with being shorter?' she asked.

Havers peered around her locker door. 'Looks OK to me. That shirt suits you.'

'I'm in court this morning, remember?'

'Ahhh, it's Cary Grant Philpott, is it? In that case you'd better take the skirt up about a foot, keep him awake!'

A short time later, Havers breezed into the office with the pile of photocopying Tennison had asked her to do. 'We'll have to wait, the machine's in use.' Tennison exploded. 'Tell whoever's on the bloody thing to get off it, I must have the stuff before I go to court!'

Havers beamed good-naturedly. She was used to Tennison's outbursts and knew better than to answer back. She had once, and regretted it; Tennison had a very sharp tongue. A perfectionist herself, Tennison expected the same diligence and professionalism from everyone else. Her pinched, angry look warned Havers that she was brewing a real explosion.

'I'll nip down and see if it's free, boss, OK?'

'Like now, Maureen, would be a good idea!'

Havers couldn't resist a little dig. 'OK, boss, but DCI Shefford's team have sort of got priority. They arrested someone yesterday for the Della Mornay murder, so the Paxman record's being challenged again. DCI Shefford's lads have started the countdown.'

Tennison frowned. The name of the victim, Della Mornay, rang a bell, but before she could ask any questions Havers had ducked out of the door. She chewed her lips, drummed her fingers on the desk. 'Come on, why do I know that name . . .?' She remembered, then; in the Flying Squad two years ago she had brought Della Mornay in for questioning, but for the life of her she couldn't remember what the case was. Something to do with a pimp who had beaten up one of his girls . . . Della was a tough little bitch, blonde and rather pretty. She had refused to give evidence against the man. The fact that she had once interviewed the victim made Tennison all the more angry that she had not been given a chance to handle the case. Mike Kernan, the Superintendent, was going to hear about this.

*

Tennison closed her office door and turned just as Sergeant Otley bumped into her.

'Oh, sorry, ma'am.'

'I hear you've got a suspect, that right?' She meant to sound just interested, but she could not disguise the sarcasm.

'Yep, brought him in yesterday lunchtime. Word's out that the ink won't be dry on the warrant before the boss charges him. The DNA result was bloody marvellous.'

'Yeah, and such good timing! I heard there wasn't much else happening.'

Otley shrugged. This was the one he didn't like, the know-all who had been prowling around for the past eighteen months. He had studiously avoided any contact with her, just in case he was roped in to work with her.

'I wouldn't say that, ma'am. The team's pretty tough, John Shefford drives us hard.'

She turned, without agreeing, and he watched her push through the swing doors in her neat jacket and skirt. As the doors slammed behind her, he gave her the finger.

Kernan toyed uneasily with a felt-tipped pen as he listened to Tennison's complaint. He had never liked her, had been against her joining AMIT from the word go, but she had been more or less forced on him. She had more experience than at least one of the other DCIs, who was already on his second case. He cleared his throat and replaced the cap carefully on the pen.

'You want a transfer, is that what this is about?'

'No, I want to be given a chance. I was available for the Mornay case, but DCI Shefford was called in from leave to take it over. I want to know why I have had not so much as a sniff of anything since I've been here.'

Kernan opened his desk diary and noted that he had a lunch appointment before replying, 'It was my decision. Shefford knows the area and he once arrested the victim on a prostitution charge. She was also one of his informers . . .'

'I knew the victim too, sir. I've been checking my old records and I brought her in for questioning two years ago . . .'

'I'm sorry, I was unaware of that . . .'

'Are you saying I would have got the investigation if you had been aware of it, sir?'

'Look, I'll be honest. Shefford's one of my best men . . .'

'I know that, sir, but he's just finished that big case and he had been given two days' leave. It was a long and difficult case, he needed to rest. I could easily have attended the court session today and handled the investigation, but I was overlooked. All I want to know is, why, and is this going to continue?'

Kernan looked at his watch. 'As you said, you had to be

in court. According to the roster you were not available, but when you are you will have your chance, along with the other four officers . . .'

'DCI McLear is on a murder case right now, sir. He has nowhere near my experience, he came here six months after me. I notice his desk isn't loaded with petty fraud and tax evasion cases. I have had nothing else since I arrived.'

'Look, Jane, if you want a transfer then put in for it through the right channels.'

She was spitting mad, but managed to control herself. 'I don't want a transfer, I want to do the work I have been trained for, and I want you to give me your word that I will not be overlooked again.'

Kernan gave her the same speech he had spouted at her the last time she had complained, and she sighed. She had the distinct feeling that he couldn't wait to get her out of the office. She looked down at her shoes and seethed as he continued, 'It takes time, Jane. If you are not prepared to wait then perhaps you should consider asking to be transferred. As I have said to you before, we all appreciate your record, and your obvious abilities . . .'

'But you are not prepared to let me put them into practice, right?'

'Wrong. Just bide your time, don't rush things.'

'Rush, sir? I've been here eighteen months.'

'I've said all I intend saying at this point. I am sorry you feel the way you do, but until a case comes up that I feel is right for you, then ...'

'Then I carry on as before, is that what you were going to say, Mike? Oh, come on, don't fob me off again. You gave me the same speech last time. You know I've been treated unfairly; all I'm asking for is a chance to show you, show everyone here, what I'm capable of.'

'You'll get it, I give you my word.' Kernan looked pointedly at his watch. 'Now, I'm sorry, but I have to get on. Just be patient, I'm sorry I can't be more positive, and your turn will come.'

She walked to the door, depressed that she had failed yet again to convince him.

'Thank you for your time!'

As the door closed behind Tennison, Kernan leaned back in his chair. A few more months and she would leave of her own accord. He had never liked working with women and knew that his men felt the same way. All the same, he knew she was right. She was a highly qualified officer, it was just something about her, about all the high-ranking women he had come across. Maybe it was simply the fact that she was a woman.

Tennison had missed breakfast in the rush to get Joey ready, but her anger seemed to have sharpened her appetite. She decided to have a bite to eat in the canteen.

She ate alone, eavesdropping on the rowdy conversation from the next table. DI Burkin was cracking a joke about somebody being trapped on a mountain when the 'bing-bong' went. He and DI Haskons were wanted in Administration. They stood up, laughing. Young DC Dave Jones, newly transferred from Cardiff, turned from the counter with his loaded tray to see the two DIs heading towards the exit.

'You want me along?'

Burkin pointed a finger and Jones's eager face fell. 'You always interrupt my jokes, Daffy. Give yourself fifteen, then get down to the Incident Room.'

Tennison watched in amazement as Jones tackled the vast amount of food he had piled on his tray; sausages, eggs, chips, baked beans, a heap of toast and two puddings with custard.

'Brunch, is it?' she asked, pleasantly.

'No, ma'am, I missed my breakfast because I had to go over to the labs for the guv'nor.' He stuffed a huge forkful of food into his mouth.

'You're on Shefford's team, then?'

Unable to speak, Jones nodded vigorously.

'I hear he's going to charge the suspect this morning, is that right?'

Jones wiped his mouth on a paper serviette. 'Yes, ma'am, he and Sergeant Otley are with the Super now. It looks good, the Sarge said.'

Tennison sipped her coffee. 'Have they found the car? I hear your suspect says his car's been stolen?'

Jones had timed his eating badly; again, he could only nod. He was relieved when the 'bing-bong' went; this time it was for Tennison.

She drained her coffee cup and picked up her bag of groceries. Passing Jones, she smiled. 'See you.'

'Yes, ma'am.'

Several officers, some of them uniformed, acknowledged her as she made her way to the door. There was an air of embarrassment; no one seemed to like her, but her rank of DCI demanded respect.

Jones waited until she had left before he burped loudly, which was received with a smatter of applause, then he continued eating at a frightening rate. He didn't want to miss the big moment. The Sarge had told him it was a dead cert that they'd charge Marlow, and Paxman's record would be smashed.

It was Maureen Havers who had put out the call for Tennison, to tell her that the photocopier was now out of order, so she was still unable to do the stuff Tennison needed for court. She asked if she should take it to another station or wait until their own machine was repaired.

Tennison dropped her bag on the desk. 'I don't believe this place, can't they get a bloody mechanic to fix it? What the hell's wrong with it, anyway?'

'Someone used the wrong type of paper and it's all jammed inside. We're trying to find the guilty party, ma'am, but it's really fouled up this time.'

Tennison rolled up her shirt-sleeves. 'Right, I'll fix it myself, at least it'll keep me occupied for a while. We'll take all the copying, and that stuff on my desk is for the shredder, let's do something useful . . .'

With their arms full of paper, they passed the open door of the Incident Room. The men were standing around in groups, with DI Burkin in the centre telling another of his shaggy dog stories.

'I hear they're charging the suspect. You heard anything, Maureen?'

Havers had to jog to keep up with her. 'Yes, ma'am, they'll break the record. There's a booze-up in the pub, whole station'll be there. Kitty's over a hundred and fifty quid already.'

Tennison squatted to peer inside the photocopier. 'Fucking thing's jammed all right, look at the mess! How do you open it up?'

Havers knelt beside her to read the instructions on the side of the machine. 'It says here, lift lever A, release spring . . .'

Tennison pushed her aside. 'I'll do it, get out of my light . . . Now then, pull what where?'

She yanked the lever and the machine split itself in two. 'Oh, shit, now what?'

'How about waiting for the mechanic, ma'am?'

Tennison froze her with a look. 'I've started, so I'll continue . . .'

For what seemed an age, the only sounds in the office were the ticking of the clock and the flick as Kernan turned the pages of Marlow's file.

'Christ, what a stroke of luck, John, bloody marvellous. What about the blood on the jacket?' He looked from Shefford to Otley, approvingly.

Shefford grimaced. He had a weird tingling in his left arm, all the way to his fingertips. He flexed his hand, rubbed the wrist.

'Willy's working his butt off. Should . . . should come through any time now . . .' The pain was shooting down his arm now, and his chest felt as if it was being crushed . . . 'It was the size of a pinprick, they're waiting for it to expand at the labs, then we can check . . . Oh, Jesus . . .'

The pain was so bad it made Shefford fight for air. Kernan looked up, concerned. 'Are you OK, John?'

'I dunno,' Shefford gasped, 'I've got . . . like a cramp in my arm . . .'

He went rigid as a new spasm of pain hit him. He snorted, and Kernan saw blood oozing from his nose. There was a terrible look of fear in his eyes.

The pain seemed to be blowing him apart, like the

bomb he had felt ticking inside his head. It was blowing up, he was blowing up! Rubbing his arm frantically, he snorted again and the blood poured down his chin. Then he pitched forward, cracking his head on the edge of Kernan's desk.

The Super was already picking up the phone, shouting for a doctor, an ambulance, as Otley grabbed Shefford and tried to ease him back into his chair. But the man was so big that Otley staggered under his weight.

Shefford's body suddenly relaxed and his head lolled on Otley's shoulder. Otley cradled him in his arms, shouting hysterically for an ambulance ... Kernan ran round the desk to help him lower Shefford to the floor. They loosened his tie, opened his shirt, and all the while Otley was saying over and over, 'S'all right, John, everything's OK, just stay calm ... Don't move, guv, it's all being taken care of, ambulance is on its way ...'

The photocopier throbbed into life and shot out three crumpled sheets of sooty paper. Tennison gave a satisfied sigh and stood up, brushing at the black specks on her hands.

'Right, Maureen, try it with a sheet we want to shred, just in case it eats it.'

It seemed that a herd of elephants suddenly charged down the corridor outside. Tennison opened the door and stepped back to avoid being trampled as the stretcher-bearers raced along. They passed too swiftly for Tennison to see who their patient was under the oxygen mask.

The corridor suddenly filled with people, propping doors open, running to follow the stretcher. Word went round like wildfire; John Shefford had collapsed.

Tennison hurried into her office to watch the ambulance in the street below, but found the window space already occupied by two WPCs. She slammed the door.

'Get away from the window, come on, move it!'

WPC Hull whipped round. 'Sorry, ma'am, but it's DCI Shefford . . .'

'Well, peering out of the window isn't going to help him! Come on, move over, lemme have a squint!'

Tennison could see the ambulance with its doors open, the stretcher being loaded. She turned back to the room.

'OK, back to work. The copier's been repaired, and we may not have a lot of work to do but we might as well clear the desk. You never know, I might be needed!'

She meant it as a joke, and it was taken as one, because they didn't know then that Shefford would never regain consciousness. He was dead on arrival at hospital.

When the panic had died down, Tennison sat alone in her office and pondered . . . She was sorry Shefford was ill, of course she was, but someone had to take over the investigation. This time Kernan had to give her the job; everyone else on the rota was busy.

Deeply shocked, Otley shut himself in the gents' toilets and wept. He couldn't face anyone, and was unable to carry the news back to the men waiting in the Incident Room. He had lost the best friend he had ever had, his only real friend.

When he was able to face the men he found them sitting in stunned silence. He tried to tell them more, but all he could say was, 'It's Tom's birthday today, it's his son's birthday . . . I bought him a magic set, and . . .' He wandered over to his desk. There at the side was the big package, the train set he had taken so long to choose. He stood staring down at it. The men, deeply shocked, didn't know what to say.

Otley's voice was barely audible. 'We were going to set it up, surprise Tom. It's from Hamley's . . .'

DI Burkin, head and shoulders taller than his skipper, slipped an arm around him. The big officer's tears were streaming down his face, but Otley had no more tears. He clenched his fists, shrugged Burkin away.

'Right, let's nail this bastard Marlow! We do it for our guv'nor, we break the fucking record, agreed?'

It was down to Superintendent Kernan to visit Sheila Shefford. Otley had agreed to accompany him, but

Kernan didn't know if it was such a good idea, the man was so distressed. In the end he decided to take DI Burkin along. No matter which way you looked at it, it was tragic.

Anticipating a harrowing time with Sheila and her family, Kernan's mood was not receptive. When Jane Tennison asked for a few minutes with him his first reaction was to refuse, but she had insisted it was important.

When he realized what she wanted he stared at her in disbelief. He was still in shock himself and he turned on her, ordering her out of his office. But she stood her ground, fists clenched.

'Look, please, I'm sorry if I appear heartless, but all I am doing is offering to finish the investigation. John was ready to charge the suspect and someone has to take over, he's not going to be well enough. We can't hold Marlow much longer, we'll have to apply for a three-day lay-down, but either way someone has to take ...'

Kernan gripped her tightly by the elbow. 'The man's not even cold! For God's sake, I can't make any decisions now. When I do, you will be the first to hear. Now *get out of my office* ...'

'Cold?' She stared at him. 'He's *dead*? But he can't be ...'

'I didn't realize you hadn't been told. John was dead when he reached the hospital. Now will you get out?'

Appalled, she shook her head as if to clear it, drew a

deep breath, then plunged on, 'But you will have to make a decision, sir, and I am offering to step in right now. I can familiarize myself with the case tonight, and if charges . . .'

'I said I would consider your offer, Jane.'

'No, sir, you said you couldn't make any decisions right now. I think, however, a decision has to be made, and fast. You can't back out of this one, you know I am here. I am available and I am qualified. Someone's got to prove that bloody survey's a load of bullshit. You pass me over on this one and I warn you . . .'

Kernan's face twisted with barely controlled anger. 'You don't warn me, Chief Inspector, is that clear? Now you and your feminist jargon can get out of my bloody office before I physically throw you out. A friend, a close friend and associate of mine died in this room this afternoon, and I am just on my way to tell his wife and children. Now is not the time . . .'

'When is the time, sir? Because we don't have any to spare – if Marlow's not charged very soon he will have to be released. I am deeply sorry for what happened to John, please don't insult me by thinking otherwise, but at the same time someone has to—'

'Please leave *now*. Don't tell me my job. I will not be forced into making a decision I will regret at a later date. Please leave my office.'

*

Maureen Havers hiccuped through her tears and Tennison put an arm around her shoulders.

'Do you want to go home, Maureen love? You can if you like, there's not much to do.'

Havers wiped her eyes. 'I'm sorry, I'm sorry, but he was always so full of life, and only today I heard him laughing, you know that big laugh of his ... He said ... he said he'd beaten Paxman's record!'

Leaving it that Havers could go home if she felt like it, Tennison left for court.

Superintendent Kernan called a two o'clock meeting with Commander Geoff Trayner to discuss the situation, particularly Tennison's request to take over the Marlow case. Neither man liked the idea, even though the file on the desk proved she was fully qualified and her ex-boss in the Flying Squad had given her a glowing recommendation.

Tennison had been with the Flying Squad for five years, and had taken a lot of flak from the men. Unlike two of her female colleagues in a similar position she had stayed her course. Her report noted that she had been offered a position training female officers because of her previous experience working with rape victims and her instigation of many changes which had been adopted by rape centres all over the country. She had turned the offer down, not wishing to go back into uniform, and had subsequently been transferred to AMIT. She was, as they were well aware, the only female DCI attached to a murder squad; with someone of her record it would be very difficult to bring someone in from outside to take over.

Kernan drummed his fingers on the desk. 'The men won't like it, you know that, but as far as I can see we don't really have a choice. There's no one free on AMIT except her. I've checked locally, and of the usuals I know Finley's in Huddersfield, Smith and Kelvin are still tied up on that shooting last week in Shepherd's Bush ... And she's got a mouth on her, I don't want her creating a stink. She as good as threatened to resign if she was overlooked again.'

'She's one of these bloody feminists, I don't want any flak from that angle. We'll give her a trial run, see what happens, but if she puts a foot out of line we'll have her transferred and get her out of our hair. Agreed?'

Kernan nodded and slapped Tennison's file closed. 'I'll get her in to see you, and I'll break it to the men.' He pressed a button on his intercom and requested Tennison's immediate presence.

'DCI Tennison's in court today, sir,' his secretary replied.

'Hell, I'd forgotten ... Let everyone know I want her the moment she comes in.'

Jane Tennison was lucky for once. The jury was out by two-fifteen and she was away. Still upset by John

Shefford's death, she drove straight to the building site where Peter was working.

Peter was in his hut, talking to one of his workmen. Jane held herself rigid and waited until the man was gone, then rushed to Peter and sobbed her heart out.

It was a while before she was calm enough to make much sense, but he eventually pieced the events of the day together. He put his arms around her; it felt so good to have him to come to that she started crying all over again.

'You know, from everything you've said, this Shefford was well-liked, it must be a shock to everyone. Perhaps you should have given it a few days.'

He bent to kiss her cheek, but she turned away. 'You don't understand,' she snapped, 'Marlow will be released tomorrow unless we charge him. If they want extra time they have to have someone to take it before the magistrate, someone who knows what's going on. If the magistrate doesn't think there's enough evidence to hold him, he'll refuse the three-day lay-down.'

Peter didn't really care if they released Yogi Bear, but he made all the right noises. At last she blew her nose and stood up, hands on hips.

'If those bastards choose someone else to take over, you know what I'll do? I'll quit, I mean it! I'll throw in the towel, because if I don't get the case – I mean, with Shefford dead it leaves only four on the AMIT team, and I know the other three are working, so they'd have to bring in someone from outside. And if they do, I quit. Then I'll take them to a fucking tribunal and show them all up for the fucking chauvinist pigs they are! Bastard chauvinists, terrified of giving a woman a break because she might just prove better than any of them! I hate the fuckers . . .'

Tentatively, Peter suggested that they go home early, have a relaxing evening, but she shot back at him, 'No way, because if they should call me and I'm not hanging by that phone, then the buggers have an excuse.'

'Use your bleeper.'

She grinned at him, and suddenly she looked like a tousle-headed tomboy, 'You're not going to believe this, but I was so pissed off I left it at the station.' Then she tilted her head back and roared with laughter. It was a wonderful laugh, and it made him forget the way she had snapped at him.

That was the first time he became aware of the two separate sides of Jane Tennison; the one he knew at home, the other a DCI. Today he'd caught a glimpse of the policewoman, and he didn't particularly like her.

The moment Tennison reached her office the telephone rang. She pounced on it like a hawk. She replaced the receiver a moment later and gave it a satisfied pat. She took a small mirror from her desk drawer and checked her appearance. She suddenly realized that Maureen Havers was sitting quietly in the corner.

'Wish me luck!' she said, and gave Havers a wink as she opened the door.

Havers sat at her neatly organized desk and stared at the closed door. She'd seen Tennison's satisfaction and knew something was going down. *Wish me luck?* She put two and two together and knew that Tennison was going after John Shefford's job. She was disgusted at Tennison's lack of sensitivity; she seemed almost elated.

Havers picked up the phone and dialled her girlfriend in Records. 'Guess what, I think my boss is going after Shefford's job ... Yeah, that's what I thought, real pushy bitch.'

Chapter Three

Otley was the last to arrive in the Incident Room. He apologized to the Super and received a sympathetic pat on the shoulder.

The room was filled with palpable depression; there was a heaviness to every man. Some of them couldn't meet Otley's eyes but stood with heads bent. Only yesterday they had been laughing and joking with their big, burly boss. Shefford had been loved by them all and they took his death hard.

Kernan cleared his throat. 'OK, I've gone over all the reports on the Marlow case and it looks in good shape. I think, when I've had time to assess it all, we can go ahead and charge him. But until that decision is made, and I know time is against us, I am bringing in another DCI to take over. You all know Detective Chief Inspector Tennison . . .'

A roar of shock and protest drowned his next words, and he put up a hand for silence. 'Now come on, take it easy, just hear me out. As it stands, I reckon we'll have to try for a three-day lay-down, so I want all of you to give Inspector Tennison every assistance possible. Let her familiarize herself with the case, and then we can charge Marlow . . .'

Otley stepped forward. 'I'm sorry, sir, but it isn't on. Bring in someone from outside, we don't want her. We've been working as a team for five years, bring in someone we know.'

Kernan's face tightened. 'Right now she is all I have available, and she is taking over the case at her own request.'

'She moved bloody fast, didn't she, sir?' Otley's face twisted with anger and frustration, his hands clenched at his sides.

DI Haskons raised an eyebrow at Otley to warn him to keep quiet. 'I think, sir, we all feel the same way. As you said, time is against us.'

'She's on the case as from now,' Kernan said firmly, unwilling to show his own misgivings. 'I'm afraid I can't discuss this further. She will assess the charges; just give her all the help you can, and any problems report back to me. Thank you . . .' He got out fast to avoid further argument, but he heard the uproar as he closed the door, heard Otley calling Tennison a two-faced bitch, a cow who couldn't wait to step into a dead man's shoes. Kernan paused outside the room, silently agreeing with him. But the investigation was at such an advanced stage, they wouldn't be stuck with Tennison for long.

The Commander's voice was gruff as he briefly outlined the procedure for Tennison to familiarize herself with the Marlow case and to do everything necessary to ensure that he was charged. He told her abruptly to take it easy with Shefford's team, who had been working together for so long that they would not welcome an outsider. He didn't actually say, 'especially a woman', but he hinted as much. 'The Superintendent will give you every assistance, so don't be afraid to use him. And . . . good luck!'

'It would help if he could handle the application for the three-day lay-down,' Tennison replied, and the Commander agreed.

They shook hands and Tennison said she would do everything within her power to bring the case successfully to court. It was not until she was back in her own office that she congratulated herself, grinning like the Cheshire Cat because, at last, she had done it. She, DCI Tennison, was heading a murder case.

Late that afternoon, still stunned by his guv'nor's death, Bill Otley was clearing Shefford's desk. He collected the family photographs and mementos together and packed them carefully into Shefford's tattered briefcase. Finally he picked up a photo of Tom, his little godson, and looked at it for a long moment before laying it carefully on top of the others.

He snapped the locks on the case, hardly able to believe that John wasn't going to walk in, roaring with laughter, and tell them it was all a joke. His grief consumed him, swamping him in a bitterness he directed towards DCI Tennison, as if she was in some way responsible. He had to blame someone for the hurting, for the loss. He hugged the briefcase to his chest, knowing he now had to face Sheila and the children, he couldn't put it off any longer. Maybe it would be best if he left it till the weekend, and in the meantime he'd keep John's briefcase at the flat along with his shirts and socks . . .

He was still sitting at his desk, holding the case, when DI Burkin looked in.

'She's checking over the evidence, you want to see her?'

Otley shook his head. 'I don't even want to be in the same room as that slit-arsed bitch!'

Tennison was ploughing methodically through all the evidence on the Marlow case. The ashtray was piled high and a constant stream of coffee was supplied by WPC Havers. She was just bringing a fresh beaker and a file.

'Deirdre, alias Della, Mornay's Vice record, ma'am.

The reason they gave for not sending it before was that King's Cross Vice Squad's computer records are not compatible with Scotland Yard's, or some such excuse.'

Flicking through the file, Tennison took out a photograph of Della Mornay and laid it beside the photos of the corpse. She frowned.

'Maureen, get hold of Felix Norman for me and find out how long he'll be there. Then order me a car and tell DC Jones he's driving me. I want to see the body tonight, but I need to interview the landlady first. And ask for another set of dabs from the victim, get them compared with the ones on Della Mornay's file.' Leaving Havers scribbling furiously, she walked out.

All the items from Della Mornay's room that Forensic had finished with had been piled onto a long trestle table. It was a jumble of bags of clothes, bedding and shoes. There was also a handbag, which Tennison examined carefully. She made a note of some ticket stubs, replaced them, then pulled on a pair of rubber gloves and turned to the clothing taken from the victim's body. The bloodstains were caked hard and black. She checked sleeves, hems, seams and labels.

Engrossed in what she was doing, she hardly noticed WPC Havers enter.

'Ma'am? Ma'am, DC Jones is waiting in the car.'

Tennison turned her attention to the filthy bedclothes.

The smell alone was distasteful, and she wrinkled her nose.

'Dirty little tart . . . Tell Jones I'll be with him in a few minutes. And tell all of Shefford's team that I want them in the Incident Room at nine sharp tomorrow morning – all of them, Maureen, understand?'

DC Jones sat in the driving seat of the plain police car. He had left the rear door open for DCI Tennison, but she climbed in beside him.

'Right, Milner Road first. What's your first name?'

'David, ma'am.'

'OK, Dave, put your foot down. I've got a hell of a schedule.'

Della's room was still roped off. Tennison looked around and noted the fine dusting left by the Scenes of Crime people, then used the end of her pencil to open the one wardrobe door that still clung to its hinges. She checked the few remaining items of clothing, then sat on the edge of the bed, opened her briefcase and thumbed through a file.

DC Jones watched as she closed the case and turned to him. 'Will you bring me two pairs of shoes . . .'

She spent a considerable time looking over the dressing-table, checking the make-up, opening the small drawers. By the time she seemed satisfied, Jones' stomach was complaining loudly. He suggested it was time to eat. Tennison paused on her way downstairs and looked back at him.

'I'm OK, but if you can't hold out, go and get yourself something while I interview the landlady.'

When Jones got back to the house he found Tennison sitting in the dirty, cluttered kitchen in the basement, listening to Mrs Salbanna moaning.

'The rents are my living, how long will you need the room for? I could let it right now, you know!'

Tennison replied calmly, 'Mrs Salbanna, I am investigating a murder. As soon as I am satisfied that we no longer need the bedsit, I will let you know. If you wish you can put in a claim for loss of earnings, I'll have the forms sent to you. Now, will you just repeat to me exactly what happened the night you found Della Mornay? You identified her, didn't you?'

'Yes, I've told you twice, yes.'

'How well did you know her?'

'How well? You're jokin', I didn't know her. I let a room to her, that's all.'

'How often did you see her?'

'As often as I could, to get the rent off her. God forgive me for talking ill of the dead, but that little bitch owed me months in rent. She was always late, and it gets so if you throw her out on the street you'll never get the money back, right? She kept on promising and promising . . .'

'So you saw her recently?'

'No, because she was in and out like a snake. I hadn't seen her for . . . at least a month, maybe longer.'

'But you are absolutely sure that it was Della Mornay's body?'

'Who else would it be? I told you all this, I told that big bloke too.'

'And that night you didn't hear anything unusual, or see anyone that didn't live here?'

'No, I didn't come home till after eight myself. Then, because I'd had such a time with my daughter – she's had a new baby, and she's already got two, so I've been looking after them . . . Well, by the time I got home I was so exhausted, I went straight to bed. Then I was woken up by the front door banging. I put notices up, but no one pays attention. It started banging, so I got up . . .'

'You didn't see anyone go out? Could someone have just left?'

'I don't know . . . See, it's got a bit of rubber tyre tacked on it to try and stop the noise, so if they didn't want to be heard . . . But it was just blowing around in the wind, it was a windy night . . . I told the other man all this.'

Tennison closed her notebook. 'Thank you for your time, Mrs Salbanna.'

Tennison stopped off at Forensic on her way to view the body, and sat in silence while Willy Chang explained the complex details of the DNA test that had resulted in George Marlow being picked up on suspicion of murder. She looked at the slides.

'There was a big rape and murder case up in Leicester. They did a mass screening, every man in the entire village, and they got him. The semen tests took weeks to match, but in the case of such a rare blood group it's much easier to define. He's an AB secreter and belongs to group two in the PGM tests, so it narrows the field dramatically. We've been doing test runs on a new computerized cross-matching system, just using the rarer blood groups, for experimental purposes. Your man was tested in 1988, and was actually on record.'

'So you got a match from the computer, out of the blue?'

'Yes. When we got the read-out it was mayhem in here, it was such a freak piece of luck.'

'So the computer is infallible, is it?'

'Not exactly, it'll give you the closest match it can find. We have to confirm the results with our own visual tests on the light-box. Want to see it?'

Tennison was shown two sets of negatives that looked like supermarket bar codes, with certain lines darker than others. The black bands on each matched perfectly. She made some notes, then asked to use a telephone.

She placed a call to her old base at the rape centre in Reading and requested the records of all suspected rapists charged as a result of DNA testing. She wanted to see how the judges had reacted, if they had allowed the DNA results to be the mainstay of the evidence.

Felix Norman slammed the phone down as a corpse, covered by a green sheet, was wheeled into the lab. Five students, all masked, gowned and shod in white Wellington boots, trailed in after the trolley.

He gestured for them to gather round, then lifted the sheet. 'Well, you're in luck, this is a nice fresh 'un. I'm gonna have to leave you for a few minutes, but you can start opening it up without me.'

He picked up a clipboard and strode out to where Tennison and Jones were waiting. Greeting them with nothing approaching civility, he led them to the mortuary. At the far end of the rows of drawers he stopped and pulled on a lever, releasing the hinge, and slid out the tray with 'D. Mornay' chalked on it.

Before removing the sheet from the body, Norman reeled off a list of injuries from the clipboard, including the number and depth of the stab wounds.

'I hear you had a lucky break with the forensic results. Your suspect has a very rare blood group?'

Tennison nodded, waiting for him to draw the sheet back. He did so slowly, looking at DC Jones' pale face.

The body had been cleaned, the blonde hair combed back from her face. The dark bruises remained and the gashes on the head were deep and clear. Tennison frowned, leaning forward.

'Pull her out further, will you?'

Norman drew the drawer out to its fullest extent. Tennison walked around, peering at the dead girl's face, then turned to DC Jones.

'Shefford identified her, didn't he?'

'Yes, ma'am, and her landlady, Mrs Corinna Salbanna.'

Tennison made a note on her pad, walked back again, then leaned in even closer. She stared for a long time before she asked to see the wounds on the torso. Norman pointed out the incisions, then indicated the deep weals on the tops of the arms.

'These seem to indicate that she was strung up. We'll do some tests with weights ... And here, on her wrists, you can see the marks of the ropes, tied so tightly they left imprints, the mark of her watch strap too, see ...'

'Where's the cut? Small cut on her hand?'

'Here.' He showed Tennison the corpse's right wrist. 'Small, but quite deep. Would have bled a fair bit.' He continued reading from his notes. 'Extensive bruising all over the front of the body, plus a good deal around the genital and anal areas, but nothing on the back or buttocks.'

Tennison nodded and again peered closely at the victim's face, then turned to DC Jones.

'I asked for another set of prints, will you make sure they're on the way, and the set from Della Mornay's file.'

Jones shifted his weight and muttered that he'd check it out. 'We already have a set, ma'am.'

Tennison snapped back, 'I need another set, and fast.'

Norman looked at his watch. 'My students are waiting, Inspector.'

Tennison was frowning. She turned again to Jones. 'Go and check on those prints now, Jones.' Then she addressed Felix Norman. 'I've got a few more questions I can ask while you work, OK?'

Norman sighed, covered the corpse and closed the drawer while Tennison added to the notes she had made during her inspection, then he led her into the dissection room.

For the next few minutes, Tennison watched as Norman, with apparent relish, helped a student remove the specimen's heart.

'That's it, ease it out . . .'

Jones returned and stood at Tennison's side. 'Prints are organized, ma'am.'

She ignored him and continued scribbling in her note-book. Jones watched Norman and his students as they worked on. Blood dripped into buckets set at each end of the trolley, and the stains on their gowns and rubber gloves made them appear ghoulish. On one lens of Norman's half-moon spectacles there was a clear finger-print in blood. DC Jones' stomach turned over.

Tennison seemed intent on her notes. She did not so

much as glance at Jones, who hadn't spoken for some time.

'How soon can you do the weight tests? I need to know exactly how she was strung up.'

'My dear lady,' Felix replied, 'we'll do them as quickly as we can, and you'll be the first to hear, though I'd have thought you had enough on your suspect to bang him up for life.'

He turned to the student and gave a helping hand as he opened the heart.

'Look at this, Inspector. This poor bugger's veins were so clogged up it's a wonder he lived as long as he did. Classic English breakfast causes this; bacon, fat . . . You like a cooked breakfast, Inspector?'

Tennison glanced around the room; Jones had disappeared. She smiled to herself.

The students clustered around Norman and took notes as he went on, 'Liver very dodgy, see just by the size . . . I hear through the grapevine that those wankers over at the labs can't even find the winder from the victim's watch. They've got fifteen square yards of carpet, combing it inch by inch. Right, now let's have a look at his testicles . . . Hmmm, well-endowed gent.'

Tennison knew she had as much as she was going to get. 'Thank you for your time, Professor Norman. As soon as you can on the—'

'You'll have my report, Inspector, but you should give

us the time to do our job properly. And next time, gown-up, you know the rules.'

He turned to pierce her with his gimlet eye, as though she were one of his students, but she was gone.

When the Western finished at midnight, Peter switched the television off, poured a fresh cup of black coffee and carried it to the dining area. As he set it down by Jane's elbow she looked up, her eyes red-rimmed with fatigue.

'Thanks, love. I just have to wade through this mound, then I'll come to bed . . .'

'Maybe you'd be better off having a sleep now and getting up early?'

'You must be joking, I'll have to get up at five as it is, to plough through that lot on the chair.'

Peter planted a kiss on the top of her head, went back to the bedroom and settled down to sleep. In the end, Jane didn't come to bed at all.

As Tennison entered the Incident Room at nine the next morning, the men fell silent. They watched her as she walked to the table and sat in the chair their guv'nor had occupied the day before. She could feel their hatred; it prickled her skin. She had not expected such open animosity and it threw her slightly.

She kept her eyes down, concentrating on her notepad,

then took out her gold pen and carefully unscrewed the cap. She raised her head.

'By now you are all aware that I am taking over from DCI Shefford, and I would like to take this opportunity to say how saddened and deeply shocked I am by this tragedy. John Shefford was a well-liked and highly respected officer.' She met the gaze of each man in turn as she spoke; several of them couldn't hold her eyes, one or two others, notably Otley, glared back, challenging her silently.

'I am not attempting to step into his shoes; I am the only available DCI and as such I shall appreciate all the co-operation and assistance you can give to enable me to grasp all the details of the investigation and bring it to a successful conclusion. WPC Havers will be assisting me, and she will give you details of everything I need. I will work around the clock . . . You wanted to say something, Sergeant Otley?'

Otley was standing, rigid with anger, tight-lipped. 'Yes, ma'am, I know you asked for this case specifically . . .'

She lit a cigarette and gazed at him, coldly. 'If you don't like it, put in for a transfer, through the usual channels. That goes for the rest of you; anyone who wishes to move can put in a formal request. Until then, I'm afraid you're stuck with me.' A murmur of resentment went around the room, but she ignored it. 'I'm asking for some more man-power. We've got more officers joining the team today, including Maureen Havers and four WPCs to assist with the paperwork.'

She picked up some items from the desk and began pinning them on the big notice-board. There were two photographs and two sets of fingerprints, highlighted with red and green arrows. She pointed at them as she spoke.

'Now, here's the really bad news. The photo on the right is Deirdre "Della" Mornay; on the left is the murder victim. Here are the prints taken from the corpse, and these are the ones from Della Mornay's Vice file. There are nothing like the sixteen points of similarity needed for a match. The victim's clothes are all from expensive designers such as Giorgio Armani, not Della's line at all. Della's shoes are all English size five; our victim took six and a half, from Bond Street.'

She looked around as they took in the implications of what she was saying. Otley was stunned; he was aware of just how well Shefford had been acquainted with Della.

Tennison went on, 'We have obviously wrongly identified the victim, which makes our suspect's statement, in which he names the girl he picked up as Della Mornay, inadmissible. If we went to court with this, the case would be thrown out. Someone's been bloody careless. The officer who interrogated Marlow . . .'

Recovering quickly, Otley went on the attack, interrupting her. 'You know it was John Shefford! Are you tryin' to destroy him before he's even buried?'

She stared him into silence. 'What I want to know is how come Marlow named the victim as *Della* when the warrant gave her proper name of Deirdre? I'm told you did not state her name at the time, you just arrested him on suspicion of murder. In the tapes of his first interrogation by Shefford, Marlow insists not just once but three times that he did not know the victim, but at the end of the second interview he refers to the victim as Della Mornay. In his written statement, made that night, he again denied knowing her. In his third statement he is calling the victim by name! This would be thrown out of court, especially as Marlow's lawyer was in the room and witnessed his denials. The cock-up is therefore down to us. DCI Shefford made a gross error in wrongly identifying our victim, just as he did in giving the name to George Marlow.'

Otley frowned but kept quiet as she continued, 'I want new statements all round, and we'll get it right this time! So get them all in again and find out where Della Mornay is now, and get the victim's clothes and shoes checked out. Our priorities are to find the real Della Mornay and to get an ID on the body.'

She paused, stubbed out her cigarette and lit another. She was wiping the floor with them, and they knew it, hated it. No one said a word as she took a sip of water, then went on.

'So we move like hell. We haven't a snowflake's chance

of getting the three-day lay-down, so if we don't come up with something today, Marlow will have to be released.'

She waited, hands on hips, for the howl of protest to die down. 'I'm afraid it's a fact of life! OK, anyone have any queries? No? What about Marlow's car, the brown Rover? Anything on that yet? I want it found. Right, that's it for now.'

The room was eerily silent as she passed them on the way out, but the moment the door closed behind her there was an explosion of cat-calls and abuse.

Otley thumped the table she had recently vacated. 'Fucking tart! She was after this before he was out of the bloody station! She was in with the Super almost before he was dead, the bitch! I'll give her queries, the hard-faced tart!'

'What about Marlow's car, Bill?'

Otley turned on Burkin. 'You heard her, cow wants it traced, so we trace it! Christ, how much evidence does she bleeding want, for God's sake? We got him, he did it! An' she's runnin' around familiarizin' herself, the stupid cunt!'

In the corridor outside the Incident Room, Tennison leant against the wall, eyes closed, breathing deeply to calm herself. It had been a tremendous effort to keep her cool in front of the men.

Once she was in control again, she headed for the lift to the Super's office.

The men dispersed to their appointed tasks in dribs and drabs. DC Lillie said quietly to his partner, Rosper, 'If the car was nicked, we ain't gonna find it. It's been stripped down by now.'

Rosper's pug-nosed face broke into a grin. 'Eh, you ever see that advert wiv the monkeys? Bleedin' funny . . .'

Otley and Jones were left alone in the room. 'What do you think, Skipper?' Jones asked.

'That tart's gunning for John. Well, let her try it; she bad-mouths him and I'll see her knickers are screwed . . .'

The phone interrupted him. He grabbed it. 'No, she's not here. Yeah? Yeah! Right, I'll send someone over. Thanks!'

He hung up and gave his first smile of the morning. 'That was Forensic. The spot of blood we got off Marlow's shirt cuff, the one they've been growing, matches the victim's! We got the bastard now . . .'

'This is a right bloody mess,' said Superintendent Kernan. Tennison ran her fingers through her hair and Kernan continued, 'For God's sake don't let the press get wind of it. Can you handle it? DCI Hicock, from Notting Hill, is available now.'

'I can handle it,' Tennison snapped. No way would she relinquish the case to Wild Bill, even if she had to hang on to it by her teeth. 'I need more men, preferably from outside. If we have to let Marlow go, we'll need someone with surveillance expertise.'

'I'll see what we can do. Are you going to see him now?'

'I want a little chat with Marlow, off the record ... OK?'

'Watch yourself, Upcher's a tough bastard.'

Tennison shrugged. 'But I bet he's not down in the cells now, is he?'

Kernan shook his head. 'Seems to me that Marlow wouldn't have hired Upcher unless he was guilty. His type cost.'

'We still can't prove he was ever in the bedsit. It's strange that there's nothing, not a single shred of evidence ...'

'Forensic's still working on it?'

'Yes,' she said, standing up. 'They are, at their own pace.'

As soon as she left, Kernan picked up the phone. 'Put me through to the Commander.'

Before seeing Marlow, Tennison listened again to a short stretch of tape from his interview with Shefford. Then she was ready to face the suspect for the first time.

Marlow had been left to kick his heels in an interview room for some time, sitting in silence, watched by a uniformed PC. DI Burkin was sitting in the corridor outside, reading the paper. He was a well-built man, a prized member of the police boxing team, and his slightly battered face showed traces of his career. He rose to his feet when DCI Tennison approached.

'Sorry to keep you waiting. It's Frank, isn't it?'

Burkin nodded and jerked his thumb towards the interview room. 'He's got coffee, and he doesn't smoke.'

Tennison was taken aback by Marlow's handsome looks; the photographs in his file had given her completely the wrong impression. He resembled an old-time movie star, not exactly Valentino, more Robert Taylor. His blue-black hair was combed back from his face, high cheekbones accentuated his jawline. His amber eyes and long, dark lashes beneath thickly arched brows would be the envy of any woman.

He glanced at the uniformed officer for permission to stand, then rose to his feet. His clothes were well-cut, rather formal; a blue and white striped shirt with a white collar highlighted his dark good looks. His suit jacket hung neatly on the back of his chair.

'Please stay seated, Mr Marlow. I am Detective Chief Inspector Jane Tennison, this is Detective Inspector Frank Burkin. I suppose you have been told that the DCI in charge of this investigation . . .'

Marlow interrupted her in a low, husky voice with a slight northern twang. 'Yes, I know. I'm very sorry, he was a nice man.' He glanced at Burkin, then back to Tennison, placed his hands together on the table and half-smiled; a dimple appeared in his right cheek.

Tennison returned his smile involuntarily. 'You have been very co-operative, Mr Marlow, and I'm sorry to have to question you all over again. But you must understand that in taking over the case I need to know everything . . .'

'Yes, I understand.'

Tennison was furious with herself because her hand was shaking as she placed Marlow's statement and her notebook on the table. 'Would you just tell me, in your own words, exactly what occurred on the night of Saturday the thirteenth of January?'

Marlow began quietly, explaining that he had drawn some money from a cash dispenser in Ladbroke Grove. He was about to return home when he saw her standing outside the tube station, obviously touting for business.

'I'm sorry to interrupt, but who was standing?'

'Della Mornay!'

'Oh, you knew her, did you?'

'No, I didn't know her name, never saw her before. He told me, said it was a tart by the name of Della . . . He told me.'

'Who, exactly, told you the girl's name?'

'Inspector Shefford.'

'OK, George, go on. Tell me what happened next.'

'I got into my car and drove past her, slowly. She came to the window, asked me if I was looking for someone. All I said was maybe, it depended how much. She said it was twenty-five pounds for full sex. If I wanted ...'

Looking up, Tennison caught his strange, beautiful eyes. He looked away, embarrassed.

'Go on, Mr Marlow. Twenty-five pounds for full sex ...'

He cleared his throat and continued, 'Masturbation fifteen. I agreed to pay the twenty-five, and she directed me to some waste ground beside the ... the Westway, I think it is. We got into the back seat. We ...' he coughed. 'We did it, then she asked me to drop her back to the Tube. Then, as she climbed over the seats into the front she caught her hand, her left hand, on my radio. It's got a sort of sharp edge, and it was only a little nick, but I wrapped my handkerchief around it ...'

'Er, sorry, George, you just said, "She cut her hand on my radio"?'

'Yes.'

'Which hand?'

He frowned and raised his hands, looking from one to the other. 'Her right hand, yeah ... It was her right hand, because my radio's between the seats. It's got a sharp edge.'

He indicated the spot on his own wrist – exactly where the small cut was on the wrist of the corpse. 'You can take the radio out, it's portable. They're always being nicked out of cars, round where I live.'

He paused for a second and sighed. 'You found my car yet?'

Tennison shook her head. 'Go on. She cut herself?'

'Yeah. I gave her my handkerchief, wrapped it round her wrist. It's got my initial on it, G . . . Then I paid her, drove her back to Ladbroke Grove station. When I dropped her off, the last I saw of her she was picking up another punter. It was a red car, I'm not sure which make, could have been a Scirocco. I didn't kill her, I swear before God that was the last I saw of her. Then I drove home, got back about half-past ten, maybe nearer eleven . . .'

Tennison had been reading his statement as he talked. It was not word for word, but slightly abbreviated, as if he was getting used to repeating only the pertinent facts. 'You saw a red car stop. Was it facing towards you or in the opposite direction?'

'Oh, it was coming towards me. I was going down Ladbroke Grove towards Notting Hill Gate.'

'So you would have dropped her on the pavement opposite the car? Or did you swerve across the road and deposit her on the other side?'

'Oh, I crossed the road. Then when she got out I drove straight down to the Bayswater Road.'

'You live on the Maida Vale/Kilburn border, wouldn't you have gone the other way? It's a quicker route, isn't it?'

'I suppose so. I never thought about it, really. I went straight along to Marble Arch, into Edgware Road and straight to Kilburn to get a video.'

'Have you picked up girls in that area before?'

Marlow shook his head and looked down at his hands. 'No, and I wish to God I hadn't picked this one up either, but . . .'

'But?'

He looked up, and again she was caught by the strange colour of his eyes. 'She was very attractive, and I thought, why not . . .'

'George, had you picked this particular girl up before?'

'No, and I must have been crazy, after what happened up north. But I paid for that. I was drunk, and I swear to you she came on to me, I swear I was innocent . . . I served eighteen months, and when they released me I swore I wouldn't mess around with other women.'

'Mess around? It was a little more than that two years ago, wasn't it? You were also charged with aggravated burglary.'

'Like I said, I was drunk. I just snatched her handbag . . . It was a stupid thing to do, and I lived to regret it.'

'So you never knew this girl you picked up?'

There was a tap on the door and Sergeant Otley peered through the window. Irritated, Tennison went out to talk to him.

'The lab came through, that speck of blood on his

jacket, it's the victim's. Thought you'd like to know. Oh, and the Super wants to see you.'

'That's it? Nothing else? They can't place him in the bedsit?'

Otley shook his head. Tennison said, very softly, 'Not enough . . .'

She turned and went back into the room, leaving Otley cursing to himself.

'How much more does she need, for Chrissake . . .'

Tennison spent another three-quarters of an hour with Marlow. At the end of that time she stacked her files and notebooks and thanked him for his co-operation. Seemingly intent on putting her things away, she asked, as if it was an afterthought, 'You drove home, Mr Marlow? Is that correct?'

'Yes.'

'Do you have a garage? Did you put the car in a garage?'

'No, I left it outside my flat. There's a parking bay, under cover, for residents. They say they can't find it, has it been stolen, do you think? Only, I should get on to my insurance broker if it's true.'

Without replying, Tennison turned to walk out. He stopped her.

'Excuse me, am I allowed to leave yet?'

'No, I'm sorry, Mr Marlow, you are not.'

Tennison was exhausted, but she hadn't finished yet by a long chalk.

Burkin had been falling asleep. He snapped to attention when Tennison knocked to be let out.

'Marlow can go back to his cell. Then I need a search warrant for his flat. We'll go together,' she told him.

'Right, ma'am . . . I'll get the warrant.'

'Meet me in the Incident Room ASAP.' Tennison went down the corridor almost at a run.

For once the Incident Room was fairly quiet. Otley was sitting staring into space when Burkin joined him.

'She interviewed Marlow, then she went to see the Super.'

Otley smirked. 'An' she'll be interviewing all afternoon, I got girls comin' in from all over town. Keep her out of our hair!'

He fell silent as Tennison walked in with a big, sandy-haired man and introduced him as DI Tony Muddyman. 'Tony will be with us as from tomorrow. I've given him the gist of the case, but you'll have to help fill in the details.'

Otley had met him before and wasn't too sure about him, but several of the others greeted him like a long-lost cousin.

'Anything on Marlow's car?' Tennison asked Otley.

'No, not yet. There's a roomful of girls waiting for you.'

'What?'

'All known associates of Della Mornay. You asked for them to be reinterviewed and they're comin' in by the car-load. There were seventeen at the last count . . .'

'I haven't got time to interview them! Why don't you take their statements and leave them on my desk?'

To cover his fury, Otley crossed the room to the notice-board and pinned up a large poster. It advertised a benefit night for DCI Shefford's family.

'Is this the list of girls reported missing?' Tennison had picked up a sheet of paper from his desk.

'Yeah, it's got "Missing Persons Report" on the top hasn't it?'

'Cut it out, Sergeant.'

'One in Cornwall Gardens, another in Brighton, one in Surrey looks promising . . .'

'Fine, I'll take them, shall I?'

'Why not, I've got seventeen slags to interview.'

'Should have staggered them!' Tennison retorted. She beckoned Jones to her side. 'Can you check if there's a handkerchief among Marlow's things. He said he bandaged the victim's hand with it, initial G on the corner.'

She reached for the phone as it rang. 'Tennison . . .' Peter was calling her; she gave a quick look around the room. Only Jones was close by, thumbing through the log book and shaking his head.

'OK, put him through.'

She turned to face the wall while she spoke, unaware that Otley was mimicking her behind her back, to the amusement of the men.

'I'm sorry, I can't really talk now, is it important?'

Burkin was waiting for her at the door. Otley strolled over to him.

'What's goin' on, are we chargin' Marlow?'

'You're joking ...' Over Otley's head, Burkin called, 'Ma'am, we've got the search warrant!'

'What's this for?' asked Otley.

'Marlow's flat, now we're looking for a handkerchief,' replied Burkin contemptuously.

With a promise to call Peter later, Tennison put the phone down and joined Burkin. As they left, Otley was at it again.

'Yeah, a bloody handkerchief, for that snot-nosed cow! Doesn't she know we've only got ten hours before that bastard has to be released?'

As Tennison and Burkin mounted the steps towards flat 22, the curtains of number 21 twitched.

Burkin knocked on the door. They waited a considerable time before they heard a lock turn and the door was flung wide open.

Moyra Henson glared at them, then looked to Tennison, who was sizing her up fast. It was the first time she'd seen Marlow's common-law wife. She knew Moyra was thirty-eight years old, but she looked older. Her face had a coarse toughness, yet she was exceptionally well made-up. Her hair looked as if she'd just walked out of the salon, and her heavy perfume, 'Giorgio', was strong enough to knock a man over at ten yards.

'Yes?' Henson snapped rudely.

'I am Detective Chief Inspector Tennison . . .'

'So what?'

Tennison was noting the good jewellery Moyra was wearing; expensive gold bangles, lots of rings . . . Her nails were long and red. She replied, 'I have a warrant to search these premises. You are Miss Moyra Henson?'

'Yeah. Lemme see it. Your lot shell out these warrants like Smarties, invasion of privacy . . .'

She skimmed through the warrant. Tennison clocked her skirt, the high heels and fluffy angora sweater with the tiger motif. Miss Henson might come on as a sophisticated woman, but she was a poorer, taller version of Joan Collins, whom she obviously admired judging by the shoulder pads beneath the sweater.

'I would like to ask you a few questions while Detective Inspector Burkin takes a look around.'

Moyra stepped back, looking past Tennison to the broad-shouldered Burkin. 'I dunno why he doesn't move in, he spends enough time here.'

Tennison was growing impatient. 'Could we please come in?'

Moyra turned with a shrug and walked along the narrow hall. 'I don't have much option, do I? Shut the door after you.'

The flat was well decorated and exceptionally clean and tidy. The cosy sitting-room contained a three-piece suite which matched the curtains and a fitted carpet.

Tennison looked around. 'This is very nice!'

'What d'you expect, a dump? George works hard, he earns good money. Found his car yet, have you? It's down to you lot, you know. This estate stinks, somebody must have seen him being taken away and nicked it.'

'I'm sorry, I can't give you any information on that. Really, I'm just here to have a chat with you. You see, I'm taking over the investigation. The previous Inspector died, tragically.'

'Good! Less of you bastards the better. Oi, what's he up to? Hey, sonny! You can put that laundry back, that's my dirty knickers! Are you some perverted crotch sniffer?'

'How do you feel about your boyfriend picking up prostitutes?'

'Wonderful, it gives me a friggin' night off!'

'I admire you for standing by him while he was in jail.'

'That bitch asked for it! She was coming on to him, and he'd had too much to drink . . .'

'Was he drunk when he came home on Saturday night?'

'No he was not!'

'And he arrived home at what time?'

'Half-past ten. We watched a video, then we went to bed.'

Tennison took a photograph from her briefcase and laid it on the coffee table, facing Moyra. 'This is the girl he admitted to picking up, admitted having sex with in his car. Now look at her.'

'What am I supposed to do, have hysterics? I feel sorry for the girl, but he only fucked her! Half the bloody government's been caught messing around at some time or other, but their wives have stuck by them. Well, I'm doing the same. Now, if you've finished wrecking my flat, why don't you get out of here?'

'I haven't finished, Moyra. Just one more question; did you know Della Mornay?'

'No, never heard of her.'

'Never?'

'No.'

'And George didn't know her, you're sure of that?'

Moyra folded her arms. 'I have never heard of her.'

Tennison put her notebook into her briefcase. 'Thank you for your time, Miss Henson.'

While she waited for Burkin to finish, Tennison had a good look around the flat. There were no handkerchiefs with the initial 'G' on the corner, either in the bedroom drawers or the laundry basket. Enquiries at the laundry Moyra had told them she used came to nothing.

103

The flat was very much Moyra's and only her things were in evidence; pots of make-up, knick-knacks, magazines. Just one small corner of the dressing-table held a neat, old-fashioned set of bone-handled brushes with George's initials in silver. Moyra, who followed them from room to room, told them they had belonged to his father.

Tennison was struck by the neatness of Marlow's clothes in the wardrobe. They took up only a quarter of the space, the rest of which was crammed with Moyra's things. His suits were all expensive, in tweeds and greys, nothing bright, and the shirts were of good quality.

The small bookcase in the lounge contained paperbacks, mostly by Jackie Collins, Joan Collins and Barbara Taylor Bradford. It was as if Marlow didn't really live there. Tennison looked again; there were a few thrillers that were more likely to be his, such as James Elroy and Thomas Harris, plus a hardback edition of *Bonfire of the Vanities* that she guessed belonged to him.

Finding nothing of interest, Tennison and Burkin left to start checking on the missing girls. They headed for Cornwall Gardens to question a Mrs Florence Williams.

Sergeant Otley had a feeling this was a good one, which was why he and Jones were there instead of Tennison. The report had only been in a few hours, but the description matched their victim.

The basement area of the flat in Queen's Gate,

Kensington, looked as if a cat-fight had taken place in the dustbins, spewing rubbish among the broken furniture and bicycles that cluttered the approach to the door.

Otley peered through the filthy window. 'Are you sure this is the right address, Daffy?'

'Yeah. Knock on the door, then.'

'Christ, place looks like a dossers' pad, you seen in here?'

Jones shaded his eyes and squinted through the iron grille over the sash window. 'I thought this was a high-class area?' he muttered.

'It is,' snapped Otley. 'And shut your mouth, someone's coming.'

The door was opened by a tall, exceptionally pretty girl with blonde hair hanging in a silky sheet to her waist. She was wearing pink suede boots, a tiny leather mini-skirt and a skimpy vest.

'Yes?'

'I am Detective Sergeant Otley, this is Detective Constable Jones. You made a missing persons report?'

'Oh, yeah, you'd better come in. It might all be a dreadful mistake, you never really know with Karen, it's just odd that Michael hasn't seen her either . . .'

Otley and Jones exchanged glances as they followed the leggy creature into the dark, shambolic hallway.

'Trudi! Miffy! There are two policemen . . .'

The blonde turned to them and pointed to an open

door. 'If you want to go in there, I'll get them. They're in the bathroom.'

The room contained a large, unmade double bed with two cats fast asleep in the middle of the grubby sheets. The furniture was a mix of good antiques and fifties junk, but the room was as much a mess as the rest of the flat. On the fireplace wall a large, moth-eaten stag's head hung at a precarious angle, with door-knockers hanging from its antlers.

'Do you want coffee or tea?' The blonde hovered in the doorway.

'Cup of tea would be nice, thank you.'

'Indian, China or herbal?'

'Oh, just your straight, ordinary tea, love, thanks.'

Jones perched on a wicker chair until he noticed one of the legs was broken and it was propped on a stack of books. He moved a heap of clothes from a winged arm-chair and sat down.

Otley whispered, 'What a bloody dump! Place looks as if it's not been cleaned in years.'

Jones flipped open his notebook. 'The girl that came in to the station is Lady Antonia Sellingham . . . So if Trudi's in the bathroom with Miffi, unless that's another cat, the blonde's a titled aristo. Typical, isn't it?'

Cornwall Gardens was a total waste of time. Edie Williams, reported missing by her mother, Florence, was a thirty-five-year-old mental deficient with a passion for watching trains at Euston Station. She had returned home that morning.

Otley sipped from the cracked mug of terrible-tasting tea, prompting the three girls to remember exactly when they had last seen their flat-mate, Karen. It was quite normal for her to spend several days at a time with her boyfriend, Michael Hardy, but he had been away, skiing. Antonia at last decided she had not seen Karen since Friday – no, Saturday.

'Do you have a photograph of her?'

'Oh, yes, lots. There's her modelling portfolio, would you like to see that?'

Miffy, a short, plump girl with a wonderful, chortling laugh, bounced out of the room. Lady Antonia asked if the police were worried that something had happened to Karen. Otley didn't reply but made a note of Karen's boyfriend's name and phone number. He glanced at Jones, whose eyes constantly wandered back to Antonia's legs.

The doorbell rang and Antonia strolled out, pausing to ask if anyone would care for more tea. None of them showed fear for Karen; they did not really believe that anything could have happened to her, it was just a bit odd that no one had seen her around.

Miffy returned and shrugged her shoulders. 'Can't find it, but we have got some photos of when we were in

St Moritz, they'd be the most recent. I'll see if I can find them.'

She went off again in search of them as the leggy Antonia returned with a large cardboard box. 'It's my new pet, a chinchilla. Would you like to see it? It's just adorable . . .'

Before Jones could take up the opportunity to get closer to Antonia, Miffy came back with a large, expensive-looking album. She flipped through the pages, then stopped.

'Oh, here's a goodie, this is Karen.'

Otley took the book, stared at the photograph, then silently passed it to Jones. The atmosphere in the room changed in an instant; the girls picked up on the glance between the two officers. Suddenly they were afraid.

'Is something wrong?' Has something happened?'

Otley sighed and passed Jones his notebook, in which he had jotted down Michael Hardy's details. 'Could DC Jones use your telephone? And I suggest you get your coats, ladies. We'll need you to accompany us to the station.'

The girls left the room. Jones hovered. 'Er . . . Who do I call, Skipper?'

Otley gave him an impatient stare. 'You call the boyfriend, and we pick him up on our way back to the station.'

'Oh, right! His number's in the book, is it?'

'In the book in your friggin' hand, you fruit!'

*

The house in Brighton was a late Victorian building with a fish and chip shop on the ground floor. Elaine Shawcross, daughter of the proprietors of the shop, had been missing for ten weeks. Her parents were upstairs in their flat; while Tennison went to see them, Burkin ordered fish and chips for them both.

As he carried them back to the car he was surprised to see Tennison leaving the house. She climbed into the car and slammed the door.

'I've salted and peppered them, ma'am, did you want vinegar?'

'Yeah, I'd like to smother that Otley's head in it, might make his hair grow. Either Detective Sergeant Otley needs his friggin' head seeing to, or he's deliberately sending me on a wild goose chase. Give us me chips, then!' She crammed chips in her mouth and continued, 'He's pissed off with me because he's back at the station interviewing hundreds of toms! Ha, ha, ha!'

As they drove back towards London, Tennison stared out of the window. 'That snide bugger Otley did it on purpose! Sending us all the way down here, he's just stirring it at every opportunity.'

Burkin did not respond, and she gave him a sidelong look. 'So, Frank, what do you think of Marlow?'

'I'm sorry, ma'am?'

'I said, what do you think of the prime suspect? George Marlow?'

Burkin shrugged. He stopped the car at a red light and she could almost see the brain cells working as he chewed his lips.

'Well, spit it out! You do have some personal thought on the matter, don't you?'

'Yes, ma'am.'

'So, tell me . . .'

'Well, I think he did it. There's something about him, I don't know what, maybe just intuition. But I think he's our man.'

She lit a cigarette and Burkin opened his window. She felt the cold blast of wind, inhaled deeply and wound her own window down. Burkin promptly closed the one on his side.

Tennison gave him a sidelong look. 'Draught too much for you, is it?'

'No, ma'am, just thought it might be too much for you!'

She stared out of the window, talking more to herself than to him.

'You know, being a woman in my position is tough going. I mean, I have intuition, but it's probably very different from yours. As a man, you feel that Marlow did it. Are you saying that your intuition tells you that Marlow is a perverted sexual maniac? Because this girl was tortured, strung up, beaten and raped . . . And you just *feel* it's George Marlow?'

'It's more than that, ma'am. I mean, he had sex with her.'

'So? That doesn't make him the killer. You've got to find the gaps, the hidden areas. His common-law wife is his alibi; she stood by him before, when he was convicted of a serious sex assault. He snatched the woman's handbag, knocked her about a bit, then he freely allowed them to take samples for DNA testing to see if they could find anything else against him. They didn't, so it was his first offence. His girlfriend must have gone through hell over that. No matter how hard-faced she seems, she's still a woman! She was betrayed by him, but they both used the excuse of drink. He had been drinking, and a lot of men do things when drunk that they'd never consider doing when sober, right? But our killer is a cold-blooded, calculating man. He scrubs his victim's hands . . .'

'Well, I agree with what you're sayin', ma'am, but there is something about him . . .'

'You can't bloody charge a man because there's something about him! You can only do that with evidence, proof, and we have not got enough proof to hold George Marlow.'

The radio crackled and Tennison went to answer it, saying, 'Maybe this will be it, fingers crossed!'

Control patched through a call from Forensic. It was Willy Chang, though Tennison could hardly tell. His voice was breaking up over the air.

'Inspector? We've *crackle* the carpet, every inch of

crackle, crackle ... have nothing. There's not one shred of evidence to prove your man was ever there. We'll keep at it, but I'm not hopeful.'

Tennison leaned back in her seat. 'Well, that confirms it. As I was saying, we have nothing, not a hair, a fragment of material, to put Marlow in that bedsit. She was covered in blood, but we've got not so much as a pinhead on a pair of his shoes ... How did he get her in there and walk away without so much as a single stain?'

'But there was one, ma'am, on his sleeve.'

'Ah, yes, but he has a plausible explanation for that. The only thing that might possibly finger him is his car. If he killed her in his car he has to have left something ... And by the by, Burkin, would you stop calling me "ma'am", makes me feel like a ruddy queen. I like "boss" or "guv'nor", take your pick. Kingston Hill coming up on the right ...'

Otley led the three bewildered girls and the handsome, tanned young man to the canteen, pushing the door open to allow them to pass in front of him. Michael Hardy paused politely, and Otley waved him on, taking a good look at the boy's high-heeled cowboy boots and heavily studded biker's jacket. But it was the ponytail that got him; his eyes gleamed.

'Take the ladies to a table, sir, at the far end out of everybody's way, and I'll arrange some refreshments.' He watched, shaking his head, as the four of them seated themselves, then turned to the counter.

The two canteen workers were about to haul the shutter down, but he scuttled over. 'Hang about, Rose! I want four coffees for this lot, on the house. I'll get you a docket later.'

The other woman walked off in a huff, not even attempting to serve him. The charming Rose muttered to herself as she turned to the steaming urn and drew four cups of pale brown liquid, banged them on the counter. Otley loaded them onto a tray. 'Thanks, darlin'!'

He plonked the tray on the table, slopping the contents of the cups, and told them they would have to wait for Inspector Tennison to return. Then with a brief apology he wandered off.

He passed Maureen Havers, who had stopped to chat to DC Lillie.

'Have you heard, they're bringing in Hicock to replace her?'

Otley's ears flapped. 'What was that? Hicock?'

'Yeah, I got it from the Super's secretary.'

Otley nearly danced for joy. 'Great! Now we need a get-together, get a report done . . .'

DI Muddyman joined them. 'What am I missing?'

'Word's out that they're bringing in Hicock, Tennison's gonna get the big E . . .' Otley beamed. 'We better give them a little assistance, I'll get a vote of no confidence going. That'll teach the pushy bitch.'

He was almost rubbing his hands in glee as he headed out of the canteen. DC Lillie was more interested in the group of girls in the corner. He nudged Jones.

'Eh, I thought all the toms were downstairs? I wouldn't mind interviewing that lot. Who's the puff with the pony-tail?'

Jones prodded Lillie in the chest. 'They're the victim's flatmates, you prat!'

'What, you got an ID on her?'

'Not official, we gotta wait for the Queen Mother! Skipper's sortin' it out, sent her off to Brighton.'

The men laughed amongst themselves, while Karen's four friends waited and waited for someone to tell them why they had been brought in, tell them anything at all. Officers came and went, but no one approached them. Michael was growing impatient, but he realized the long wait meant something terrible had happened. No one answered his questions, no one would tell him if Karen had been found.

'Was it Coombe Lane, ma'am?'

'Yep, should be off to the left ... Yes, this is it. Oh, yeah, very posh.'

Tennison licked her fingers, then sniffed them. They smelt of fish and chips. She took a perfume atomizer from her bag and sprayed herself quickly.

They cruised slowly along Coombe Lane and stopped

at a barred gate with a sign, 'The Grange'. Tennison hopped out to open it. The tyres crunched on the gravel drive and they both looked around, impressed.

The Tudor-style house, all beams and trailing ivy, stood well back from the road. There was a golf course behind.

'Obviously loaded, and no doubt Otley has sent us on another wild goose chase,' commented Tennison. 'OK, we both go in – and straighten your tie, Burkin!'

Large stone eagles and huge urns of flowers and ivy flanked the heavy oak door. There was an old-fashioned bell-push and, next to it, a modern plastic bell.

The deep bellow of a large dog was the first response to Tennison's ring. She stepped back and waited, hearing footsteps on a stone-flagged floor. Then the door was opened wide.

'Major Howard? I am Detective Chief Inspector Tennison and this is Detective Inspector Burkin. Do you think we could ask you a few questions?'

With a slight frown he replied, 'Yes, of course. Do come in.'

They followed the major through the echoing hall into a vast drawing-room with french windows overlooking a rolling, immaculate lawn. There were oil paintings and ornate statues in abundance, elegant sofas and chairs covered in rose silks. Even Tennison could tell that the thick, sculptured Chinese carpet was worth several years' salary. The whole place smelt of money.

A little over-awed, Tennison watched the major closely as he apologized for his shirt-sleeves and put his jacket on over his dark green cords and checked shirt. Tall and well-built, he had obviously been a very handsome man in his youth. Now, with iron-grey hair and a back straight as a die, he still exuded the sort of easy charm that comes with total confidence.

He turned to DI Burkin. 'Sit down, Inspector. Now, what can I do for you? Is there something wrong?'

Tennison stepped forward. 'Thank you, sir, I'll stand. I am Detective Chief Inspector Tennison. I hope we will not take up too much of your time, but we are enquiring about your daughter. She has been reported missing?'

The major looked surprised. 'By whom?'

Tennison was annoyed at herself for having to check her notebook. 'A young man by the name of Michael Hardy. He gave this address.'

The major frowned. 'Well, I hope this isn't some practical joke, that's her boyfriend. My daughter Karen doesn't actually live with us, she shares a flat with some girls in Kensington. I'd better call my wife, see if she can get to the bottom of this. Reported missing? Are you sure? I haven't heard the first thing about it. To be honest, I thought it was about Karen's car. She got a new Mini for her birthday and her parking tickets are always being sent here. We've had some fair old arguments about that. But please, I won't be a moment, excuse me.'

As soon as he was out of the room, Tennison walked across to the grand piano on which stood a number of family photographs. One, in a particularly large frame, showed a girl holding the reins of a pony and smiling into camera. She would be about ten years old. The next photograph was of a family Christmas, with everyone in paper hats roaring with laughter. Tennison's heart started thumping and she moved along to the photo that had caught her eye.

The beautiful, sweet young face, the wondrous hair . . . She was the epitome of youth and health, a smiling, vibrant, free-spirited girl. Tennison turned slowly towards Burkin.

'We've found her . . .'

Mrs Felicity Howard handed Tennison two large, professional photographs of her daughter, taken in the past year. They confirmed Tennison's suspicion. The major, knowing without being told that something was dreadfully wrong, moved to his wife's side and held her gently.

Quietly, Tennison said, 'I'm sorry to have to tell you that I believe your daughter may be dead. It will be necessary for one of you to come with us to identify the body.'

The major sat without speaking throughout the journey. He sat stiffly, staring straight ahead. Tennison did not attempt to make conversation; when she had radioed in to say that she was bringing Major Howard to identify the victim, she lapsed into silence.

Otley, Jones and Muddyman spent the rest of the afternoon interviewing prostitutes and call girls for the second time. They were all unhelpful, uncooperative, and one or two even had the cheek to complain about loss of earnings.

None seemed able to recall when they had last seen Della Mornay. It seemed that she was reasonably well-liked, but no one admitted to mixing with her when not on the streets.

The story was the same from the pimps and the patrons of the clubs and cafés frequented by Della Mornay. By late afternoon there was no evidence of any recent sighting of Della; it appeared that no one had seen her for weeks. At last, one very young girl volunteered the information that a friend of Della's, known only as Ginger, had contracted Aids and returned to Manchester. Perhaps Della had gone to visit her.

A few girls hinted that Della had the odd S & M client, but when asked for names their faces went blank; the reaction was the same when Otley enquired if anyone else had ever been picked up by any of Della's special clients. No one was interested.

Otley was gasping for a cup of tea, or something

stronger, but the canteen was closed. He jerked a thumb at Muddyman and winked. Muddyman followed him out.

'Let's take a little break. We can use the office, she won't be back yet.'

Two of the tarts he had interviewed passed him on their way out. They waved; he gave them the finger.

'You know,' he said viciously, 'when you start talkin' to them all it makes my skin creep. They're like an alien species, opening their legs for any bastard that'll pay up. I'd like to get a water cannon, wash the lot of them off the streets.'

Muddyman shrugged. 'Well, if the Johns weren't there they wouldn't be on the streets in the first place. Hose them and you've gotta hose the guys doin' the kerb-crawling after their skinny, dirty little cunts.'

Otley opened the office door carefully and looked around; it was empty. He closed the door softly behind them.

Tucked at the back of one of his desk drawers was a half-bottle of whisky. He unscrewed the cap and offered it to Muddyman.

'Fuckin' toms, I tell you, we had this Marlow done up, we'd have sent him down if it wasn't for that bitch Tennison. Now we got to crawl through the gutters, makes me puke.'

'Maybe the one we found wasn't a tom?'

'Bullshit! She was in Mornay's flat, why else was she there, you tell me that? Don't give me any crap because she was wearing designer knickers, I've had girls come in dripping with mink, wearing high-class gear, but they're all the same, open the legs, drop in yer money!'

Muddyman thought it best to keep quiet as Otley was really sounding off. His face was twisted with anger and pent-up frustration.

'My wife, the most decent woman you could ever wish to meet, never done a bad thing in all her life, died of cancer, screamin' in agony. She was goodness itself, and she was a bag of bones. These slags, tartin' around, passing on filthy diseases . . . Why my wife? That's what I ask myself over and over, why does a decent woman die like that and they get away with it?'

Wisely, Muddyman decided there was no answer to that. Instead, he enquired for the third time what they were going to do about the three girls and Michael Hardy.

'What d'you think, we keep them here until ma'am comes back. I get their statements, I can't whip 'em over to the morgue, she's got a family . . . We wait, but it'll be worth it, because it's all going down on my report sheet!'

'The canteen's closed, Skipper, they're in one of the interview rooms – not the one with the tarts. They've been here for hours, an' I think Lillie's taken a fancy to the tall blonde one!'

Muddyman was referring to the youngest member of

the team, DC Lillie, nicknamed Flower. He took the brunt of their wisecracks when Jones wasn't around.

Otley sucked in his breath and prodded Muddyman's chest. 'I'm doin' the report, an' I know how long they've been here, OK? When the canteen reopens we'll wheel 'em back up, an' you tell Lillie no chattin' up the blonde Puss in Boots, savvy?'

Muddyman bristled. Sometimes Otley got right under his skin, seeming to forget who was the senior officer. But he replied, 'I savvy, Sarge!'

In the mortuary, the wait for the body to be brought out seemed interminable, yet it was no more than a few minutes. The major stood in the small waiting room, tense and unspeaking.

After putting out a DO NOT DISTURB sign, Felix Norman opened the door of the waiting room and gestured to Tennison that everything was ready. He held the door open as Tennison led the major out, followed by Burkin. They formed a small group around the open drawer where Karen lay covered with a green sheet. Tennison looked at the major.

'Are you ready?'

He nodded. His hands were clenched at his sides as the sheet was drawn back.

'Major Howard, is this your daughter, Karen Julia Howard?'

121

He stared as if transfixed, unable to raise his eyes. He did not attempt to touch the body. Tennison waited.

After a long, terrible pause, the major wrenched his eyes from the body.

'Yes, this is my daughter,' he whispered.

His work forgotten, Otley was still holding forth to Muddyman. The only way to get rid of Tennison, who he instinctively associated with the tarts, was a vote of no confidence. He had spread the word to any who would listen, and was sure the team would back him. Suddenly, he remembered that he had intended to see the Super to tell him they thought the victim had been identified.

Tennison had many questions she needed to ask the major, but before she could phrase the first one, he said bluntly, without looking at her, 'How did my daughter die? I want to know the facts. I want to know how long she has been dead, and why I have not been contacted before this. I want to know when I can have my daughter's body, to give her a decent funeral . . . And I want to know who is in charge of this investigation . . .'

Tennison interrupted. 'I am in charge of the investigation, sir.'

He stared at her, then looked at Burkin. 'I am a personal friend of Commander Trayner, I must insist on speaking to him. I do not . . . I will not have a woman on this case, is that clear? I want to speak to the Commander ...'

Tennison sighed. 'I am in charge of this investigation, sir. If there is anything you wish to discuss with me, please feel free to do so. I assure you we will release your daughter's body as soon as it is feasible. The only problem is if you want to have her cremated ...'

'Cremated? Good God, no, a Christian burial is what I want for my daughter ...'

'Then the delay should be minimal, Major. I'll see to it personally,' Tennison promised. 'I think perhaps the questions I need to ask you can wait until you have had a chance to recover. I will arrange for a car to take you home ...'

'I want to speak to Commander Trayner. If I didn't make myself clear in the first place, woman, then let me repeat to you, I refuse ... I will not have ... I will not have a female in charge of this case.'

Tennison was about to reply when Burkin caught her eye. He gripped her elbow and whispered, 'Leave the room, let him cry, leave him ...'

She allowed herself to be steered from the room. She stood in the corridor, angry at first, then looked through the small glass panel in the door. She could see the major; he slammed his fist into the top of the bare table.

'I have many friends, I know many people who could take over this investigation ...' Then he disintegrated like a helpless child, his body sagged and he held out his arms, in desperate need of comfort from anyone, a stranger, even the Detective Inspector . . .

Gently, Burkin held the heartbroken man as he sobbed his daughter's name over and over.

Tennison felt inadequate and ashamed of herself for being so eager to question the major. In his grief and rage he had turned to the young Inspector, not to her. For a long time he wept in Burkin's arms.

Listening to him, Tennison was flooded with sympathy.

Eventually the door opened and Burkin emerged.

'He's ready to go home now. I'm sorry, ma'am, if I was rude, but I could see the old boy was . . .'

'You were quite right, Frank. Don't worry about it.'

He started back into the room, then paused and turned. 'Oh, Sergeant Otley wants you at HQ.'

'Did he just call you?'

Burkin evaded her gaze. 'Came in while we were in Brighton. Karen's boyfriend and flatmates have been brought in for questioning. Sorry . . .'

'I see! In future, pass on any information immediately, no matter the circumstances. I'll go there now, you see to the major. Was there anything else?'

Burkin shook his head. She watched him closely as she said, 'Otley stirring it up, is he? Next thing, he'll be going for a vote of no confidence.'

His sudden flush was enough to tell her she'd hit the nail on the head.

Burkin had been greatly moved when the major, with a tremendous effort, had pulled himself together and said he was ready to go home, ready to tell his wife, and that he would be available the next morning to answer any questions. He had even asked Burkin to apologize to Inspector Tennison on his behalf for his rudeness.

As Burkin helped him out to the car the major's back was ramrod straight. He shook the younger man's hand and was gone to break the news to his wife.

Chapter Four

Otley was furious to discover that Tennison had beaten him to it; her report on the identification of the murdered girl was already on Superintendent Kernan's desk. He couldn't think for the life of him how she had managed it.

It was out of order for Otley to come direct to the Chief Super but, knowing how the Sergeant felt, Kernan said nothing. He waited; Otley was still hovering.

'Something else, Bill?'

After a moment's hesitation, Otley blurted out that the men felt that Tennison wasn't sufficiently experienced. 'It's out of control, guv! The big interview room's full of toms bein' questioned for the third time, and not one's seen hide nor hair of Della Mornay. The Incident Room's full of blokes sitting around waiting for her . . .'

'Is this a consensus?'

'We all feel it, guv. She's just not right, she's not handling the men at all well. She's smug, she doesn't fit in, we all feel it. We've only got a few hours left, and the way she's going we'll have to let him go!'

Kernan pursed his lips and nodded a fraction. 'It's not entirely up to her, the situation's under constant review. Leave it with me, Bill, OK?'

Arnold Upcher sorted through some documents, then pushed them across the desk to Chief Superintendent Kernan.

'I thought these might interest you. They're cases from the last three years where the evidence depended solely on DNA tests. You can see for yourself, in every instance the judge threw the case out. I think my client and I have been most patient; if you have any further incriminating evidence then we'll discuss it, but I am not prepared to let him stay here another night if you cannot substantiate your suspicion of murder. And that's all you're holding him on – suspicion. It's not on; he has a solid alibi, he has been co-operative and totally honest with you. Come on, Superintendent! You've got the wrong man.'

Convinced that the Super was going to take Tennison off the case, Otley watched with a gleam of triumph in his eye as she entered the Incident Room, obviously harassed and sweating, with Burkin at her heels.

'Anything on Marlow's car yet?' she demanded.

Ken Muddyman answered her from the far side of the room. 'Not yet, ma'am, but we've got you a slot on the Shaw Taylor programme!'

'That's a good idea!' She heard Lillie sniggering behind her but ignored him.

'I was joking, ma'am!'

'I'm not! Laugh away, DI Muddyman, but time's almost up and Marlow's lawyer's with the Super now. Get on to the Press Office . . .'

Muddyman couldn't work out if she was kidding or not. Lillie interrupted them.

'Ma'am, Records sent this in, about Moyra Henson. She was picked up for soliciting fifteen years ago. I dunno if it's of any interest, but she's been on the dole for four years.'

'You never know. Stick it on the file.'

Otley chipped in, 'We've got twenty-two statements from the toms, and there's more of 'em upstairs. Nothing worthwhile yet. Plus her boyfriend and flatmates are waiting to be interviewed. What's goin' on, are we gonna charge him?'

It was coming at her too fast; Tennison floundered for a moment.

'I'd better see the girls first. Keep the Super off my back for a while. And I want to see everyone in here when I'm finished.' She looked around the room to see who was there. 'Ken, you'd better organize a WPC for the girls . . .'

Otley perched on the edge of his desk, watching with delight while she tried to cope, and failed.

'There was something else . . .' Tennison continued. 'Oh, the identification. Her name's Karen Julia Howard.'

'We know,' said Otley.

'Oh . . . yes, of course you do. Right, I'm off.'

Following her, Ken Muddyman minced from the room, camping it up and blowing Otley a kiss as he went. The hoot of laughter could be heard all the way down the corridor.

The three girls' vagueness about Karen was infuriating; Tennison terminated the session after half an hour. By that time she knew that Karen had often spent days, even weeks, at her boyfriend's flat, but the couple had recently had a disagreement and had not seen much of each other since. When Karen had not returned for a couple of nights they presumed she had made it up with him.

On the other hand, Miffy conjectured, Michael obviously didn't make contact because he thought Karen didn't want to see him, but eventually he had called round. Discovering that no one had seen Karen, and she wasn't with her parents or any other friends, Antonia had reported her missing.

The last time the girls had seen Karen she had driven

off in her white Mini to Ladbroke Grove for a modelling job. It was a knitwear advert, she had told them. She had taken her large portfolio and her Filofax. Perhaps Karen's agent would know the name of the firm.

The girls constantly looked at each other as if to confirm every detail. A couple of times they broke into tears; Tennison was patient with them but she kept pushing for the information she needed.

'Was there any mention of a new man in her life?'

They could think of no one. Miffy, her eyes red from crying, believed that Karen had loved Michael more than she pretended, but got fed up because he was a bit possessive.

'So they used to argue about it, did they?'

'Just sometimes. You know, she wanted to let her hair down a bit, but they had been going out together for years . . .'

'Did she drink a lot?'

'Oh, no! She didn't drink at all, or smoke. She was a fitness freak, always dieting, and her room at the flat was a no-smoking zone.'

Tennison stubbed out her fifth cigarette of the session, not that she was counting. 'What about drugs?'

They shook their heads in unison, Tennison thought a little too eagerly.

'You mean never? Not just a little grass or speed?'

Lady Antonia twisted her hands in her lap. 'Karen

didn't like drugs, hated any of us having stuff in the flat. She wouldn't touch anything like that.'

'Not even coke? Did she use cocaine?'

'No, honestly. We've known each other for years, since school, and she got quite uptight about that sort of thing.'

Tennison sighed. 'OK, so what about Michael, she was a virgin as well, I suppose?'

Lady Antonia crossed her long legs and fiddled with the top of her boot. 'That was her business, I have no idea what she did in private.'

'Now it's my business, love. Karen was found in a prostitute's room, and I have to find out how she got there. Come on, what do you take me for? Are you trying to tell me that four girls, living in the same flat, never even mentioned sex?'

Lady Antonia pursed her lips. 'I don't think you have any right to ask us that sort of question.'

Tennison was getting more irritated by the second. 'I have every right, as I said before. Anyway, that's it for now, but I might need to talk to you all again before you leave. This officer will show you the way back to the canteen, go and have some coffee.'

Lady Antonia faced Tennison. 'I am going to complain about the way we have been treated, as if we were criminals. And we don't want to go back to that awful canteen. Please would you call my father, if you need to speak to us we are perfectly willing, but we have been here for . . . we really . . . I would like to go home.'

Tennison never took her eyes off the girl's face. The bravado disappeared fast, and Antonia blinked back the tears. 'Please, let us go home. We've been here for hours.'

Tennison pursed her lips. 'Antonia, isn't it? Yes? Well, all I can do is apologize for keeping you here for so long. You are free to go at any time, but I need to question Michael Hardy. As you all came together, perhaps you'd like to leave together. I'll order you a car. Your girlfriend has been brutally murdered, we are just trying to find out how she came to be in that bedsit . . . OK? And any assistance you can give us, give me, is really appreciated. So have a cup of tea or coffee, anything, just for a while longer . . .'

She watched the round cheeks flush, and the girl blinked rapidly. Her whole face seemed to be moving, trying to say something, but unable to form the words. Then she burst out, 'She was always happy . . .'

Antonia left the room, and Tennison could hear her sobbing outside in the corridor. She felt dirty, her hands were grubby, and she sniffed her armpits then made a quick exit for the locker room. Next was Karen's boyfriend, Michael Hardy, and though she was sure he was innocent he had to be checked out, eliminated completely. To do that she was going to have to be tough.

The cold water felt good as she splashed it on her face. She washed her hands, scrubbed them, then stared into the soapy water. The killer had used a wire brush on the victim's hands, scratched them raw . . .

Michael, obviously distraught, was sitting with his elbows on the table and his head in his hands. His voice was muffled. 'I can't believe she's dead, I can't believe it . . .'

'You said the reason you hadn't seen Karen was because you'd had a row, is that right?' Tennison asked him.

'I agreed not to see so much of her . . .' he stopped, too choked to continue.

'She was murdered, Michael, and we found her in a prostitute's bedsitting room. Now, take a look at this photograph and tell me if you've ever seen this man, ever seen Karen with him. Come on, Michael, look at the photograph.'

He raised his head and stared at the mug shot of George Marlow. 'No, I've never seen him.'

'OK, now what I need to know is when you last saw or spoke to Karen.'

He coughed and ran his hands over his ponytail. 'I, er, I phoned her, the day before I went to Switzerland. The fifth of January.'

'Did you call her from there? While you were away?'

'No . . .'

'And you came back when?'

'I came home on the thirteenth, a week early. There wasn't much snow about.'

Tennison sat slightly straighter in her chair. 'Did you see her when you got back?'

'No. I went round to her flat yesterday. Miffy said Karen wasn't at home, they'd presumed she was with me. Then I called her parents' house. The housekeeper told me Karen hadn't been home since Christmas, so I rang round a few other friends. When I ran out of places to look for her, I went to the local police station and told them.'

'When was that?'

'Er, first thing this morning. I just said no one had seen her lately.'

'Ah, so we got two separate reports . . . Now, Michael, her car, the Mini. Have you any idea where it might be?'

'No . . .' he thought for a moment. 'It wasn't outside the flat.'

All through the interview, Tennison was aware of a lot of coming and going outside. Faces popped up in the small window, but no one knocked. One of them was the Super, but he waved at her not to bother. She found it all distracting, so it was almost a relief when Michael burst into tears and she was able to pace around the room for a few moments.

Eventually Michael blew his nose in his handkerchief. Tennison sat down again.

'So let's get back to this argument you had with Karen.'

'It wasn't really an argument, it was just . . . just that she decided we were getting too involved, she wanted more time to herself. I agreed, but we didn't argue.'

'But you didn't like it?'

'No, I wanted to marry her. But she was only . . . she . . .' His eyes filled up and he turned away, shrugging his shoulders helplessly as his voice cracked, 'She was only twenty-two years old . . .'

'So, you agreed not to see so much of her. Did you find out if there was someone else?'

'No, she didn't have anyone else.'

'How can you be so sure?'

'Because I know . . . She would have told me if there was something . . . someone else. I'm sorry . . .'

'So you don't think she had other boyfriends?'

'She had a lot of acquaintances, men friends, but most of them I knew. She didn't have anyone else, wasn't seeing anyone else.'

'But you were in Switzerland, maybe she met someone else while you were away?'

He shook his head and looked at the table. Tears trickled down his face and Lillie felt even more sorry for him. The boy kept looking at Lillie as if he could stop Tennison's stream of questions.

'Did you and Karen have a good sexual relationship?'

Michael's voice was a whisper. 'Yes.'

'Did she like anything ... unusual? Was she a bit kinky?'

'No.'

'Do you know if she took drugs?'

'She didn't drink and she didn't take drugs.'

'Do you?'

'Pardon?'

'I asked you if you take drugs, do you use hash or cocaine?'

'I have ... but not recently.'

'Did you score it?'

'How do you mean?'

'Did you buy it for yourself? Go out and score from people?'

'No ... when I say I've used ... I was offered some cocaine once, and grass quite a few times, but I've never bought any. Do you mean do I go out to a dealer?'

'Yes?' He shook his head.

'Michael, are you sure? We found Karen in an area where a lot of drug dealers hang out. You sure she wasn't using anything, or maybe going to get some for you?'

'*No!*'

'Did she pick up men?'

'*No! No* ... Karen would never ... Karen ...'

He started to sob, hunching his shoulders, and Tennison leaned closer.

'Tell me, Michael, come on. If she was scoring for you

136

it would make sense of where we found her, why we found her!'

Michael stood up, shaking with anger and grief, his face red with frustration. '*No!* She was a sweet, innocent girl, and you're making her out to be something dirty, something sick! You disgust me . . .'

'Sit down, Michael, *sit down*! Come on, now. You said that on the night of the thirteenth of January you . . .'

He gritted his teeth. 'I was at my parents' house, I went straight from the airport. We had dinner and I stayed the night. I've told you this, I've told you this three times!'

Tennison closed her notebook. 'Yes, you have, and thank you for being so co-operative. If you'd like to have a wash there's a gents' just along the corridor, and then DC Lillie will take you up to the canteen.'

He was slumped in his chair, silent. He didn't look up. She walked to the door.

'You can go, Michael, and the girls are free to go with you. Thank you . . .'

Tennison leaned back and lit another cigarette as Michael followed Lillie along the corridor, standing aside to allow Superintendent Kernan to pass. The Super stopped at the door of the interview room.

'Anything?'

Tennison shook her head. 'No,' she replied wearily, 'her

car might give us a clue, if we can find it. None of them know where it is.'

'Sergeant Otley reckons you've got enough to charge him.'

She stood up and faced him. 'Detective Sergeant Otley is wrong.'

Kernan shut the door. "What do you want to do?"

She pushed her fingers through her hair. 'We have to release him, we can't hold him any longer. In my opinion we don't have enough to make it stick . . . Let him go!'

At six-fifteen, Chief Superintendent Kernan left the Commander's office and spoke briefly to Tennison. He had agreed to the release of George Marlow.

Reluctantly, Tennison went to the interview room and told the men the bad news.

'We will keep at it until we have the evidence to arrest him and keep hold of him.'

Otley, as tired as everyone else, shouted that it was lunacy, Marlow was guilty. Tennison didn't even attempt to argue, but when Otley stood up in front of everyone, jabbed an aggressive forefinger at her and told her that if Marlow killed again it would be down to her, she snapped, 'That's enough, Sergeant! I've taken a lot of flak from you, but I've had you right up to here! You start acting like bloody cowboys and this is what happens. This investigation has been a cock-up from the word go. If anyone should be yelling and pointing the finger, it should be me! You all fucked up, so now we take it, we eat it, and start again from scratch. I want us on that bastard night and day. We'll get him back and we'll keep him. Now, I don't know about anyone else, but I need some sleep, so let's take a break. Tomorrow we'll reassess everything we've got.'

She packed her briefcase and left. Only a few murmured 'goodnights' marked her departure, but she was too tired to care.

Burkin and Jones remained at their desks, but the atmosphere in the room was thick with fatigue. Everyone was knackered, but above all, they felt defeated. Marlow had beaten them.

Otley sat for a few moments, devastated. He had been so certain that they had Marlow.

When his phone rang it took him a second to recognize the sound. He answered automatically, then sat bolt upright. 'Yeah, I got that! Thanks, mate, I owe you one!' He jumped up and ran from the building.

It was drizzling as Tennison unlocked her car. She chucked her case inside and sat for a moment, trying to raise the energy to drive home.

The rain increased to a downpour as she drove slowly

out of the car park and past the main entrance to the police station. George Marlow stood there with Upcher, waiting for a taxi. A cab pulled up, and as they stepped from the doorway Marlow spotted Tennison. He ran in front of her car, then to her window. Upcher put out a hand as if to stop him, but he ignored it and tapped on the glass.

'Excuse me . . . Excuse me, miss!'

She did not want to face him, but there was no way out of it. She lowered the window.

'I'd just like to say thank you, I really appreciate it. I knew you'd help me.'

She looked once again into those wide, amber eyes. She said nothing, just gave him a stiff nod of her head and raised the window again. She didn't see Otley run out of the station towards her until he shouted to her. Then he saw Marlow stepping into the waiting taxi and stopped dead. He stood in the rain as the taxi did a U-turn and slowly headed back towards him. As it passed he could see Marlow's face pressed against the window, smiling.

Otley tapped on the passenger window of Tennison's car, gestured for her to open the door. He climbed in and shook his head, showering her with water, and wiped his balding head with a crumpled handkerchief.

'Is this important, Sergeant?'

'Yes, ma'am. I just got a call from DS Eastel at Sunningdale. They've found another one, about two hours ago. He's given me the tip because her hands are tied behind her back and she's been stabbed and beaten. He reckons, from our description, that it's Della Mornay.'

By the time Tennison and Odey reached Sunningdale golf course it was after eight. They were directed away from the clubhouse towards a crescent of exclusive houses. There were many cars parked at one end, where a narrow, private gateway led directly onto a small wooded area at the perimeter of the golf course.

A uniformed officer in a shiny black cape dripped water over their identification as he checked it, then sent them towards arc lights which had been placed around a nearby bunker on which the silhouettes of a few men could be seen. As Tennison drew nearer she could see more men sheltering beneath the trees.

Otley strode ahead, his shoulders hunched against the downpour. The ground was a shifting mud bath and Tennison gave up picking her way among the puddles. Her shoes were already sodden. As she reached the group on the bunker she found Otley already deep in conversation with his friend, DS Eastel.

Eastel shook her hand, then turned to a man taking shelter beneath the trees. 'He was walking his dog. The rain must have washed some of the soil away, exposing her arm. The dog made a pretty good job of digging her up. You want to take a look?'

Tennison stared at the dog-owner, who was obviously agog at what was going on. His dog still strained on his lead, barking continuously.

Neither Eastel nor Otley assisted her up the muddy bank and she slithered the last two feet. She clutched Eastel's arm to stop herself falling.

Eastel handed her a long stick. 'Take a look, see if you can make out her features, but keep off the sheeting if you can. They're almost ready to lift her.'

Tennison craned forward and gently lifted the matted hair away from the girl's face. Everyone stopped what they were doing to watch as Tennison peered at the pitiful face of the victim. She crouched down, then knelt on the plastic sheeting for an even closer look. The stench of decomposed flesh made her nostrils burn, but she forced herself to study what she could see of the girl's profile, trying to match it with the photographs of Della Mornay.

Eventually she let the hair fall back into place and accepted help to rise to her feet. She slithered as she tried to climb the bank and Eastel gave her a hand.

'I can't be a hundred per cent sure, but I think you're right. It looks like Della Mornay.'

The body was eased onto the plastic sheeting and lifted onto a stretcher, face downwards. The rain still pelted down as four men carried the stretcher up the bank and passed directly in front of Tennison. She stepped back to let them by, then asked them to wait a moment; she could see the rope that bound the corpse's hands. She turned to Otley.

'Is it the same rope?'

'I don't know, ma'am, but I think if she is our girl we should have her sent to our patch, get Felix Norman on it.'

Tennison nodded. Despite the mud she could see marks on the victim's arms, deep weals that looked similar to those on Karen Howard.

'Yes, get Felix. I'll go back to the station and wait for him to contact me, but I want him out here tonight.'

Otley nodded agreement. He watched as they carried the body away. 'You should never have released Marlow. Any money on it, that bastard did this one as well.'

She bristled. 'I had no option but to release him. If he's guilty, I'll get him back.'

'There's no *if*, you know it, we all know it. Why d'you think my guv'nor was so desperate to book him? He *knew* . . .'

'Like I said, Sergeant, when I've got the evidence we'll make an arrest, and this time we'll go by the book. This time there'll be no cock-ups!'

'Yeah, you do that, love! Go by the book, and if he kills again you can say, "I hadda stick to the rules!" That bastard is guilty, and my guv'nor knew it!'

'If he knew so much why did he foul up the way he did? Don't give me that bullshit! Right now it's the last thing I need. And you tell me, if a male officer of my rank had taken over this team, would you call him "love"?'

'I'm sorry, ma'am, slip of the tongue. But if you blacken my guv'nor's name, you start raking up the dirt on him, then . . .'

'Then what?'

'If you were a man I'd punch that snotty look off your face, I'd do it and wouldn't give a shit about the consequences. Right now I'm off duty . . .'

Tennison wanted to shriek, but she controlled the impulse to land a punch on Otley's sharp nose. She snapped, 'I don't give a damn whether you are off or on duty, Sergeant Otley. If Shefford hadn't been so damned eager to try and beat that bloody stupid Paxman's record, then maybe he wouldn't have fucked up!'

Otley looked at her with loathing. 'There was never any such person as Paxman, ma'am, it was a joke. The guv'nor just made it up to gee the lads up a bit, there was no record. If you'd known him you would have sussed that out! Just as he sussed that George Marlow was our man. He even reckoned Marlow'd done a girl up north . . .'

Tennison turned quickly to face Otley. 'What did you say?'

'The boss reckoned Marlow had done a girl up north, years ago. That's why he wanted him nailed, wanted him banged up. And if he bent a few rules, so fuckin' what?

Because Marlow's gonna kill again . . . and when he does, it's down to you and your fuckin' rules and your precious book.'

She clenched her fists to control her fury. 'You're telling me that Shefford believed Marlow had killed before? And said nothing? Is that what you're saying?'

Otley backed off, shrugged his shoulders. 'I'm not saying anything. I got a lift back with Eastel, I'm on my way . . .'

Tennison followed him. 'If what you say is true, why isn't it in the records? Or in Shefford's memos? Why?'

'As I said, ma'am, it was just supposition. He died before he could take it any further, he died, ma'am, remember? That's how come you're here!'

'I want your report on my desk first thing in the morning. And Otley, I've told you before, if you don't like working for me, then you can put in for a transfer.'

He stared at her and she was taken aback by the loathing in his small, dark eyes. 'You mean like the rest of the lads? Fine, I'll think about it. Good night.'

As he stomped off, Tennison became aware that their conversation had been overheard. She gave Eastel a cursory nod of thanks, then turned back to repeat her thanks to the officers still searching the area. She was very close to the edge of the bunker; she teetered and lost her footing, landed on her backside in the mud. There were sniggers. Two uniformed men jumped to assist her and she gave a grin. It was all she could do under the circumstances.

'Ah, well, they say mud's good for the complexion!'

It was the wrong thing to say and she knew it as soon as it was out. No one laughed; they had all seen the body of the girl, stripped, tortured and covered in the filthy, slimy mud.

Chapter Five

At ten o'clock Peter put a pizza in the oven as it didn't look as though Jane would be home. While he was eating it she phoned to tell him not to wait up as she had to go over to the morgue. She sounded tired and depressed.

'Things bad, are they, love?'

'Yeah, you could say that. We found another girl tonight. I'll tell you all about it in the morning.'

He knew she must be exhausted, she couldn't have slept for more than thirty-six hours, but he couldn't help feeling slightly irritated as he put the phone down. He was having a tough time at work himself; things were going from bad to worse and he needed someone to sound off at. He had tendered for a major building project that would have put him back on his feet financially; had gone in as low as possible, but had been pipped at the post.

He sat down to finish his pizza, which he'd overcooked and was hard as a rock, but he ate it anyway. Then he ploughed through his accounts, getting more depressed by the minute.

He was on the edge of bankruptcy and there seemed no way out. His share of the proceeds from the house had virtually been swallowed up by maintenance payments and business debts. He slammed the books shut and opened a bottle of Scotch.

A few minutes later the phone rang again. It was his ex-wife, asking if Peter could have their son to stay for the weekend now that he was settled. The thought cheered him up; Marianne had never been keen to allow Joey to stay overnight. His few Saturdays with the boy had left him feeling low.

'If he could maybe stay next weekend? Would that be convenient?'

'Yeah, sure! I mean, I'll have to sort it out with Jane, she's very busy at the moment, but I'm sure it'll be OK.'

'How's it going with the new woman in your life, then?'

'Going fine, Marianne.'

'Good. Oh ... Nearer the time for the baby, early days yet, but later on perhaps Joey could stay longer. It'd help me out, and it's good for Joey to get to know you.'

'Marianne ...'

'Yeah?'

'Marianne . . . Look, were you trying to tell me something the other day?'

'When?'

'Come off it! When you told me you were pregnant . . .'

'Oh, that! No . . . why, what's the matter?'

'Nothing,' he replied shortly, 'OK, talk to you soon.' He wanted her off the phone, he wanted to think . . .

'All right, then, bye!'

He put the phone down, absently. He didn't like her saying that he should get to know his own son, but it was more than that. He was trying hard to remember the date, the time he had gone to the house to pick up some of his things. Yes, it must have been about the time he had moved into Jane's . . .

Then it all came back to him; Steve not being there, Marianne a little tipsy . . . He knew it was madness, but when she wrapped herself round him the way she used to, teasing him, there had been no stopping . . . It could be. He knew her so well, that look . . . Or was she just trying to wind him up for some obscure reason? Was she jealous of Jane, angry that he was getting himself together? Could she be that small-minded? He tried to dismiss it, but the thought kept returning.

There were always so many things he should have said, things that should have been said months ago, but he never had. He never mentioned her new husband, who had once been his friend; the pain and humiliation of that betrayal were still too fresh. He found himself wishing that Jane would come home, and wondered how to tell her that his son might be coming to stay, not just for the odd weekend, but perhaps for weeks at a time.

In the Incident Room, Tennison was munching on a sandwich as her tired eyes searched the notice-board. The tickets for Shefford's benefit night were selling well. Her eyes came to rest on Karen Howard's face.

She heard a door bang and jumped, then got up to see if Otley had come back after his drink with Eastel. It might be a good time to attempt to iron out the ill feeling between them and to question him further about the other murder, the one 'up north'. She went through to the room Otley shared with the two DIs, but there was only the night cleaner emptying the wastepaper baskets.

The only thing on Otley's desk was a framed photograph of a rather austere-looking woman standing by a cherry tree, a white Yorkshire terrier at her feet. Tennison wondered if Otley had, as he said, put in for a transfer. She wiped the remains of her sandwich from her fingers and opened the top drawer.

There were a few photos of Shefford and his family, which made her feel guilty for snooping, but she continued. In the third drawer was a familiar file; Della Mornay's

Vice record . . . She knew her copy was on her desk; the cover was almost identical, but a bit more dog-eared and perhaps a shade darker.

As she pulled it out a paper-clip caught onto the sheet beneath it. She took the whole lot out and detached the clip; underneath was a small red 1989 diary with thin cardboard covers. It had been doodled on and covered with cartoon faces, but the remarkable thing about it was the name, ornately decorated in felt-tip pen: Della. She knew there was no record of a diary having been found at Della's bedsit.

Tennison carried her finds back to her own office and flipped through the little book, slowly. It contained mis-spelt notes, appointments for hospital checkups, lists of cash against rent and expenditure. One entry read 'New dress, new shoes, streaks'. There were a number of pages missing throughout the year; they had been roughly torn out, in some cases leaving chunks of paper behind.

Was there also a diary for 1990? Tennison went back and searched Otley's desk again, but found nothing apart from a near-empty whisky bottle.

She left everything as she had found it, apart from the file and diary, collected her copy of the file from her desk and returned to the Incident Room. She laid the two files side by side on the desk and began to compare them, fighting to keep her eyes focusing.

*

The box room felt airless. Tennison tossed and turned, got up to open the window. She had decided to sleep there so as not to wake Peter.

She lay down again, but kept seeing Della Mornay's face and hearing Otley's voice as he told her that Shefford had believed there was another murder ... Going over and over her conversation with Sergeant Otley she dozed off at last.

At five-thirty in the morning Peter shot out of bed. He could smell burning.

He rushed into the kitchen and checked that everything was off, then followed his nose along the hallway. On the radiator near the door was Jane's raincoat; the back was singed, leaving a large, dark brown stain.

He looked into the spare room. The window was wide open and Jane lay sprawled face down, arms spread wide. He felt as if he was intruding and he gently closed the door, afraid to wake her.

At six-thirty Peter brewed coffee. He was due on the building site by seven. He carried a cup into the spare room.

'Jane ... Jane!'

'What ... What? *What?*'

'Hey, it's OK, it's me. Brought you some coffee. There's more in the pot, but I've got to go.'

'Oh, shit, what time is it?'

'Just after six-thirty.'

'Oh, God, I've got to get cracking. I've got to ... I've got ...'

She flopped back on the pillow. 'I am knackered, completely and utterly knackered ...'

'So's your raincoat. You left it on the radiator in the hall and it's singed. I'll have a look at the heating when I get home tonight, shouldn't get that hot.'

'Oh, I turned it up, my coat was sopping wet.'

'Well, it's dry now ... What time will you be home tonight?'

'Oh God, don't ask me.'

'Well, I am. I've hardly seen you for three days. I was thinking you might like to have dinner somewhere.'

It was the last thing she could think of. Still half-asleep, she gulped her coffee and flopped back on the bed.

'Do you think it would be OK if Joey came over, stayed the weekend? Marianne phoned last night ...'

'Yeah, sure. You don't have to ask me, and I promise I'll try and get back by, say, eight? Is that OK?'

He leaned over and kissed her. 'Tell you what, call me when you're awake, then if you know for sure you'll be free I'll book a table at Bianco's, OK?'

'Sounds good to me ...'

Tennison was showered and dressed, her hair washed but not dried, and on her way to the station by seven-thirty.

She thought her raincoat smelt a bit off, but hadn't noticed the dark stain on the back . . .

For once the Incident Room was empty, so Tennison spent some time in her own office, checking the work rota for the day. Then she skimmed through the surveillance report on Marlow. Each shift consisted of four men; two occupied an empty flat opposite Marlow's and the other two a plain car.

The team reported little movement; after work Marlow had visited a video club and then gone straight home, remaining there with Moyra for the rest of the evening. There were one or two photographs of him leaving the flat; Tennison stared at his handsome face and noted again how well dressed he was. There was still no trace of his car, the brown Rover.

It was eight-thirty; the men would start to arrive soon. She fetched herself another mug of coffee and lit her fifth cigarette of the day. At eight-forty-five she gave up waiting and set off for the mortuary.

She was just getting into her car when she saw Jones arrive on his moped. She yelled across the car park, 'About time too, Jones! Come on, we're going to the mortuary!'

Mumbling about having had no breakfast, Jones climbed into her car, still wearing his crash helmet.

*

Felix Norman turned the sheet back carefully. 'She took one hell of a beating, poor little soul. Died about six weeks ago, so we won't get any results on vaginal swabs. Lots of blood, I've sent samples over to the forensic girls. She's got similar wounds to your first victim, made by a long, thin, rounded instrument with a razor-sharp point. All the wounds are clean, and hellish deep. Could be a screwdriver, but it's longer than the weapon used on the other victim.'

Tennison was wearing a mask, but the stench of the body combined with the disinfectant fumes made her sick to her stomach. 'Any hope of getting anything from beneath her nails? You said she put up a struggle?'

'Well, she did that all right, but she had false nails. A couple have snapped clean off, and three are missing altogether. She has deep scratches on her hands, similar to the other one – her hands were scrubbed.'

Tennison nodded. 'And what about the marks on her upper arms, are they the same?'

Norman nodded but, as always until he had made out his report, he would not commit himself. 'They're similar. I've not compared them as yet, so don't quote me. Maybe he strung her up to clean her, I won't know until I've made more tests. He seems to have gone to great lengths to remove any traces of himself.'

He drew the sheet back from the corpse's face, revealing the side Tennison had not seen before. She had to turn away.

'Cheek smashed, jaw dislocated . . .'

'Can you give me any indication of his size? I mean, is he a big man, or . . .'

'I'd say he was medium height, five ten, maybe a little more, but he's very strong. These lower wounds were inflicted with one direct lunge, those to the breasts and shoulders are on an upward slant, which again indicate that she was strung up . . .'

Tennison swallowed, trying to remove the taste of bile from her mouth. 'Off the record, then, and I won't quote you, you think we're looking for the same man?'

Norman chortled. 'Off the record, and I mean that because I've worked my butt off to give you this much, until bloody two o'clock this morning . . . Yeah, I think it might be the same man. But until I've had more time, you mustn't jump the gun. It was a different weapon, longer, but the same shape.'

Tennison patted his arm, then turned to the row of seats by the doors. DC Jones was sitting there, looking very pale. As she watched, he put his head between his knees. Norman suddenly snapped his fingers and dug a hand into his back pocket.

He brought out a screwed-up bundle of notes. 'Eh, Daffy, I've got to give you some money, boyo!'

Jones looked up. 'Don't mind if you do,' he managed to reply.

'For the benefit night, man. What was it, a pony?'

Jones looked completely blank.

'Sorry, forgot you're an ignorant Welsh git! Twenty-five quid, was it?'

Jones nodded, still confused and sick. Norman handed him the cash with a flourish.

Tennison said cheerfully, 'OK, if you're feeling better, DC Jones, you can drive me back to the station.'

'Yes, ma'am. Sorry about this, but I was up half the night. The wife cooked a curry, must have turned my stomach. Sorry!'

She smiled and winked at Norman as she removed her mask. 'You'll call me with anything I can quote? And ... thanks for coming out to Sunningdale. Bye!'

Jones followed Tennison through the main doors into the station, on his way to Forensic, and noticed the stain on her raincoat. It was in a most unfortunate position, as if she'd sat in something nasty. Embarrassed, he would have let it go, but WPC Havers, coming out of the Ladies', spotted it.

'Oh, boss, just a minute ...'

'Whatever you've got, it'll have to wait.'

Havers blushed. 'It's your coat, you've got a terrible stain on the back!'

Tennison pulled her coat round to look. 'Oh, bugger, it singed! I got soaked last night and left it on the radiator. Can you take it and sponge it down, see if you can do anything with it? It's a Jaeger, really expensive ...'

While Havers inspected the coat, Tennison looked at Jones. 'It's in a pretty unfortunate position, wouldn't you say, Jonesey? What did you think it was, menstrual cycle? Or curry tummy?'

He flushed and replied, 'I didn't notice it, ma'am.'

Tennison snorted. 'Oh, yeah, pull the other one! Thanks, Maureen.'

At nine o'clock George Marlow, looking extremely smart, left his flat and made his way to the paint factory he worked for. His shadows kept watch on both entrances to the building.

The main part of the factory with the massive vats for mixing the colours was as big as an aircraft hangar. The narrow lanes between the vats stretched from one end of the building to the other. The offices were ranged along the far side and all the windows looked out over the factory floor.

There were some outrageous stories spread among the workers about some director or other who had been caught giving his secretary a seeing-to on the desk. The embarrassed man discovered, too late, that he had neglected to draw the blinds. The entire factory had viewed the deflowering of the poor woman, Norma Millbank, who was so mortified that everyone had seen her thrashing on the desk-top that she quit her job on the spot. Since then the workers had lived in hope, but the blinds were usually kept lowered. But the offices were known from then on as the 'Fish Tank'.

The office George Marlow used when he was in London was at the far end. He shared it with three other salesmen, one of them a fresh-faced boy called Nicky, who had only been with the firm for sixteen months. A huge chart nearly covered one wall, and the men vied with each other to plot their progress in brilliant colours, like bolts of lightning. The bulletins were a great encouragement and stirred up the competition, not just among the four men in Marlow's office but all the salesmen. Every month there was a bonus for the highest sales, and George Marlow won it as often as not. He was known as the champion.

Marlow prided himself on being number one, and yet he was a very generous man with his contacts. He had trained and helped young Nicky Lennon, giving him introductions and special hints. Nicky was working on his accounts when the word went round that George Marlow had been picked up and charged with murder, and that he was on the factory floor right now!

They all knew that he had been in prison for rape, and that his job had been held open for him. When he had returned to work he had thrown a big champagne party, inviting all of them to ask anything they wanted, to discuss it and get it out in the open. He talked of his trial, the prison, and still he claimed he was innocent.

It had taken him a few months and some obvious ill-feeling and embarrassment before he was again the champion, accepted and fighting to regain the best-salesman sash. Never mind the bonus, it was the sash he wanted, and he won it fair and square the year he returned. He also won the respect of his colleagues, and because he was such a good worker and always ready to give assistance to the others, no one ever mentioned his spot of trouble.

Marlow was a known collector of jokes, he could out-joke the professionals and keep on going. He was the man who knew everyone by name, their wives and their sisters, their troubles. There was always a special joke, and one their mothers could be allowed to hear. The secretaries flirted with him, a few had even dated him, he was so attractive, but Moyra was a strong woman who made it known that he was her man.

The men loved Moyra, because she was as good as Marlow with the wisecracks, and they socialized quite a lot, although Marlow's frequent trips north meant that they had few close friends as a couple. There were occasional dinners and parties at the factory.

When Marlow crossed the factory floor, the cat-calls and shouts that usually filled the cavernous building were ominously missing. Secretaries appeared around the sides of the vats, then vanished. Marlow could see police everywhere he looked, talking to the paint mixers, the sales personnel, the accountants ... He couldn't find a joke inside him even if he tried.

He kept his head down and hurried towards the Fish Tank. He was pink with embarrassment, hearing the whispers following his progress, and he was glad to make it to his office, especially when he found it empty. He peered through the blinds, wondering why they were doing this to him. Echoing footsteps hurried past his window, the distant giggles made him sweat. Was he dreaming it, or were they all watching him, whispering about him?

It was no figment of his imagination. As the morning wore on it grew worse, and no one came to his office. The worst moment was when he spotted young Nicky, who stared at him with unabashed distaste, so obvious that Marlow thought he was joking. When he approached the boy he turned his back and walked away. Not one person spoke to him or looked him in the face.

He sat in his office and typed out his own resignation, as the group's secretary insisted she was too busy. He licked the envelope and stuck the flap down, then went to see the manager. But Edward Harvey was in a meeting with all the salesmen. Marlow could see them through the window; as he walked in they fell silent. He went straight to Mr Harvey and handed him the envelope.

'It's just a conference about the new paint for European

distribution, George, not your territory, but you can stay if you want.'

At least when Harvey spoke to him he looked him in the eye, even though he was lying. When Marlow walked out they started to talk again, a low hubbub at first, but it grew louder. The blinds were lifted a crack and they watched him, the champion fallen from grace. This time he had fallen too far to be picked up.

Marlow hurried among the paint vats, then turned towards the offices. He shouted, and his voice echoed around the factory floor.

'I didn't do it, you bastards!'

DC Rosper and WPC Southwood followed Marlow as he hurried from the factory. Southwood suddenly nudged her partner as she saw DI Muddyman waving to them from the main entrance.

'He's just quit his job,' Muddyman said as he came close. 'I was just interviewing that little cracker from their accounts department, and he handed in his notice. Instructions are to keep on him, OK?'

Rosper turned this way and that. Marlow was nowhere to be seen. 'Where the hell is he?'

Southwood pointed. Way up ahead, Marlow was just crossing the main road, heading for the tube station. Rosper and Southwood took off at a run.

*

When Jones returned from booking Della's clothing into Forensic, Otley took him aside. 'Look, my old son, she's tryin' to rake up the dirt on our old guv'nor, so stick with her. You're young an' a good-looking lad; try an' get into her good books. Anything you find out about the old slag, report back into my shell-likes.' He tapped his ear, and continued, 'We're lookin' for anything to needle her, know what I mean? We want her off this case . . .' He clocked Tennison heading towards them and shut up.

Tennison was talking fast. 'She was naked, hands tied behind her back, dead approximately six weeks. Like Karen, she wasn't killed where she was found. You'll get all the info as soon as I do. The rope's not the same type, but the knot is! We're going to have to talk to all those toms all over again!'

The Incident Room door opened and Otley waltzed in, closely followed by the Super. All twelve people in the room turned their heads to look.

Kernan gestured to Tennison to continue, then found a chair at the back of the room.

'Right, what you got, Muddyman?' she asked.

'Marlow's made several visits to Chester Paints, the last one this morning while I was there. He's just quit his job.'

'What was he doing in the first week of December? Was he in the London area?'

'Yes, it's a pretty slack period in the paint trade, he didn't go on the road again until . . .' He flicked through his notes, but Tennison was off on another track.

'So we've established that Marlow was in London for both murders. Is there anything on his car yet? No? What about his neighbours?'

'My lads have questioned most of the ones in the block. He seems to be pretty well-liked, uses the local pub regularly. Several people remembered the car, but couldn't say when they last saw it.'

'You'd better turn your attention to Sunningdale. I want the biggest team you can muster, do all the houses bordering the golf course. Someone must have seen him, or at least the car. It's a collector's item, and an unusual colour, so go out there and ask them.'

The meeting broke up. As the room emptied, Otley said to Tennison, 'Did you arrange for the release of Karen's body? The morgue said they were finished, everyone else has finished with her, Pathology and Forensic. It was all waiting on you, and her parents have asked God knows how many times . . .'

'I'm sorry, yes, I've finished with her. Will you arrange it?'

Otley pursed his lips. 'Not my job, but if that's what you want . . .' Kernan came up behind Tennison. 'I'll see you in your office, OK?' Tennison didn't have time to reply. Otley and Kernan walked off together and she gazed after them. She was going to look for one of those gigantic wooden spoons, and present it to Otley.

George Marlow inserted his key in the front door and pushed. The door opened about two inches and stopped dead; the chain was on.

He rang the bell and waited; nothing happened. 'Moyra? Moyra! Let me in!' he called. He had to ring and shout again before the door eventually swung open.

As Marlow walked into the hall, Moyra stuck her head out of the door and looked around, saying loudly, 'That old cow next door is going to do herself a mischief one of these days, glued to that bloody door all day!'

Suddenly she looked across at the block of flats opposite, stared for a moment. Then she unbuttoned her blouse, crossed the walkway and opened it wide.

In the surveillance flat DI Haskons, bored rigid, had been chatting on the radio with the two officers in the unmarked car. He sat bolt upright.

'Well, chaps, I think she's spotted us – I don't suppose anyone got a shot of her titties?'

Tennison found the Super sitting at her desk. Otley was with him. She asked Kernan about the press release.

'So we're not mentioning the weals on the arms this time either?'

'No, I kept it to a minimum.' He flicked a glance at Otley. 'Your decision to release Marlow could backfire ...'

Tennison was furious, but she kept her temper. 'My decision? You backed me up, have you changed your mind?'

Kernan ran his fingers through his hair and said to Otley, 'You want to give us a minute?'

'No, I want him to stay ... sir.'

'OK ... The consensus seems to be that this case is getting a little heavy for you to handle.'

Tennison couldn't hold back. 'Bullshit! I can—'

'Just let me finish, will you?'

'I'm sorry, sir, but I want to ask the sergeant a question.' She turned to face Otley. 'How well did Detective Chief Inspector Shefford know Della Mornay?'

Otley replied with a shrug, 'He knew her, nobody ever denied that. She was an informer ...'

'So you agree he knew her well?'

Otley flashed a puzzled look at Kernan and shook his head.

Tennison banged on, 'Why did DCI Shefford wrongly identify the first victim?'

'Because they bloody looked alike,' snapped Otley. 'Her face was beaten to a pulp!'

'You knew her too, didn't you? Then why wasn't it realized until after I took over the case that the body identified as Mornay was, in fact, Karen Howard?'

'What's this got to do with anything?' Kernan demanded impatiently.

Tennison opened a drawer and slapped two files on the desk. She stood directly in front of Kernan.

'When I took over the case, I requested Della Mornay's file from Vice. I was told that the delay in sending it was due to the computer changeover, leading me to believe that DCI Shefford had not had access to the records. I was mistaken.' She slapped the file. 'He did have it, but it was not recorded in the case file.'

'This is a bloody waste of time!' Otley protested, uneasily.

'Is it? Here's the one I received from Vice. And here's the one Shefford received. Two supposedly identical files, but in mine there was no mention of Della Mornay being used as an informer, no record of the fact that DCI Shefford was her arresting officer when he was attached to Vice.'

Otley pointed to the files. 'I don't know anything about that, but I do know that you've got some personal grudge against a man that was admired—'

Tennison cut him short. 'Shefford was so damned eager, even desperate, to make an arrest, judging by this ...' She stopped, realizing her voice had climbed almost to a shriek. She went on more calmly, 'I still want to know, if both you and Shefford knew Della Mornay personally, how the body was wrongly identified.'

Otley stared at her with loathing, tried to face her

down. But she had him backed into a corner; his eyes flicked from side to side as he said, 'Why don't you leave it alone! The man is dead!'

Tennison pointed to two photographs on the wall. 'So are they! Karen Howard and Della Mornay! So explain this, Sergeant . . .'

Opening her desk drawer again she produced Della Mornay's diary. 'It was in your desk along with the original Vice file.'

Otley had no reply to make. Kernan thumped the desk. 'What the hell is going on?'

'This, sir, is Della Mornay's diary, not tagged, not logged in. There are pages missing, obviously torn out.' She turned to Otley and asked icily, 'Do you know what happened to those pages?'

'I can explain about the diary. I gave it to John . . . er, DCI Shefford. I presumed he would have . . .' He dropped his gaze to the floor. 'I found it when I was clearing out his desk. He must have removed the pages.'

Through gritted teeth, Kernan whispered, 'Jesus Christ!' He looked at Tennison. 'You realize what this means? You are accusing a senior officer of doctoring evidence.'

'Marlow made two statements. In the second one he stated that he picked up *Della* Mornay. He has to have got her name from Shefford. Yes, I know what I'm saying. If I discover any further irregularities . . .'

'Any so-called irregularities, Chief Inspector, you bring

straight to me. I will decide if the matter is to be taken further.'

'Until I have verification that both women were murderd by the same man, I'd like to keep the discovery of Mornay's body under wraps.'

'Marlow still your main suspect?'

'Yes, sir. I want him kept under pressure, round-the-clock surveillance. I know it's expensive, but if he's killed twice ...'

Kernan nodded, and she continued, 'I'd also like to handle the press releases myself from now on, sir – reporting to you, of course.'

She had won, and she knew it. She walked out and left them there, closing the door quietly behind her.

There was a moment's silence. Otley just stood there, still looking at the floor, waiting for the explosion.

'You bloody idiot! She's effing wiped the floor with the lot of you! You were lucky this time, she let you off the hook, not me!'

Otley dug into his pocket and brought out his wallet. 'It was just the days John went to see her, nothing to do with the case.'

His face set, Kernan held out his hand. Otley laid a few crumpled pieces of paper on his palm.

'He was fond of her ...' When he looked up, Kernan was gone. He turned to face the photograph of Della on the wall. 'He was very fond of her.'

*

George Marlow was looking at the TV guide in his *Evening Standard*. He paid no attention to the large photograph of Karen Howard on the front page.

'You're home early,' Moyra commented from the doorway.

'Did you get a video?' he asked.

'Yeah ... The cops've been here again, they took the rest of your shoes. I said they'd better bring them quick or you'd be selling paint in your stockinged feet.'

'No I won't,' he answered, 'I quit today before they could sack me.'

Moyra walked to the window, the tears pricking her eyes. She moved the curtain slightly to look across at the dark windows of the surveillance flat.

'Bastards! You'd think we were the spies, the way they carry on. I'm keeping the chain on the door all the time now. They've had all our keys, and I don't trust them. They could have had them copied ...'

He looked up. He couldn't say anything to comfort her, and she was trying hard not to cry as she said, 'It's getting me down, George, like we're prisoners ...'

'I'm sorry ...' He put his hand out for her, but she held back, folding her arms.

'Moyra, don't you turn against me. No one said a single word to me in the factory, except Edward Harvey, and even he didn't want to look me in the eye ... I love you, Moyra, but I don't know how much more of this I can take.'

'I have to take it too, George. With you not earning, what are we going to do?'

He stood there looking forlorn and his voice cracked as he said, 'I won't let them beat me, I'll find another job . . .' He shook his fists in the air in frustration and yelled, 'I didn't do it, I didn't do it! So help me God, I didn't do it . . .'

The telephone rang and he nearly jumped out of his skin. He stared at it as it continued to shrill.

Moyra sighed. 'I'll get it. If it's another of those filthy bloody perverts . . . And those kids next door . . .'

She picked up the phone but said nothing for a second or two, then, 'Oh, hallo, Doris . . . Yes, just a minute.'

She turned to George. 'It's your mum, it's a payphone.'

He shook his head, unable to face speaking to her.

'You'll have to talk to her, come on, love.'

He pulled himself up and took the receiver. Moyra was astonished that he could sound so bright.

'Hallo, Mum! I'm fine, yeah. How's your hip? It is?' He whispered to Moyra, 'She's only using one stick now!'

He listened a while, then answered, 'Thanks, Mum, I wish the cops felt the same way. You know what they're like . . . I'm sorry, they're talking to everyone I know.'

Moyra watched him closely until he put the phone down and stood there, dejected.

'You never even mentioned you've no job, you should have told her.'

'It wasn't necessary.'

'It will be when you can't pay for her "residential home".' Moyra couldn't keep the sarcasm out of her voice.

'I'll manage, man with my experience can always get work. Things'll be OK, I'll go and see her. Will you get me the perfume she likes?'

Moyra wanted to weep; his whole life was turned upside-down, and hers, and he was asking her to buy perfume.

'She must have a drawer full.'

'I like to take her something, you know that. I'm all she's got.'

'You're all I've got too, George!'

He gave her a sweet gentle smile, showing his perfect teeth, his slanting, wonderful eyes. She loved him to bursting sometimes.

'I'll get us a cup of tea.' She didn't mean to sound abrupt, it just came out that way.

When Jane arrived home that night, later than she had promised, she wanted nothing more than a hot bath and to crash out.

As she walked into the bedroom, Peter took one look at her face. 'I suppose you don't want to go out to eat? Want me to get a takeaway?'

'Oh, yeah, but first I want a shower.'

'I booked a court, didn't the message get to you?'

She looked at him and realized that he had been play-ing squash. 'I'm sorry, love, I've been in and out of the station. I meant to call, but I kept getting waylaid.'

'You gonna be waylaid over this dinner?'

'What? The takeaway?'

'No, I told you, I asked you for a date when I could invite Frank King and his wife, and Tom and Sheila, to dinner. I told you.'

'I know, and I haven't forgotten. I've even arranged for Pam to come over tomorrow to help me sort out the menu!'

'Well, there's no need to go mad!'

'With my culinary expertise, darlin', I doubt it, but I'll have a go.'

He tipped her chin up and kissed her, looking into her eyes. 'It's important to me. I lost out on a contract; if I pull off this deal with Frank King we'll set up a partnership. He's got a big yard, employs fifty guys, and then Tom sup-plies the paint. We cut costs all round. I don't know if they want me with them, but it'd be a big plus for me, so the dinner's important.'

'I know, it's no problem, but my hunger is! Lemme have a shower, you get the nosh.'

The hot water felt good. Wrapped in a big towelling dressing gown, Jane switched on the television and lay on the bed to watch it. She could have gone to sleep there and then, but Peter arrived with the Chinese takeaway. She could hear him banging around in the kitchen but didn't have the energy to get up and help him.

The telephone rang and Peter appeared at the door. 'If that's for you to go out, I quit! *I quit!*'

It was Jane's mother on the line to remind her of her father's birthday and to invite her to a small party. Jane covered the mouthpiece and called to Peter, 'Pete! Pete, it's Mum! Are you free next Monday? It's Dad's seventy-fifth and she's having a little do! Pete?'

Peter brought the tray with the cartons of food and a bottle of wine. 'Sounds OK,' he said.

Jane listened to her mother carrying on about her sister Pam's pregnancy and pulled a face. 'Pam's got water retention!'

Already tucking in to the food, Peter gestured that it would get cold.

'Mum, I'll have to go, we're just having dinner. Yes! I'll be there, and Peter . . . OK . . . Give Pop my love!' She put the phone down. 'Dear God, don't let me forget Dad's birthday card, remind me to send it off.'

It was almost ten. They settled back to watch TV as they ate, but Jane had no sooner lifted the fork to her mouth than the phone rang again. She pushed the tray away.

'I'll get it.'

Peter continued eating. He could hear excitement in Jane's voice, then her laughter. At least it sounded like good news. She came back into the bedroom, beaming.

'Guess what, I'm going to be on TV!'

'What? I thought *Opportunity Knocks* was defunct?'

'Ho, ho! No, I'm going on *Crime Night*, the police programme, and I will be the first female murder officer they've ever had on!'

'Oh, great! Finish your dinner, the crab and noodle's good.'

Jane twirled around, suddenly no longer tired. 'I pulled every string I could muster. Mind you, the Chiefs got to give the go-ahead, but he can't refuse. I mean, to date we've got bugger all, but I know this'll bring us something, I just know it. I'm gonna get that bastard ...'

'When is it?'

'The twenty-second, they need a while to organize the mock-up film, and I've got to put together all the evidence we can use ... Oh, shit! It's Dad's birthday!'

'Well, maybe they can have it another day?'

'Don't be stupid, the programme goes out at the same time every week ...'

Peter threw his fork down. 'I didn't mean the bloody TV programme, I meant your Mum could change the party night!'

'Oh, sorry. It'll be OK, I'll just have to make a late entrance.'

'I'm not that dumb. Do you want to finish your dinner or not?'

'No, I'm not hungry.'

'Fine, then I'll clear away.'

He snatched up the tray. As he passed her she put out a hand. 'I'm sorry, I guess I'm not hungry.'

'That's OK, suit yourself, you usually do!'

'What's that supposed to mean?'

'It's Saturday night, Jane. I thought that just for one night, just one, you wouldn't be on the bloody phone!'

She sighed and flopped back on the bed. She was so hyped up about the TV programme that she hadn't given Peter a thought. But by the time he came back into the room she was sitting cross-legged, with that tomboyish grin he liked so much. For a moment he thought it was for him, but then she clapped her hands.

'I am going to nail him, Pete, I know it!'

'I'm going to the pub, see you later.'

When Peter got home she was asleep. He stumbled around the bedroom in the dark, cursing as he stubbed his toe. Past caring if he woke her up, he threw himself into bed and thumped his pillow.

Half-asleep, she rolled towards him and muttered, 'I'm sorry, Pete, but I get so tired . . .'

He looked at her shadowy face, then drew her into his arms. 'You're gonna have to start making time for us, Jane, you hear me?'

'Mmmm, yeah, I know . . . and I will.'

'Is that a promise?'

'Yes. I love you, Pete.'

She was asleep again, her head resting on his shoulder. He eased her gently back to her side of the bed and then turned over. He was more than worried about his business, and he needed the deal with Frank King to come off. He knew he wouldn't be able to keep afloat for much longer, he'd be bankrupt.

Moyra eased the bedroom curtain aside. She could see the small red dot of a police officer's cigarette. There were two of them; bored with sitting in the car they were taking a breather, walking around the estate. She let the curtain fall back into place.

'There's two of them still prowling around outside, George!'

Marlow lay face down on the bed, his naked body draped in a sheet that just covered his buttocks. He was lean, taut, muscular.

He banged his pillow. 'Just ignore them.'

'It's tough, they're outside day and night, and I know there's another two in the flat opposite us. I've seen them, I know they're cops, and they've got a camera.'

'You'd think they'd have better things to do with ratepayers' money.'

'Yeah, but it makes my skin crawl. And her from next door is in and out, talking to everyone! I feel everybody looking at me when I go out. Bastards, this is harassment! I'd like to get them, the bastards. Why?'

'They've got nothing better to do. It's the way they work, look at the way they treated me over that other business. They stitched me up over that! I just hope to God they find some other sucker and lay off us.'

'You hope! Jesus Christ, am I going nuts?'

'Then come here . . . Take your dressing gown off and come to bed.'

Moyra slipped off her Marks and Sparks satin robe. It was sexy, like the old film stars used to wear. Beneath it was a matching nightdress with thin ribbon straps.

'You look good, Moyra. That colour suits you, and it looks expensive.'

'Yeah, well, it was cheap, like me!'

'Don't say that! Come here . . .'

She sighed and sat on the edge of the bed. She wanted to cry, she wanted to bang on the window and scream at the pigs. 'I don't feel like it, George.'

'Then just lie with me, let me hold you.'

He took her gently in his arms and rested his head on her breast. She stroked his hair.

'Why, George, why did you pick that bloody girl up?'

'Because . . . because she was there, Moyra, and if you think I wouldn't give anything to turn the clock back . . . I wish to God I'd never picked her up.'

'But you did.'

He propped himself on his elbow and traced her cheek with his fingers. 'I know I did, and I know I have to make it up to you, but if I swore to you now I'd never have another woman you wouldn't believe me. I've always told you, I've never lied to you, Moyra, never! I don't cheat on you like some guys would. I don't screw your friends.'

'What friends? I don't see anyone, especially not now. They can't get away from me fast enough.'

'I'm sorry . . .'

'I know, love . . .'

'I love you, Moyra, and if you ever left me, and I know you have every right, but if you were to finish with me . . .'

'I'm here, aren't I? I'm not going any place.'

She turned to him then, and he kissed her, a sweet, loving kiss. His beautiful eyes were so close that she could feel the long lashes on her cheeks. He covered her face with childish kisses, her lips, her eyes . . . She tried not to cry, but her body trembled.

'Oh, no, please don't cry, Moyra! Please don't cry!'

'I love you, George, I love you, but sometimes I just can't cope, and I don't want to lose you . . . You'll have to promise me, no more girls, please . . . please!'

He rolled onto his back and stretched his arms above his head. 'OK.'

'Promise me?'

He smiled and turned to her, cupping his head in his hands. 'I promise, Moyra Henson! And after the trouble I'm in, do you really think I would? I'll tell you something, I don't think I could, and I'm not joking. It's made me impotent, I can't do a thing!'

She pushed his chest and giggled. 'Wanna bet?'

He caught her to him then, hugging her tight, with his wonderful, gurgling laugh. 'Oh, my darling, I am a lucky man!'

Chapter Six

Karen Howard's coffin was completely smothered beneath wreaths of flowers, many of them from sympathetic people who had never even met her.

The funeral drew considerable media attention. Television news cameras followed the grieving parents and friends as they left the church. Tennison held back from the crowd and gestured for Jones and Otley to join her as Major Howard turned towards her.

He thanked them courteously for coming, and suggested that they might like to join the family at their home after the burial. Tennison thanked him for the invitation but declined. He seemed not to hear her, being more intent on sheltering his wife from the prying eyes of the reporters as he helped her into their car. Felicity Howard wore a wide-brimmed hat which only partially concealed a face etched with grief.

All Tennison could think of was how did a respectable girl like Karen end up in a sleazy tart's hovel. There was no hint of her being addicted to drugs, the usual reason someone like Karen did a bit of ducking and diving.

She spoke quietly to the two officers. 'I'll have to make a move. You go to the graveside and then back to the station, OK?'

Jones nodded and gave her a quick grin. 'Break a leg!'

She gave a short laugh and eased herself away from the mourners towards her parked car. Otley watched her departure with a smirk; a moment later he was approached by a newscaster seeking further news of the murder investigation. He replied that there was none, and that they would be informed as soon as anything developed.

The media had still not linked the Karen Howard case with the murder of Della Mornay. The report of the discovery of the body of a prostitute on Sunningdale golf course had merited only half a column in the nationals, and Tennison wanted it to stay that way. The press release had simply identified the victim and included a routine appeal for information.

The make-up department at the television centre was a small room off the main studio floor. Tennison had spent a busy hour with the producer, discussing the questions she would be asked and running through the mock-up of

Karen's last known movements; now that she was sitting in Carmen rollers and protective gown, with no one to talk to, she had time to worry. She began to sweat; it was six-thirty and the programme would go out live at eight-fifteen. Would she make a fool of herself? Would she stutter? The more she thought about it, the more nervous she became.

The PA to the floor manager came in to go over a few last-minute notes. He reminded her that she was to pause after the third question to allow for the footage of the funeral that had taken place that afternoon. Two officers from her team were already in the telephone control room, running through the hot-line procedure before relaxing for a while in the hospitality room. As the time drew closer, Tennison found herself longing to join them. Her mouth was dry and she kept clearing her throat, but she wouldn't accept anything alcoholic. She clutched a glass of water and went over and over the questions and answers, knowing how important it was to get it right. She was very conscious of being the first female officer in her position ever to appear on the programme, and she couldn't foul it up.

Jane's father was sitting right in the centre of the sofa opposite the television, his hand on the remote control. Her mother was settling her grandchildren for the night, or trying to. They were dashing up and down the hall of the flat, screaming their heads off. She was getting a headache.

Jane's sister, Pam, yelled at them to be quiet and go to bed, but they paid no attention to their mother. Their father, Tony, glared at her over the evening paper and she told him to go and see to them. Peter, sitting on the arm of the sofa, gave the harassed Tony a wink and opened a bottle of wine.

'Can I give you a refill, Mr Tennison?'

'Thanks ... Everyone should get in here, it's going to start in a minute.'

Peter poured the wine. The birthday cake and champagne were all on hold for Jane's arrival. Mrs Tennison came rushing in with more plates of sandwiches.

'Peter, check he's got the right channel for the video, she wants us to record it.'

Her husband looked daggers at her. 'Just come in and sit down, she'll be on in a minute.'

Peter looked at the video machine. 'Are you on the right channel, Mr Tennison?'

The *Crime Night* theme started and everyone took their seats. Mr Tennison, ignoring Peter's question, turned up the volume on the TV and sat back. 'Right, no talking ...'

All of John Shefford's team were gathered around the bar, off the main hall where the benefit dinner was to take place. The MC stood in the doorway, bellowing himself hoarse.

'Take your seats for dinner, gentlemen, please! Dinner is now being served, please take your seats for dinner . . .'

No one paid him the least attention, especially Sergeant Otley, who was leaning over the bar tugging at the sleeve of the harassed barman.

'Is the TV set up in the back? I want to see the start of the programme.'

Dave Jones nudged him. 'Come on, let's go and eat. Someone'll have taped it.'

Otley shrugged him away. 'Go on in, we're on the centre table. I'll be a few seconds, go on . . . Oi, Felix! you want a quick one before we go in?'

Felix Norman had appeared in the doorway, still in his overcoat. 'I can't find a bloody parking space!' he yelled.

The MC had got hold of a microphone and his voice boomed, 'Please take your seats, gentlemen, dinner is now being served!' He was obviously under pressure from a row of aged waitresses who were giving him foul looks. 'Please go in to dinner!'

At last there was a slow surge into the main hall where the tables had been set up around a central boxing ring. Norman downed his double malt and grinned at DI Muddyman.

'How's our man? I hope he's not been in here; he can't

box and drink. When I was the amateur middleweight champion of Oxford, did I tell you, I had ten bouts . . .'

Someone yelled, 'How many years ago was that now, Felix?' Everyone had heard of his boxing prowess, sadly cut short by a hand injury, and no one paid any further attention in the crush as they all tried to get into the main hall at once. Superintendent Kernan was laughing at some joke, the tears rolling down his cheeks, and Otley whistled to him, pointing towards the hall.

'We're on table six, Mike, right up against the ring!'

As the men sorted themselves out and filtered into the hall, Otley scuttled round the bar and headed for the back room, where there was a small portable TV set. A little unsteadily, Otley propped himself near the door, and was squashed against the wall as the barman came through with a crate of bottles.

Tennison was on screen. Otley squinted. 'That's her, she's on! What's she think she's come as, Maggie Thatcher?'

He inched further into the room to get a better view. As he had organized the benefit night he had been propping up the bar since six-thirty, and the small screen made his eyes water. He could see six of Tennison, six of the bitch! And one was bad enough.

Tennison paused on cue for the footage of Karen's funeral. She was in fact coping very well. She was now half-way through her discussion with Brian Hayes; she was clear, concise and very direct.

'We know Karen left the offices of the MacDonald Advertising Company soon after six-thirty on the evening of the thirteenth of January this year. She told the people she was working with that she was going home to her flat in Kensington. No one was seen to meet her. She turned left into Ladbroke Grove, towards the side street where she had parked her white Mini.'

The picture cut to Brian. 'Karen Howard never returned to her flat. Were you in Ladbroke Grove that night, Saturday the thirteenth of January, at around six-thirty? Did you see Karen?'

Again the picture cut. The screen showed WPC Barbara Morgan, dressed in the dead girl's clothes, walking away from the film company's offices.

As Jane was no longer the centre of attention, her mother got up from her seat to get a glass of wine. She was told to sit down again and not interrupt the programme. She gave Peter a look and pointed to the video machine, whispering, 'Is it on the right channel, Peter?'

Mr Tennison pounded on the arm of the sofa. 'Be quiet!'

'Jane's not on, and I was just asking if you'd checked it's on the right channel.'

'I *have*! Now be quiet!'

Mrs Tennison sighed. The recreation of the dead girl's movements meant nothing to her; she was a stranger.

*

Major and Mrs Howard were sitting in front of their television set, holding hands tightly. The major had not wanted his wife to see the programme, but she had quietly insisted. They had been told so little, they knew only the bare essentials about the death of their beloved daughter.

WPC Barbara Morgan was wearing a blonde, shoulder-length wig and a jacket similar to the one worn by the real Karen on the night she had been murdered. The jacket had never been traced. The WPC also wore sheer black stockings, a leather mini-skirt and identical black ballet pumps. She actually carried Karen's own portfolio containing her modelling pictures.

On screen, Barbara Morgan began acting out the last known movements of Karen Howard. Walking casually along Ladbroke Grove, she headed towards the Mini.

The major and his wife watched the last known movements of their daughter, the last hours of her life.

'She looks like her.' The major's voice was very low and he gripped his wife's hand more tightly.

'No,' Felicity said, 'Karen was prettier.'

The tears streamed down her cheeks as WPC Morgan turned a corner into a side street, stopped by a white Mini and unlocked it. After putting the portfolio in the back she sat in the driving seat and tried to start the car, but the engine would not turn over.

Brian Hayes's voice accompanied the film. 'Having

arrived for work at the film studio early in the morning, Karen had left her car lights on, and the battery was flat. A man working on the building site opposite was backing his truck into the street while Karen was trying to start her car. He stated that it was almost six forty-five.'

On the screen, the driver hopped down from his cab and crossed the road to offer his assistance.

'Got a problem, have you love?'

'Yes, I think the battery's flat.'

'You need jump leads, love. Sorry I can't help, but hang on a mo.'

He called across to his mates, asking if they had any jump leads, and was told they had not. The driver suggested that he and his pals could give the car a push, but he had to return to his truck as he was blocking a van from leaving the building site.

'Thanks for your help, but I think I'd better call the AA.'

Brian Hayes's voice again took up the story. 'Karen locked her car and waved to the driver as he moved off. Then she walked back to the main road.'

George Marlow was standing directly in front of the television screen, his hands stuffed in his pockets, his face expressionless, as Moyra entered the room.

'Turn it off, George. What are you watching it for? Turn it off!'

She didn't wait for George, she turned it off herself. 'What are you watching it for?'

With a sigh, Marlow asked, 'Why do you think?'

'You tell me?'

'Because somebody out there might have the fucking evidence that'll get me off the hook, that's why. I didn't kill her, but somebody did, and they're trying to make out that it was me. I want to see if there's anything I can help them with. Now turn it back on!'

'No!'

'Jesus Christ, Moyra! You don't believe me, do you?'

'I just don't want to see her.'

'It isn't her, she's dead. That's a policewoman.'

'I know that,' Moyra snapped. 'Why don't you go out and bloody pick her up while you're at it?'

Marlow shook his head in disbelief. 'Look, how many more times? If I could turn the clock back, if there was any way I could ... but I can't. I picked that girl up and now they're saying that I killed her. I swear before God that I didn't, and maybe, just maybe, there's something in that programme that'll make me remember more. Somebody killed her, Moyra, but not me!'

'I don't want to see it.'

'Then leave the room.'

He bent to switch the set on again but she broke down. 'Why? Why did you do it, George? Why?'

'You mean why did I pick her up? Why did I fuck her?'

'*Yes! Yes, tell me why!*'

'Because she was there, and I was there, and she . . . She gave me the come-on, and she was . . . I don't know why! If I was to say to you that I'd never have sex with another woman, you wouldn't believe me. She was a tart. I picked her up, we did the business, I paid her. It meant nothing, it never means anything. I don't cheat on you, Moyra, and I never have.'

'You don't what? You don't cheat on me? *Jesus Christ, what do you call it?*'

'*Wanking off! And no, I don't call that cheating!* It's fast, clean and finished, and I pay for it.'

'You can say that again . . .'

'Yeah, I'm paying for it, I'm paying, Moyra. All I want is for them to find out who did it, find him and let me off the hook.'

Moyra snapped the TV set on. 'You want him found, what d'you think I want?'

The telephone rang. Moyra turned and looked as if she would yank it from the wall and hurl it across the room. Marlow gripped his hands together, trying to concentrate on the television.

'Don't answer it, Moyra, just leave it.'

Moyra marched to the phone. 'If this is another crank bitch, then I'm ready for her. I'm bloody ready for anyone.'

She snatched up the phone but said nothing, just

listened. Then she sighed and held the receiver out to Marlow.

'It's your mother. George, it's Doris.'

She handed the phone over, not even bothering to say hallo to Mrs Marlow. She stood with her hands on her hips, watching the way he swallowed, closed his eyes for a moment as if trying to calm himself, make himself sound relaxed.

He said brightly, 'Hallo, my old love? Mum? Eh, eh, now what's this? You crying, sweetheart?'

Moyra sighed and turned back to the TV set, arms folded, only half-listening to George's conversation.

'Yes . . . Yes, Mum, I'm watching. We've got it on. Yes, I know . . . Look, I don't want to talk about it, can I call you back? Because I want to see it! No, no . . . I was released, Mum, it was just . . . No, they don't want to see me again, no, they released me. It was a big mistake . . .'

Moyra turned the volume up and turned to George. 'Jesus Christ, they got a car identical to yours! Look, look at the TV! They're giving out your number plate! George!'

Marlow dropped the phone back on the hook and stared in shock at the screen. Moyra shouted for him to get on to his lawyer, but he slumped in his chair, hands raised helplessly. 'How can they do this to me? Why . . .? Why are they doing this to me?'

*

'Oi, Otley, what the fuck're you doin' in here? You've missed the soup and the chicken frisky ... mind, I don't blame you, we'll all be salmonellaed by tomorrow!'

Otley ignored the well-flushed Jones as he chuntered on. The barman had started the glass-washing machine, and the din from the main hall was drowning out the TV programme.

'Come on, Burkin's on first! He's matched against the Raging Bull of Reading!'

Otley pointed drunkenly at the screen. 'Look at this bull dyke, Jesus, hate her guts ... She's comin' on like bleedin' Esther Rantzen! Look, d'you believe it? And I'm tellin' you, she's really done herself in.'

Jones stared at the small screen. 'Shit, it's Marlow's car, isn't it? I mean, the make?'

'Yeah, an' if that's not an infringement of personal privacy, she's given out his fuckin' registration number!'

Otley chortled, choked and drained his glass. Tennison, on screen, was discussing the Rover with Brian Hayes, then the camera zoomed in on her face for a close-up.

'Did Karen have a handbag with her on the night she died? Her portfolio was found in her car, but no bag. There was also her Filofax; it could be that she carried it in a handbag, and it has not been found. The witness who saw her stop at a cardphone and directed her to a payphone on Ladbroke Grove couldn't tell us if she had a bag or not ...'

Otley exploded. 'Oh, that's bloody marvellous! By tomorrow mornin' we'll have every soddin' lost bag in the London area ... This bloody woman is a total fuckin' idiot ...'

On screen, Tennison was still talking. '... Telecom tell us that the coinbox was out of order that night. The AA have no record of a call from Karen ...'

The bellowing of the Master of Ceremonies cut through the singing and shouting from the main room. 'Gentlemen, in the red corner we have DI Burkin, weighing in at sixteen stone fifteen pounds, let's hear it for him ... And in the blue corner, the Raging Bull of Reading!'

Boos and cat-calls drowned Brian Hayes and Tennison. DC Jones gave up on Otley and returned to the hall to watch the fight. This was his first benefit, being the fresh man on the team, and he was having the time of his life. He seemed unaware that the orange juice was well and truly laced with vodka, but he'd know by the end of the evening. He was well on his way to getting totally plastered for the first time in his life.

Otley did not join table six until *Crime Night* was over and the fight was in the fourth round. Burkin looked very much the worse for wear, his nose streaming blood and one eye nearly closed.

During the break, Felix Norman climbed into the red

corner, screaming instructions as if he was Burkin's second. 'Keep your fists up! Up, man! You're flayin' around like a bloody oik! Hit him with a good body, then one, two, one, two . . .'

Felix was hauled out of the ring as the bell rang for the next round. Men were bellowing from the back of the room for Felix to sit down, they could not see through his bulk.

Otley cheered loudly as he poured himself a large Scotch from one of the many bottles in front of him. Kernan was whistling and thumping on the table; Otley leaned across to him.

''Ere, Tennison's done 'erself in tonight, guv! Wait till you see what she bloody went on about in the telly programme. How she wangled that I'd like to know!'

'Yeeessssss!' Kernan was on his feet, fists in the air, as Burkin landed a good uppercut to his opponent's chin. The entire room erupted and chants of 'Blood . . . blood . . . blood . . .' mingled with a pitiful request over the public address system for whoever had parked in front of the fire escape to move his car. The chanting mounted in a crescendo as Burkin staggered as if he was going to keel over, but he planted his elbow in the Raging Bull's ribs, and a small but visible head butt gave an opening for his right hand. The cheers were deafening as Burkin was proclaimed the winner.

The tinny blast of a worn-out record of *The Eye of the*

Tiger started playing for the next bout as the buckets for donations to Shefford's family were being passed around. Otley sat back in his chair with a grin like the Cheshire Cat; he knew Tennison was in the shit, knew it, because he also knew that Marlow's car had not been reported stolen. To give out his registration number on live national television was going to create a nasty scene with Marlow's legal adviser. Otley's hands itched for his wooden spoon ...

DC Jones was propped against the table, insisting on singing a solo, demanding to be let into the ring. His young face was flushed an extraordinary red, his shirt was undone ... Otley chuckled; they'd got the poor lad well and truly pissed. He stood up to give Jones a helping hand and slithered beneath the table, where he remained for the rest of the evening.

Jane drove straight from the television studios to her parents' flat. The follow-up would not go on air for another hour and a half, and she was not required to wait for the phone-in. The two officers left in charge had her number, and she was ready to act immediately on any information that came in.

Her family had waited long enough, so the champagne was open and the candles on her father's birthday cake were lit when she rang the bell, just in time to join the chorus of Happy Birthday. She had forgotten to post his card, but presented it with a flourish with the two bottles of champagne she had picked up on the way from the television centre.

Her father hugged her tightly, proud of her achievements, although he never said much about it. She kissed him while her mother looked on, surreptitiously removing the supermarket price labels from the champagne bottles, but not before she noticed they were bought locally. Jane couldn't even spare the time to buy her Dad a present!

'Well, was I OK? What do you think, did I look OK?'

She was asking generally, but her eye caught Peter's and he gave her the thumbs-up. 'Well, come on, put the video on, let me see meself!' She sat down with a glass of champagne.

Her father leaned against the back of the sofa. 'What's this Brian Hayes bloke like, then? I listen to him on the radio, you know.'

'Oh, he's great! Did you think I was OK, Dad?'

''Course you were, love. Do you want a sandwich?'

'No, thanks, I just want to see what I looked like. The second part'll be on soon.'

Peter started the video and ice skaters zapped across the screen in fast forward. Then came a snatch of *Dallas*, then back to the skating.

'Is this the video? Peter? Is it on?'

Peter straightened and flashed a look at Jane's father. 'Sorry, love, I think we recorded the wrong channel . . .'

'What! Oh, shit, no, you haven't, have you?'

The ice spectacular continued. As Peter looked on, Jane threw a beaut of a tantrum, only interrupted by the ringing of the telephone.

The second part of the programme reviewed the number of calls that had been received and mentioned further evidence in the Karen Howard case.

There had actually been ten calls connected with the murder, but only one was to prove worthwhile. Once the cranks and hoaxers had been weeded out, one caller remained. Helen Masters, a social worker, had seen Karen in Ladbroke Grove on the night of the murder; she had seen a man picking her up, a man who, she was sure, knew the victim.

It was almost midnight when two officers arrived at Miss Masters' house in Clapham to take a statement. She had seen a man she was able to describe in detail, and was sure she would be able to recognize again. She described the man as five feet nine to ten, well dressed, rather handsome, with very dark hair; she described George Arthur Marlow.

Jane and Peter argued all the way home from her parents' flat. They were still rowing when they reached their door.

Peter was furious at her behaviour; they had all been waiting for her to cut the birthday cake, but as soon as she had
arrived she had caused a terrible argument over her father
not recording the programme. Her tantrum, which was
how he described her tirade against her father, was dis-
gusting, especially when she knew that they had recorded
it at home anyway.

Jane refused to back down, it was important to her and
her father had known it.

'Do you think he did it on purpose, for God's sake?'

'That's not the point! They all knew how important it
was to me, but they didn't give a fuck! The stupid old sod
should have let someone else do it! He always gets it
wrong!' She stormed into the bedroom.

'Of course they bloody cared!' Peter slammed the front
door so hard that it sprang open again and hit him on the
shoulder. 'You arrive late, scream about the bloody telly,
then get on the phone for the rest of the night!' He
strode into the bedroom, still yelling, 'I don't know why
you bothered turning up, you're a selfish bloody cow!
He'd been waiting to see you, he's proud as punch about
you!'

'Oh, yeah? Well, I've never heard him say it. If you
must know, Mother has never even approved of me being
in the Force, when I was in uniform she used to make me
take my bloody hat off so the neighbours would know it
was me! But Pam, oh, Pam could never do anything

wrong, all she's done is produce children at such a rate she looks ten years older than she should . . .'

Peter sighed and chucked his coat on the bed. Jane's followed, so hard that it flew across the room. She kicked off her shoes and sat down grumpily on the bed.

'Actually,' said Peter, 'it was quite funny, watching you and your dad, with Torville and whatsit whizzing round on the screen . . .'

Jane grinned like the sun coming out. 'He's never got the hang of that video recorder. He taped bits of a football match over Pam's wedding film . . .' She giggled and hummed a snatch of *Here Comes the Bride*, then shrieked, 'Goal!'

She threw herself back on the bed, laughing hysterically, while Peter stood shaking his head in wonder at her sudden change of mood.

'I'm going to have a drink,' he said.

'Great, me too, and make it a large one!'

When Peter brought their drinks to the bedroom he found Jane glued to the TV screen as the opening theme of *Crime Night* faded into Brian Hayes's voice.

'I only want to see myself, I'm sure that make-up they put on me looked appalling.'

She wound the film forward and stopped it; Peter heard her recorded voice. At the same moment the phone rang in the hall. Jane jumped to her feet and hurried to answer it. Peter sat on the bed and sipped his Scotch, watching Jane on the programme sitting a little stiffly, but looking very calm and together. The screech that emanated from the hall could hardly be anything to do with that cool woman on screen . . .

She banged open the door, fist in the air. 'We've got a witness who called in after the programme. She says she saw Karen Howard picked up by a man. She says the man knew her, because she's sure he called her name . . . And, Pete, the description, she described bloody George Marlow!'

Her fist shot into the air again. 'We got him! We got him, Pete!'

Pete held up her drink. 'You wanted to see your performance? Well, you're missing it.'

'Sod that, I'm gonna pick him up tonight.'

Peter looked surprised and glanced at his watch. 'Tonight? Are you going to the station?'

'You're kidding, I'm on my way right now . . .'

It was a while before she did leave; there were hurried phone calls while she was changing her clothes. She wiped the make-up off and gave Peter a perfunctory kiss, then grabbed her bag and bleeper and was gone.

Peter continued to watch her on screen, until he grew bored and switched the video off. He lay back on the bed and sighed . . . Sometimes, more times than he cared to think about, she made him feel inadequate. But tonight he didn't just feel that way, he was also irritated by her, annoyed by her attitude, her temper, her ambition. He started counting all the emotions she aroused in him, and it was like counting sheep. There were too many, too many to remember. He fell asleep.

Chapter Seven

'I was outside Ladbroke Grove underground station,' Helen Masters was telling DCI Tennison, 'waiting to meet one of the girls from the Hammersmith half-way house, Susan Lyons. She'd absconded a few days earlier, then she called to ask me to meet her. But she was late.'

Tennison nodded. Helen Masters was a terrific witness, a social worker, calm and unruffled, with, most important of all, a retentive memory.

'Were you standing on the pavement, or in the entrance?' Tennison asked.

'Mostly in the ticket area, it was a pretty cold night, but I kept checking outside in case I'd missed her. That was when I saw them.'

'And who did you see?'

'The man, at first. I just watched him for something to do. There's a bank across the road, a few yards down, and he was standing near the cash dispenser. He had dark hair ... Then I saw Karen, the girl who was murdered. I'd seen her photographs in the newspapers, but it didn't register until I saw them in colour, on the TV programme. For a second I thought it was Susan, she's blonde too. I stepped forward ...'

'How close were you?'

'Oh, about five yards ...' She looked around and pointed to a WPC on the other side of the room. 'She was about there.'

'And then what?'

'The man over the road walked to the edge of the pavement and called to Karen.'

Tennison leaned forward and watched Helen closely as she asked her next question. 'You heard him clearly, calling her name?'

Helen nodded. 'There was quite a lot of traffic noise, but he definitely called out her name.'

Tennison relaxed a little. 'Can you tell me what he was wearing?'

'A brownish jacket, with a light shirt underneath.'

There was a brief knock on the door and a uniformed DI entered. He gave Tennison a nod. 'We're ready for you, Miss Masters,' he said.

DI Sleeth led Helen Masters to the observation room next door, explaining the procedure as he did so.

'You will be able to see them, but they can't see you, it's one-way glass. Anything you want them to do, tell me and I'll give the instructions over the address system. Take your time, and don't worry. Any questions?'

She shook her head. DCI Tennison had already told her that another officer had to accompany her for the identity parade, to avoid any suggestion of bias. Helen gave Sleeth a nervous smile and sat in the chair he indicated, facing the one-way glass and the twelve men in the line-up. Sleeth gave Helen a small wink as he tested the microphone that linked them to the identification room.

The twelve men stood in a row, facing the observation window. Each man held a number in front of him; George Marlow was number ten. They were all dark haired and more or less of a size with Marlow, and two, like him, had a deep six o'clock shadow.

'Would you all please turn to your right,' Sleeth said into the microphone.

Helen looked at each man in turn, frowning, then made another request. Sleeth announced it.

'When I call out your number, please take one pace forward and say the name "Karen" clearly. Number one, step forward please.'

Number one turned slowly and obeyed. 'Karen!'

Helen shook her head and Sleeth said, 'Thank you, number one, you may step back.' He consulted with

Helen and continued, 'Number eight, please step forward and say the name "Karen".'

The eighth man's voice was indistinct. 'Louder, please, number eight,' said Sleeth.

'Karen!' shouted number eight.

In the corridor outside the observation room, Tennison and Otley waited nervously. She was pacing up and down, smoking. The door opened and DI Sleeth came out.

'She wants a closer look,' he told Tennison, and led Helen to the main room. Tennison made no attempt to speak to her.

Otley tapped Tennison on the arm and gestured towards the observation room. It was against the rules, but she couldn't resist. They scurried furtively inside to watch.

Helen was moving slowly down the line of men. She paused in front of number two, but only for a second. She stopped at number ten, George Marlow.

'Come on, Helen, that's the one!' Tennison almost shouted in her excitement. Sudden panic made her check the sound system; it was set to receive only. She sighed with relief and whispered through gritted teeth, 'Come on, number ten, number ten . . .'

George Marlow stepped out of the line, holding his card in front of him and staring straight ahead. Tennison's spine tingled; it was as if he knew he was looking directly into her eyes.

'Karen!' he called loudly.

Tennison dragged on her cigarette as the tension in the viewing room built up. Otley leaned forward, gritting his teeth. She was staring too long at Marlow, taking too long ... He drummed his fingers on the table.

'Come on sweetheart, that's him, yes ... You've got him!'

The reception area of Southampton Row nick was a hive of activity. A woman was in tears because her Saab Turbo had been either towed away or stolen, and she swore to the desk sergeant that it had been legally parked. Two punks, wearing torn jeans and leather jackets, were being released after a night in the cells. The mother of one of the boys, a Princess Anne lookalike in a camel coat and Hermes scarf, was berating him in a voice that could have shattered glass.

'How could you be so stupid? This will ruin your chances of university! How could you do it ... Do you know how long I've been waiting?'

Three of the men from the identity parade were leaving, pocketing their eight quid expenses, and in the midst of it all DCI Tennison was thanking Helen Masters, thanking her when she could have screamed the place down with frustration.

Arnold Upcher was guiding George Marlow through the crowd, but suddenly Marlow turned back and pushed his way past the punks towards Tennison.

'Excuse me, Inspector,' he said softly, and touched her arm.

Refusing to look at him, Tennison moved quickly, through the door which led behind the reception desk, reappearing next to the desk sergeant. Marlow faced her across the broad counter.

'Inspector Tennison! You're making my life a misery! I was dragged out of bed at four o'clock this morning with no explanation. You've got people watching me night and day, tell me why? You know I'm innocent. If you've got something personal against me, tell me now, what did I ever do to you?'

Upcher, disapproving, grabbed his arm to drag him away. Tennison gave Marlow a long, hard stare, then turned her head to find two men taking great interest in the transaction.

'Inspector Tennison? *Daily Express*, can you spare us a few seconds?'

With a gesture to the desk sergeant, Tennison said, 'Get them out of here!' The reporter was moved on by a uniformed officer at the same time as George Marlow, protesting, was being manhandled out of the door by Upcher.

'She's got something personal against me! *I didn't do it! I didn't do it!*'

Scenting a story, the reporter turned his attention to Marlow.

Everywhere Tennison went that day she encountered men with sore heads and matching tempers. Burkin was the worst for wear; his triumph the night before had been paid with a cut eye and lip. Tennison found the resulting lisp irritating.

'Where the hell is Jones?' Tennison demanded. 'I need him with me.'

Otley's piggy eyes were bloodshot and seemed smaller than ever. 'Dunno, ma'am.' He was having difficulty looking his guv'nor in the face; he had just been telling everybody that their great witness had picked out a tax inspector who'd been hauled in off the street. They were all at it; every time she turned her back one of them would purse his lips and run his hands through his hair in imitation of Tennison on TV.

Three minutes later Jones arrived, belching from the Alka-Seltzer he'd just forced down himself. His head throbbed, his tongue felt like rubber and he looked very pale and shaky. Totally unsympathetic, Tennison told him not to bother sitting down, they were going out.

WPC Havers came rushing in. 'The Super wants to see you, ma'am, right away.'

'Tell him you can't find me.'

'Marlow's lawyer's with him, screaming about you

giving details of the car last night. Marlow's never reported it stolen.'

'Shit! Well, someone had better get it sorted, and before I get back. We all know how careless filing clerks can be, don't we? The Vehicle Theft Report's probably just been misfiled, hasn't it, Burkin?'

The DI was standing in the centre of the room, yawning. 'We keeping you awake?' asked Tennison.

'Sorry, ma'am, got a bit of a headache.'

'I just hope you won.'

He started to nod but thought better of it. On top of his injuries, the bevvies he had consumed after the fight didn't help.

'It was in a good cause, ma'am. I got him in the last round – at least, I think I did. Old Felix was virtually in the ring with me, he used to box for . . .'

Otley smirked. 'Made a nice little packet for the Sheffords, at twenty-five quid a ticket.'

'Yes, I know. I bought four tickets myself, I'm just sorry I couldn't be there.'

She jerked her head to Jones to follow her as she walked out. Otley pursed his lips; nobody had told him that split-arse had chipped in!

'It was George's decision to give notice,' said Edward Harvey, George Marlow's boss at the paint factory he represented. 'He was getting a lot of stick from the others. I'd never have asked him to leave, he's too good at his job, been with us ten years apart from the time he was in jail.'

'He told you all about that, did he?'

'Yes, came straight out with it. I know he was found guilty, but . . .'

'But . . .?'

'Well, he was always a bit of a lad, popular with the girls. He swears he's innocent, and I really can't see why such an attractive bloke would go and do a thing like that. He was very distressed about it.'

'You're entitled to your opinion, Mr Harvey. Now, could you show us around? If you have time.'

'My pleasure.'

Mr Harvey, a cocky little man in his fifties, showed them the well-equipped production line, stopping now and then for a word with the men on the floor.

'We employ three hundred salesmen up and down the country,' he told Tennison, while Jones all but disappeared head-first into one of the mixing vats. 'We guarantee to match any colour you want; the difficult shades are still mixed by hand.'

Tennison looked around with interest. 'George Marlow always worked from London?'

'He started with the firm in Manchester. We moved our headquarters down here in eighty-two, and George came with us, but he kept his old routes. Had all the contacts, you see, and of course they still had family and friends up north . . .'

'They? Did Marlow travel with someone else?'

'Moyra always went with him on his trips . . .'

'How far back do your staff records go?' asked Tennison.

'Since we moved here. We had a computer system installed, but we've got all the files . . .'

'Would they include the hotels your salesmen used, expenses and so on?'

'This company is run like clockwork,' said Harvey proudly. 'We like to know where our men are and what they're doing.'

'We will need to examine them,' Tennison said, clocking Jones' incredulous reaction. 'Just Marlow's, of course.'

Harvey looked puzzled, but said mildly, 'Just so long as we get them back.'

Tennison was starving when she arrived back at the station. She grabbed a sandwich and tried to eat it in her office, but she was interrupted by Maureen Havers, who had contacted the Rape Centre about Marlow's earlier victim and managed to find out who she was.

'She wanted her identity kept secret, but it's Miss Pauline Gilling, ma'am, from Rochdale. She's been having counselling after a nervous breakdown, and the people in Rochdale say it would only aggravate the situation if we started asking questions.'

Tennison spoke through a mouthful of sandwich. 'I could be in line for a breakdown myself . . .' She took a sip of coffee. 'Get back on to them and don't take no for an answer.'

She finished the rest of her sandwich and started gathering items for the team meeting. 'Oh, and Maureen, you don't know where I am if the Super asks, OK?'

They were all there. Otley was pinning black-and-white photographs of Della Mornay's and Karen Howard's bodies on the notice board. There were also blow-ups of the marks on their arms. He turned to the waiting men.

'Right, you can see the similarities of these marks. We got a DNA match on George Marlow's sperm with the blood samples from when he went down for rape, but that's no help with Della. It also doesn't help that he admitted having sex with Karen, and gave a very plausible reason, which seems to check out, for the spot of Karen's blood on his sleeve. We're sure his car's the key; find that and I reckon we've got 'im. So keep at it.'

He moved on to the photos of the bodies. 'The clearest evidence linking the girls, apart from the marks on the arms, is the way their 'ands were tied. Not the rope itself, but the knots.'

'Ah, knot the rope, eh, Sarge?' Burkin put in, still lisping.

Otley gave him the finger and replied, 'Yeah, very funny ... The knots are the same, but any boy scout could tie 'em. Now it's your turn, Inspector ...'

Tennison entered the room, munching a packet of crisps. Burkin waited while she sat down, then picked up from Otley.

'The sack that covered Della Mornay's body was the usual type of hessian, no markings, but there were traces of sump oil on it. There was also sump oil found on Karen's skirt. It doesn't mean a lot, Karen could have got it off her own car.' He nodded to Tennison. 'All yours,' and sat down.

She crunched the last few crisps and screwed the bag up, tossing it at the waste-paper basket and missing. As she bent to retrieve it they all saw the edge of pink lace. Otley, who never missed a trick, pursed his lips and crossed his legs like an old queen.

'Karen didn't put up much of a struggle,' Tennison began, spitting a piece of crisp onto her jacket and brushing it off. 'Her nails were short, clean, no skin or blood beneath them, but her hands had been scrubbed with something similar to the kind of brush used on suede shoes. Gimme Della's ...'

Otley passed her a blow-up of Della's hands and she put it up beside the others. 'I asked for this because you can see scratch marks on the backs of the hands and fingers. Now, Della did fight, and her nails, unlike Karen's, were long and false. She lost them from the thumb, index and little fingers of her right hand.'

Burkin asked, 'Did Marlow have any scratches on him when he was stripped?'

'No, he didn't. George Marlow is still the prime suspect, but we have no evidence to put him in that bedsit, no eye witnesses to link him with either Karen or Della, no mention of him in Della's diary. The list of what we don't have is endless. But if Marlow killed Della before he killed Karen, then he knew her room was empty. He might even have known that the landlady was away, probably hoped that Karen's body wouldn't be found for weeks. His mistake there was in leaving the light on. Mornay's handbag was in her room, but there were no keys.'

Always ready to needle her, Otley piped up, 'That reminds me, ma'am – handbags. We got a good selection an' they're still comin' in; blue ones, green ones, big 'uns an' little 'uns. What d'you want me to do with 'em?'

Tennison responded quite calmly, considering. 'Get one of her flatmates in, let her go over them to save time. Right, the good news is, I'm going home. Sergeant Otley will now tell you the bad news.'

As she left the room, she could hear the moan that went up in response to the bad news; all weekend leave was cancelled.

'All leave, that is, apart from 'er own. We got to check

through all that gear from the bleedin' paint factory, an' there's a lot. It's a wonder they 'aven't computerized their salesmen's bowel movements . . . Get to it!'

When he went to Superintendent Kernan's office later that evening, Otley found him sitting at his desk, writing memos. Kernan pushed his work aside and poured Otley a large Scotch.

Otley sat down, took a swig and sighed. 'We're gettin' nowhere, guv, we've 'ad nothing for days now,' he said bitterly. 'It's demoralizing, an' it's takin' good men off the streets.'

'Most of them have been on the streets, and we've still got nowhere,' Kernan replied. 'But now she's digging up unsolved murder cases on Marlow's sales routes. He covered the Manchester area, Rochdale, Burnley, Oldham.'

Otley shook his head in disgust and opened his mouth to speak, but Kernan wouldn't let him.

'And I've OKed it, so cool off, Bill. I know what you're after, but unless there's good reason for kicking her off the case, she stays put.'

'It's because she's a woman, isn't it? If it'd been any of my lads that done that cock-up on telly, given out Marlow's registration number . . . You know he never reported it stolen! There's no report in the log, and I heard his brief was in here creating about it . . .'

Pissed off with Otley's attitude, Kernan cut him short.

'Records had the report all the time, Bill. It was misfiled. She's off the hook, and so am I.' He paused to let it sink in and wagged a warning finger. 'Bill, a word of advice. Make it your business to get on with her.'

Otley downed his whisky and stood up. 'That an order?' he asked through clenched teeth.

Kernan didn't reply and he walked to the door, stopped with his back to the Super. 'John Shefford was the best friend I ever 'ad. When my wife died, he pulled me through. I miss him.'

Kernan said gently, 'We all do, Bill.'

Otley's back was rigid as he replied, 'Good night, sir, an' thanks for the drink.'

Outside the office, Otley stopped and shook out his old mackintosh, folded it neatly over his arm. *Jesus Christ, Otley, where the fuck did you get that raincoat, when you were demobbed? I'll start a whip-round, get you a decent one, fancy one of those Aussie draped jobs?* He could hear Shefford's voice as if it was yesterday and he ached with grief. He missed his friend more than he could ever put into words, especially to men like Kernan.

Maureen Havers tumbled through the double doors carrying a vast stack of files and gave him a glum smile.

'You seen what's coming in? We need a new trestle table for this lot . . . I thought you were on nine to three, Skipper? Haven't you got a home to go to?'

After a moment's hesitation, he offered to give her a hand, and as they walked along the corridor he said casually, 'Do me a favour, would you, Maureen? If anything comes in from Oldham, let me have a shufti first, OK?'

'Sure! You got relatives up there? You know, I was almost transferred to Manchester, but I failed my driving test . . .'

They passed through the second set of swing doors and suddenly Otley felt better, because he had something to do. He was off-duty, but had nowhere to go, not now John Shefford was gone.

It was a struggle for Jane Tennison to open the front door. The files she carried were slipping out of her arms, and she dropped her briefcase to save them. When she finally made it into the hall she shut the door behind her and leaned against it, exhausted but glad to be home.

Joey's voice wailed from the spare bedroom, 'Nooo-o-o-o! Daddy, don't go!'

'OK, Joe, just one more story,' Peter replied patiently.

Grateful that the door was closed, Jane tip-toed past it and into her own bedroom. She was in bed before Peter had finished the last story.

'And then, what do you suppose he did then?'

Silence. Peter peered at his son in the dim light of the Anglepoise lamp; he was asleep at last. He tucked the duvet around Joey's shoulders and sat for a moment, staring at the gleam of his ash blonde hair and the long, blonde lashes lying on his pale cheeks. He loved the boy so much, if only Marianne . . . But he mustn't think like that, the past was done, buried.

Sitting in the semi-darkness, he was unable to stop himself going over and over it in his mind; the anger and hatred, the terrible things that were said, the dragging sense of loss . . . and the last time he had seen Marianne alone. She was so flippant, sometimes he could strangle her . . . He knew he could never let it rest until she told him the truth. She was pregnant again and, from Peter's calculations, he knew that he could be the baby's father.

Jane was asleep as soon as her head touched the pillow. When Peter came to bed, needing her, needing someone, he found her flat out, snoring lightly. Suddenly angry, he threw his dressing-gown off, climbed in beside her and thumped his pillow.

She shot up, blinking in panic, then collapsed with a moan. With her eyes still closed, she mumbled, 'Whassamatter with you?'

'Every night's the same. You're exhausted, asleep before I've even cleaned my teeth . . .'

She rolled towards him and opened her eyes. 'I'm sorry, Pete.'

'You make me feel guilty if I so much as touch you. We

haven't made love for . . . I dunno how long, I hardly see you. And when I do see you, you're always knackered. Our relationship stinks!'

Tentatively, Jane put out a hand and stroked his chest. 'I love you.'

'You do? But if this —' he lifted her pillow and brought out her bleeper — 'if this goes off, I don't exist! You're always either giving someone a bollocking on the phone or buried in files.'

He switched off his bedside light, plunging them into darkness, and lay down, not touching her. Jane giggled, 'You're right! I'm sorry, I will make more time for us . . .'

He felt her moving beside him. A moment later, her nightdress flew across the room.

'There! Just to prove I'm not a frigid old bag . . .'

Peter smiled and propped himself on one elbow, reached for her.

'Daddy?' said a little voice. Framed in the light from the hall, Joey peered into the room. 'Daddy . . .?'

Pulling the duvet over her head, Jane cracked up, with laughter. 'Ignore him, he'll go away . . . Go back to bed, Joey!'

Thinking it was a game, Joey snorted with laughter and jumped on the bed, trying to pull the quilt away from her.

'Don't, Joey! Go back to bed! Joey?

He tried to climb into the bed, but Jane hung on. 'Joey, will you pass me my nightdress?'

'Why?'

'Because I don't have any clothes on, that's why.'

Peter lifted the duvet on his side. 'Come on, get in . . .'

As he snuggled down, Joey demanded in his piped voice, 'Tell me a story, about bums and titties!'

'Where did you learn those words?' Peter tried to sound angry, but Jane's sniggers didn't help.

'At school. My mummy goes to bed without any clothes on, sometimes, but sometimes she . . .'

He fell asleep mid-sentence. Peter lifted him into his arms. 'I'll just carry him back to his own bed. Jane? Jane . . .?'

All he could see was the top of her head, but he knew she was asleep. He sighed; the pair of them were out cold, but he was wide awake . . . Wide awake and thinking about Mariannc, naked, in bed with his ex-best friend.

Chapter Eight

Maureen Havers was complaining bitterly to Sergeant Otley. It was the third Sunday she had worked in a row, and she didn't like it. She dumped a pile of boxes on the desk.

'These are unsolved murders from the entire Manchester area, every location visited by George Marlow since nineteen eighty-bloody-four!'

Otley was unravelling a huge computer print-out from the paint factory. Its end trailed in a heap on the floor.

'Ma'am needs her rest, Maureen! You got anythin' from Oldham?'

She pointed across the room. 'It's on your desk, Skipper. Want some coffee?'

Otley grinned. 'Do I! And keep it comin', it looks like we got a real workload.'

The rest of the team began to appear in dribs and drabs,

looking pretty unenthusiastic about being there. Then Burkin came racing in, the only one who seemed to have any life in him. Grinning, he waved a copy of the *News of the World* under Otley's nose.

'Wait till you see this! All is avenged!'

The two sisters didn't resemble each other in any way. Jane, older by three years, was a nightmare in the kitchen. She had chosen woodwork at school instead of domestic science, and actually preferred M&S ready-to-serve dinners than anything she attempted herself.

Pam, on the other hand, loved cooking. She had done a brief stint behind the counter at Boots the Chemist, then married and produced two children. Her third baby was due within the month. She was easy-going, sweet-natured and boringly happy squashed into Jane's tiny kitchen. Sunday mornings in her household were reserved for preparing the big lunch, but she had managed to send Tony and the kids off to Hampstead Heath so she could come round and help. Yet it was Jane who was brewing the coffee, Jane who set out the cups and saucers, who had brought out the well-thumbed cookery books and was frantically searching for a suitable dish for Peter's big dinner party. Everything Pam had so far suggested had been greeted by groans from Jane; she couldn't attempt a roast, she'd never get the joint ready at the same time as all the vegetables, and she'd never made proper gravy in her life.

'For Chrissakes, Pam, just something simple that looks like it's not, easy to cook but doesn't look like it, know what I mean? I've got the starters organized, just avocados with some prawns bunged in, but it's the main course I'm worried about.'

'How many is it for?'

'There'll be six of us. It's got to be something simple, I haven't cooked for so long I don't think I could cope.'

'Tell you an easy one – fresh pasta, a little cream and seasoning, then strips of smoked salmon. Plenty of good crusty bread, and fruit and cheese to follow. Are any of them vegetarians?'

The front door banged open and Peter appeared, with the *News of the World* open at the centre pages.

'Are any of your friends vegetarian, Pete?'

Ignoring her, Peter read aloud from the paper: '"George Marlow opened his heart to our reporter. He wept, saying he was an innocent man, but the police are making his life a misery . . ."'

Jane tossed her head, thinking he was joking. 'Very funny!'

He laughed. 'I'm serious! They've got a terrible picture of you, like something out of a horror movie. Dragon Woman!' He dodged her as she grabbed for the paper, and continued reading in a Monty Python voice. '"This is the woman detective in charge of the murder investigation. To date, her only words have been 'No comment'." Should be at home with me, mate!'

Jane's next attempt to get the paper from him succeeded, but she tore it in half in the process. 'Now look what you've done!' he teased.

But she wasn't listening. Her mouth hung open as she scanned the article. She screamed, 'My God, they've got pictures of my surveillance lads!'

Still laughing, Peter was reading over her shoulder. '"Marlow states that he is being hounded by a woman with an obsession – to lock him up . . ."'

'It's not bloody funny! It's buggered everything! We can't have any more line-ups, with his face plastered all over the papers. Not to mention the boys; I'm going to have to pull them off him now their cover's blown!'

She stormed out to the telephone, leaving Pam and Peter staring at each other. Pam whispered, 'I think I'd better go.'

George Marlow walked quickly up the steps of a large, detached house in Brighton and through the open front doors. A pair of glass swing doors admitted him to the hallway.

Following the directions of the receptionist, Marlow entered a high-ceilinged, airy room with windows overlooking the sea. Several elderly people were quietly playing draughts or chess, while one or two just sat silently in armchairs, their eyes focused on a future that no one else could see.

He knew where he would find her; alone in her wheelchair by the window, gazing out towards France. He walked silently towards her, stopped two or three feet away.

In a low voice that could not be heard by the other residents, he began to sing, 'When you walk through a storm, hold your head up high . . .'

His mother turned in her chair, her face lit with joy. As her son kissed her gently on both cheeks, she picked up the refrain.

'. . . And don't be afraid of the dark; at the end of the storm there's a golden sky, and the sweet, silver song of a lark . . .'

Mrs Marlow, or Doris Kelly as she used to be known, had spent the entire morning getting ready for his visit. Her make-up was perfect, her lipstick and eye shadow perhaps a trifle overdone, but she was still a beauty, retaining a youthfulness in her face that was, sadly, not mirrored in her once-perfect body. She had grown heavy, and the scarves and beads, chosen carefully to disguise the fact, didn't help. Her tiny hands, perfectly manicured with shell-pink varnish, glittered with fake diamonds.

'Hallo, my darling!'

When he kissed the powdery cheek, he could feel the spikes of her mascaraed eyelashes. She smelt of sweet flowers. The big, china-blue eyes roamed the room as if acknowledging the other residents' prying eyes.

'Take me somewhere special for lunch, George, I'm ravenous, simply ravenous. How about the Grand Hotel? Or we can have morning coffee, I'd like that. They're so kind at the Grand.'

He gathered her things into a carrier bag and hung it on the back of her chair, then wheeled his mother out, pausing beside grey-haired, docile old women for Doris to smile and wave gaily, and elderly gentlemen who begged her to sing their favourite songs that evening.

'Oh, we'll have to see, Mr Donald ... Goodbye, William, see you later, Frank ...'

She loved the fact that even here she was a star. On Sunday evenings they hired a pianist, and she would sing. 'The old fools love to be entertained, George, but the pianist has two left hands. Do you remember dear Mr McReady? What an ear he had, pick up any tune ... But now, without sheet music, this young man can't play a note.'

She sang snatches of songs as George tucked her blanket around her swollen legs, and called and waved until they reached the end of the driveway. Then she fell silent.

'Shall we have our usual stroll along the front, work up an appetite, Ma?'

Doris nodded, drawing her blanket closer with delicate,

pink-nailed fingers. George started singing again, 'When you walk through a storm . . .' but Doris didn't join in.

'Come on, Ma, let's hear you!'

'No, darling, my voice isn't what it was.' She put a hand to her head. 'Did you bring me a scarf?'

It was high tide, and the spray was blowing onto the promenade. He parked the chair beside a bench and brought out a silk square. Folding it carefully, he handed it to her.

'Thank you, darling. I was asking Matron if we could get a better hairdresser, only I need a trim, but I don't like the young girl that comes in. Oh, she's very sweet, but she's an amateur . . .'

George watched her tie the square over her head, carefully tucking in the hair. 'You have to watch these girls, they cut off far too much . . .'

George could see the reflections of her past beauty as she tilted her head coquettishly. 'All ship-shape, am I, darling?'

He nodded, and gently pressed a stray curl into place. 'All ship-shape. Now, how about singing me "Once I had a secret love, that dwelt within the heart of me" . . .?'

Sitting in her wheelchair, wrapped in her rug, she swayed to the rhythm, her hands in the air like an old trouper. Being together like this brought the memories flooding back to both of them, and they were laughing too much to finish the song.

'You always liked the old ones best. Remember that Elvis medley I used to do?' She sat up straight and played an imaginary piano as she sang, 'Love me tender, love me true, all my dreams fulfil; for, my darling, I love you, and I always will ... That was your Dad's favourite. I don't know what he would think about this ... What does that Moyra think of it all?'

George's face fell. 'Now, Mum, don't start. Moyra's a good woman, and she's stood by me.'

He took a newspaper from the carrier bag. It was folded so that the article about him was on the outside. Managing to grin at her, he asked, 'What did you give them this photo for? I hated that school.'

Mrs Marlow pulled a handkerchief from her sleeve. 'Your Dad would turn in his grave ...'

'Don't cry, Mum, don't ... I'm innocent, Mum, I had to do something to prove it. They'll lay off me now, and I got paid a fair bit. I'll get a new job – they gave me good references. Things'll turn out, don't you worry.'

He walked to the railings at the edge of the promenade and threw the paper into the sea. When he turned a moment later to face her, his hands were in his pockets.

'Which one's got a present in?' he demanded. 'I want a song, though, you must promise me a song.'

She made a great performance out of it, finally fooling him into giving her a clue to which pocket his gift was in. He presented the perfume with a flourish and she made him bend down for a kiss. Her warmth and her love for him shone out, despite her fears.

On the way back to the home they sang, 'Why am I always the bridesmaid, never the blushing bride?', vying with each other to sing the silly bits and breaking into giggles.

Moyra was doing the ironing. While George put the kettle on he was singing 'Why Am I Always the Bridesmaid?'.

'Every time you go to see her you come back singing those stupid songs,' Moyra complained.

'That was by way of a proposal,' he said as he put coffee in their mugs and poured the boiling water. 'I reckon it's time I made an honest woman of you.'

'Not if your mother has any say in the matter; I was never good enough for you in her eyes!' Moyra retorted. 'And I notice she gave the papers that photo of you in your posh school uniform . . .'

He handed her a mug of coffee. 'Did I ever tell you about—'

She interrupted him. 'How beautiful she looked at the school prize-giving? How all the lads said she looked like a movie star? Yes, you did!'

'But I've never told you about afterwards, after the prize-giving.'

'I dunno why you go on about it, you were only at the school two minutes.'

'I walked Mum and Dad to the gates. They were all hanging out of the dormitory windows, giving her wolf-whistles. Mum was being all coy, you know, waving to the boys. She didn't want them to know we didn't have a car, that they were going to catch the bus. And then, just as we got to the gates, the wind blew her wig off. They all saw it . . .'

Moyra spluttered through her mouthful of coffee. 'You're kidding me! Blew her wig off!' She laughed aloud.

Offended, he blinked. 'It wasn't funny, Moyra. My Dad ran down the road to get it back, and she just stood there, rooted to the spot . . .' He raised his hands to his own hair. 'I didn't know her hair had fallen out. Dad helped her put the wig back on, but the parting was all crooked. Underneath all the glamour she was ugly; an ugly stranger.'

'And everybody saw it? Did she ever talk about it?'

'She never even mentioned it.'

'I always thought it was just old age, you know. I've never said anything to her, but it's so obvious. How long has she been bald, then?'

'I don't know. She still pretends it's her own hair, even to me, says it needs trimming and so on.'

'Well, what do you know! Underneath it all the Rita Hayworth of Warrington is really Yul Brynner in disguise!'

He looked at her for a moment, then laughed his

lovely, warm, infectious laugh. He slipped his arms around her and kissed her on the neck.

'Did you mean it, George? About getting married?'

He lifted her in his arms and swung her around. 'I love you, Moyra – what do you say, will you marry me?'

'Will I? I've had the licence for two years, George, and you won't get out of it.'

He smiled at her. Sometimes his resemblance to his mother took her breath away. He was so good-looking, every feature neat and clean-cut. Doris had been a real looker, and George was the most handsome man Moyra had ever known. Held tight in the circle of his arms she looked up into his dark eyes, eyes a woman would pray for, with thick dark lashes. Innocent eyes ...

'I love you, George, I love you.'

His kiss was gentle and loving. He drew her towards the bedroom.

'George! It's nearly dinner time!'

'It can wait ...'

DCI Tennison stared at the headline, furious. Then she ripped it down from the Incident Room door. She took a deep breath, crumpled the paper into a ball and entered the room.

The men fell silent, watching her. She held the ball of paper up so they could all see, then tossed it accurately into a waste-paper basket.

'OK, we've all read it, so the least said about it the better. But it's not just me with egg on my face.'

She crossed to her desk and dumped her briefcase. 'It makes our surveillance operation look like a circus.'

'Any word on what their readers' survey came up with, ma'am?' asked Otley with a snide smile. 'For or against female officers on murder cases?'

She gave him an old-fashioned look. 'Oh, you're a biased load of chauvinists, and there's thousands more like you!'

'Don't worry, ma'am,' chipped in Dave Jones, 'you could always get a job in panto!'

He was holding up the photograph of her from the paper, but it had been added to in felt-tip. She started laughing and clipped him one.

Maureen Havers walked in as he raised his hands to defend himself. She tapped Tennison on the back.

'Why me? I didn't draw all over it. It was him!' Jones pointed to Burkin, who hung his head, although he couldn't really give a fuck. When she'd gone, Jones would get a right clip round the ear hole.

Tennison turned to Havers, who told her she was wanted on the top floor.

'Oh well, here it comes. See you all later.'

Otley claimed everybody's attention as soon as she had gone. 'Right, we've all had a jolly good laugh, now get yer pin-brains on this lot. We want all these unsolved murders on the computer, so we can cross-check them for any that occurred when Marlow was in the vicinity.'

As they went reluctantly to work, Maureen Havers had a word with Otley.

'You finished with the Oldham files? Only they haven't been put on the computer . . .'

'I'll sort 'em, love. Haven't had a chance to look through them yet.'

Havers began to distribute more files around the Incident Room, which was greeted with moans and groans. Otley rapped his desk.

'Come on you lot, settle down. Sooner you get this lot sorted, sooner we're in the pub. As an incentive, first round's on me!'

But a pint wouldn't compensate for the tedious slog of sifting through hundreds of unsolved murders. Otley opened the Oldham file he had already checked over; he knew there was a problem, and now he had to work out the best way to deal with it.

The bar was full of familiar faces. At one of the marble-topped tables several of the lads were discussing the unsolved murders.

'I've looked at twenty-three cases,' Muddyman said, 'all around Rochdale, Burnley, Southport; and I've got one possible but unlikely . . .'

Rosper cut in, 'There was a woman found in a chicken

run in Sheffield. Reckon she'd been there for months. The chickens were knocking out record numbers of eggs!'

'You know they've been feeding the dead ones to the live ones, that's why we've had all this salmonella scare. Got into the eggs,' Lillie contributed.

'This woman was seventy-two, an old boiler!' Rosper chuckled.

They were suddenly all aware that Tennison had walked in. She looked around, located Jones and went to lean on the back of his chair.

'Next round's on me, give us your orders,' she told them. 'The bad news is: I'm asking for volunteers. They've withdrawn the official surveillance from Marlow, so I want four men to cover it.'

Lillie stood up. 'Excuse me . . .'

'Great, that leaves three . . .'

'I was just going for a slash . . .'

Rosper laughed and she nailed him. 'Two! Come on, undercover's a piece of cake. Two more . . .'

She handed Rosper a twenty and sent him to the bar. 'Let's get those drinks in. I'll have a large G and T.'

Lillie pulled out a chair for her. 'How did it go, boss?'

The others pretended not to listen. Tennison said quietly, 'If I don't pull something out of the bag very soon, I'm off the case.'

Her gin and tonic arrived. She thanked Rosper and he handed her back her money.

'What's this?'

Rosper shrugged. 'It's OK, Skipper coughed up.'

'Is this a truce? Ah well, cheers!' She raised her glass to them, but Muddyman and Rosper were looking towards Otley, who was sitting at the bar.

'Cheers, Skipper!' Muddyman called.

Otley turned and grinned, as if he had got one over on Tennison, even in the pub.

With a few drinks inside them they returned to the Incident Room to work. The stacks of paperwork did not seem to have diminished much, despite the busy atmosphere. The room was thick with tobacco smoke and littered with used plastic cups. Tennison, a cigarette dangling from her mouth, was double-checking and collating results.

At nine o'clock, Muddyman stood up and announced that he was going home. Many of the others started to make a move and Otley approached Tennison.

'We've got several cases that need looking into: one at Oldham, another at Southport, an' we're checking one in Warrington. Ma'am? . . .'

Tennison looked up. 'Sorry.'

'Who do you want checking these unsolved cases?'

'Oh, anyone who's been cooped up here all day, give them a break.'

'OK,' Otley muttered. He made a few notes on a pad.

'I'll do the Oldham ... Muddyman, Rosper and Lillie are on Marlow, so that leaves ... Can you take the Southport case?'

'OK, just pin it up for me.'

Otley put the list up on the notice-board and picked up his coat. As he left he passed WPC Havers.

'You'll be able to retire on your overtime, gel!'

'Night, Sarge!' she replied, as she passed some telephone messages to Tennison. 'Why don't you take a break, boss?'

'Because I've got more to lose, Maureen.' She rose and stretched, yawning, then went to examine the list on the notice-board. 'I've lost track,' she sighed.

Only three of the men were left working. 'Go on home, you lot,' she told them. 'Recharge your batteries.'

DC Caplan put his coat on and asked, 'Anyone for a drink?'

'I've had enough liquid for one day, mate,' replied Jones. 'I'll be bumping into the mother-in-law in the night, she spends more time in the lavvy than a plumber ...'

There was a metamorphosis taking place right in front of them, not that anyone noticed. DC Jones, of the polished shoes and old school tie, had taken to wearing striped shirts with white collars and rather flashy ties, similar to those favoured by DI Burkin. He was also knocking back the pints, was even the first in the bar at opening time. It was taking time, but he was at last becoming one of the lads.

As they left, still joking, Havers asked Tennison casually, 'What's with Oldham, then? He got relatives there or something?'

'What?'

'Skipper asked for anything from Oldham. I wondered what the attraction was . . . Mind if I push off?'

It slowly dawned on Tennison what she was talking about. 'He's doing it to me again!' She shook her head in disbelief and muttered a vague goodnight to Maureen, intent on getting to the bottom of it. Maureen saw her uncover one of the computers and start tapping the keyboard as she closed the door.

Tennison muttered to herself, 'Right, Otley, let's find out just what your game is! Jeannie Sharpe . . . March nineteen eighty-four . . .' She moved the cursor down the screen, read some more, then picked up the phone to make an internal call. There was no reply; she put the receiver down and went across to the large table in the centre of the room where all the files were stacked in alphabetical order. Whistling softly, she selected the Oldham file and flipped through it, then carried it back to the computer.

'Ah . . . Jeannie Sharpe, aged twenty-one, prostitute . . .' She compared the entry on the computer with the notes in the file. 'Head of investigation, DCI F. G. Neal . . .

Detective Inspector Morrell and ... DI John Shefford!'

She pushed her chair back, staring at the computer screen. Why was Otley so intent on taking the Oldham case? It had to be something to do with Shefford; it was too much of a coincidence. He had put her down for Southport with DC Jones; she snatched the list down from the notice-board. By the time she had retyped it she was seeing spots before her eyes. It was time to call it quits; but she, not Otley, was now down for Oldham.

'My car'll be here any minute! I was too tired to drive last night.' Dressed and ready for work, Jane was rushing around the kitchen. Peter, still half-asleep, stumbled in.

''Morning!'

'I got in a bit late, so I slept in the spare room. Feel this – d'you think it'll soften up by tonight?' She handed him an avocado.

'It's fine.' He stood in the middle of the kitchen and stretched. The avocado slipped from his grasp and Jane caught it deftly.

'I'll be back early to get everything ready for tonight. I'm doing what Pam suggested: pasta and smoked salmon. Prawns and mayonnaise in the avocados ... Ah!' She whipped round and jotted 'Mayonnaise' on her notepad. The doorbell rang. 'And cream. Give us a kiss. I'll see you about seven. If anyone calls for me, I'll be in Oldham.'

She left Peter standing in the kitchen. 'Oldham, right . . .' He woke up suddenly. 'Oldham?' But he was talking to himself.

Tennison and Jones followed the uniformed Sergeant Tomlins through a makeshift door in a corrugated iron fence. Tomlins was still trying to make up for his error at Manchester Piccadilly station, where he had assumed Jones to be the Chief Inspector.

'In nineteen eighty-four all this part was still running,' he said as he led them into the cavernous, empty warehouse. 'It was shut down soon afterwards, and hasn't been occupied since. The only people that came here were the tarts with their customers, and I think some still do.'

'We got the call at four in the morning, from a dosser who'd come in for the night.' He pointed to an old cupboard against a wall, minus its doors. 'He found her in there.'

Tennison inspected the cupboard. 'Actually inside?'

'Yes. The doors were still on then, but not quite closed. She was lying face down, her head that way . . . This shed was used for dipping parts; the vats used to fill the place.' He spread his arms to indicate the whole area. 'They all went for scrap, I suppose. They lowered the stuff on pulleys – you can still see the hooks – then raised them again to dry.'

Dozens of rusty hooks still hung from the ceiling.

Tennison looked around and asked, 'Hands tied behind her back, right?'

'Yes. Savage beating, left half-naked. Her face was a mess. Her shift was found outside, and her coat over there.'

They started to leave but Tennison turned back to stare at the spot where Jeannie Sharpe was found.

'Nasty place to end up, huh?'

'Well, these tarts bloody ask for it.'

She snapped at him, 'She was twenty-one years old, Sergeant!' but he was moving ahead, heaving the rubbish aside. He waited for them at the door.

'You wanted to have a word with her friends? Slags isn't the word for it . . .' He pushed the corrugated iron aside for Tennison to pass. 'We clean up the streets and back they come, like rodents.'

She let the door slam back in his face. 'Sorry!' she said.

The flat was damp, with peeling wallpaper, but an attempt had been made to render it habitable. The furniture was cheap: a single bed, a cot, a painted wardrobe and a few armchairs, and it was fairly tidy, apart from the children's toys scattered everywhere.

Tennison was sitting in an old wing-chair beside a low table on which were two overflowing ashtrays, a teapot and a lot of biscuit crumbs. She was totally at ease, smoking and sipping a mug of tea.

Carol, a drably dressed but attractive blonde woman in her early thirties, was telling her about the last time she had seen her friend Jeannie alive.

'We were all together, just coming out of the pub, our local, y'know. We'd had a few . . .'

Linda, plump and cheerful with dark hair, interrupted her. 'I hadn't! I was on antibiotics, can't drink with them.'

'His car was parked, er . . . You know where the pub is?' Tennison shook her head. 'Well, it's right on a corner, y'know, so there's a side street . . .'

Finishing her tea, Tennison suggested they go and look.

The three women stood on the corner outside the pub. It wasn't easy to tell by looking at them which were the prostitutes and which the senior policewoman.

'See, there's the side street. He was parked just there. You could only see a bit of the car,' Carol was saying.

Tennison offered her cigarettes round. 'You couldn't tell me the make of it? The colour?'

'It was dark, I reckon the car was dark, but it had a lot of shiny chrome at the front, y'know, an' like a bar stuck all over with badges an' stuff. He called out to Jeannie . . .'

Tennison grabbed the remark. 'He called out? You mean he knew her name?'

'I don't think it was her name. It was, y'know, "How much, slag?" I said to her, hadn't she had enough for one night . . .'

Carol put in: 'Ah, but she was savin' up, wanted to emigrate to Australia if she could get enough.'

'So Jeannie crossed the road? Did you see her get into the car?'

Linda replied, 'She went round to the passenger side.'

'I looked over, y'know, to see, but he was turning like this . . .' Carol demonstrated. 'I only saw the back of his head.'

Tennison stepped to the kerb and peered around the corner as Linda said, 'We never saw her again. She had no one to even bury 'er, but we had a whip-round.'

'Fancy a drink?' asked Tennison.

They piled into the pub and found an empty booth. Carol went to the bar while the locals sized up Tennison. They were mostly labourers in overalls.

Linda had produced a photograph of herself and Jeannie. 'Lovely lookin', she was. That's me – I was thinner then, and blonde. Cost a fortune to keep it lookin' good, so I've gone back to the natural colour. Set me back twenty-five quid for streaks! We used to get cut-price, mind, at the local salon, but they've gone all unisex, y'know. I hate having me 'air done with a man sitting next to me, don't you?'

Tennison opened her briefcase to take out her copy of the *News of the World*, but was interrupted by a man in dirty, paint-splashed overalls who strolled across from the juke-box. He put a hand on Tennison's shoulder and leaned down to whisper, 'I've got fifteen minutes, the van's outside . . .'

Turning slowly, she removed his hand from her shoulder. 'I'm busy right now.' He made no move to go, so she looked him in the eye. 'Sod off!'

He looked in surprise at Linda, who mouthed 'Cop!' and shot out before anyone could draw breath. Tennison carried on as though nothing had happened.

Carol returned with the drinks as Tennison placed the newspaper on the table.

'The barman says you just missed the London Express, but there's a train at four minutes past five.'

'I'll be cutting it fine . . .' Tennison checked her watch and smiled. 'Dinner party! Is this like him?' She pointed to the newspaper photo of Marlow and took a sip of her drink.

'He's a bit tasty, isn't he?' Carol commented, and glanced at Linda. 'He was dark-haired . . .'

'You thought he had a beard, didn't you?' Linda said.

'Beard? You never mentioned that in your statement.'

'She couldn't get out of the nick fast enough, they're bastards,' Carol informed her. 'An' I'll tell you something for nothing – they never gave a shit about Jeannie. We're rubbish, until they want a jerk-off! Four kids we got between us, and no one's interested in them. An' that inspector geezer, y'know, him . . .' She nudged Linda. 'I'm not sayin' any names, but . . .'

'I will,' said Linda. 'It was that big bloke, John Shefford. They got rid of him faster than a fart.'

Tennison asked, deadpan, 'What do you mean?'

'I reckon they found out about him an' Jeannie,' Carol told her confidentially. 'Next thing we knew, he was on his bike, gone to London. He was as big a bastard as any of 'em – bigger. Jeannie never had a chance: her step-dad was screwin' her from the time she was seven. She was on the streets at fourteen, an' that Shefford used to tell her he'd take care of her. Well, he never found out who killed her; they never even tried.'

'Poor kid, strung up like that, like a bit of meat on a hook!' Linda said. 'You have to be really sick . . .'

Tennison jumped on her. 'What? What did you say?'

'The dosser who found her, he told me.'

'You know this man? He got a name?'

'Oh, he's dead, years back, but he told me all about it. Hanging by her arms from a hook in the ceiling.'

It was getting late. Peter checked his watch anxiously and started to lay the dining-table. Where the hell was she?

The front door crashed open and Jane rushed in, yelling, 'Don't say a word, I've got it timed to the second. Don't panic!'

True to her word, everything was just about ready by eight o'clock, and she had put on a nice dress, though her hair was still damp. She ran quickly around the table, distributing place mats.

'Water's on, what else can I do?' Peter asked.

She stood back to look at the table. 'Right, glasses for red, glasses for white, starter plates, teaspoons . . . Napkins! Shit, hang on . . .'

She shot out to the kitchen, returning to fling a packet of paper napkins at him, then disappeared again, shouting, 'Bread, bread!'

The doorbell rang as she came back with the basket of rolls. She gave Peter the thumbs-up.

'All set! Let them in!'

Peter grabbed her and kissed her cheek, then they both headed for the hall.

When they had finished eating, Jane cleared the table and went to make the coffee, taking her glass of wine with her. The kitchen was a disaster area with hardly a square foot of clear work surface. She tidied up a little while she waited for the percolator.

Peter rushed in, obviously panicking. 'You're taking your time! Where are the liqueur glasses?'

'We haven't got any! You'll have to use those little coloured ones Mum gave me.' She drained her glass of wine. 'How's it going?'

He relaxed a little. 'Just getting down to business. Can you keep the women occupied? I'll take the tray.'

As he hurried back to his guests, Jane yawned and pressed the plunger on the percolator. The hot coffee shot from the spout, all over her dress. 'Shit!' Then she shrugged, wiped herself down as best she could, fixed a smile on her face and marched out with the coffee pot.

Frank King was obviously the dominant male, the one with the money and the big ideas. He had spread some plans on the table and was explaining them to Peter and Tom.

Frank's wife, Lisa, and Tom's wife, Sue, were sitting in the armchairs at the other end of the room, drinking apricot brandy from tacky little blue and green glasses. They were both dressed to the nines, perfectly coiffed and lip-glossed, but Lisa was the one with the really good jewellery. Jane poured them coffee.

'It's nice, isn't it? I like sweet liqueurs,' Lisa was saying to Sue. 'We spent three months in Spain last year; the drinks are so cheap, wine's a quarter of the price you pay here. Oh, thanks, Jane. Mind you, the price of clothes – all the decent ones are imported, that's what makes them so expensive.'

Jane moved on to the men. Neither Tom nor Frank thanked her for the coffee and Peter, intent on what Frank was saying, refused it.

'Like I said, no problem. Get the bulldozers in and they're gone before anyone's woken up. Don't know why they make such a fuss about a few trees anyway. So, we clear this area completely, but leave the pool, which goes with this house here. The other we build at an angle, the two of them have to go up in less than three-quarters of an acre . . .'

'What sort of price are we looking at?' Tom wanted to know.

'The one with the pool, four ninety-five. The one without we ask three fifty. That's low for an exclusive close . . .'

Leaving them to it, Jane found a small glass that Peter had poured for her on the dresser. She carried it over to the women and sat down.

She took a sip from the glass. 'Christ, it's that terrible sweet muck!' Up again, Jane fetched a wine glass and went looking for the brandy. It was on the table beside Frank's elbow, and she helped herself to a generous measure. She had been drinking since lunchtime: gins in the pub, on the train, wine throughout dinner. She was tying one on, but it didn't show, yet. She captured a bowl of peanuts and sat down again. It seemed as though Lisa hadn't stopped talking.

'She goes on and on, she wants a pony. I said to Frank, there's no point getting her one if she's going to be the same as she was over the hamster. The poor thing's still somewhere under the floorboards . . .'

Sue took advantage of the pause to speak to Jane. 'Tom was telling me you have Joey at weekends.'

Jane was searching for her cigarettes. She nodded and opened her mouth to speak, but Lisa got in first.

'What I wouldn't give to have mine just for weekends! Au pairs have been the bane of my life . . .'

'Oh, I've never had any troub—'

Lisa steamed on regardless. 'I've had German, Spanish, French and a Swedish girl. I was going out one day, got as far as the end of the drive and realized I'd forgotten something, so I went back. She was in the Jacuzzi, stark naked! If Frank had walked in . . .'

'Probably would have jumped on her!' At last Tennison had got a word in edgeways. She grinned.

Sue nearly laughed, but remembered in time that she wanted to stay in Lisa's good books. She changed the subject.

'You're with the Metropolitan Police, Jane? Peter was telling . . .'

Lisa broke in: 'Well, I'd better tell Frank to ease up on the brandy, can't have you arresting him . . .'

'That's traffic, not my department,' Jane replied, knocking back her brandy.

'Oh, so what do you do? Secretary? I was Frank's before we got married.'

'No, I'm not a secretary.' The day was beginning to catch up on Jane, or rather the tragic little Jeannie. *There was no one to bury her, so we had a whip-round . . .*

If Lisa had heard Jane's reply she paid no attention. Her

peanut-sized brain was now fixed on wallpaper, and she was holding forth about which was best, flock or fabric. In her opinion, fabric held its colour better . . .

The three men were still sitting around the table, hogging the brandy bottle. As Jane helped herself to another large one, Frank pushed his glass forward without pausing for breath.

'I put my men on the main house, Pete's men on the second, and the two of them go up neck and neck. I'm looking for a quick turnover, so we do a big colour brochure with artist's impressions and start selling them while we dig the foundations. Tom does the interiors, and we split the profits . . .'

Jane was unused to being ignored. She downed the brandy and poured another to carry back to her perch on the arm of the only really comfortable chair which, oddly enough, no one had sat in. She knocked over the bowl of peanuts into the chair and spent a few minutes eating the spilt ones from the seat, then slowly slid into it herself.

Lisa had not drawn breath, but Jane's accident with the peanuts finally brought her verbal assault course on wallpaper to a grinding halt. There was one of those classic silences among the women, during which Frank's voice could still be heard.

Lisa turned her full attention on Jane. 'I hear you were on the *Crime Night* programme?'

'That's right, I was answering the telephones, I was the

one passing the blank sheet of paper backwards and for-
wards.'

Missing the sarcasm in Jane's voice, Lisa ploughed on,
'I am impressed! I never watch it, it scares me, but I'm
paranoid about locking the house. And if a man comes
near me when I'm walking Rambo . . .' She laughed.
'That's our red setter, I'm not talking about Frank!'

Jane switched off for a moment, gazing into the bottom
of her empty glass. When she snapped to again she realized that Lisa hadn't paused once.

'But don't you think, honestly, that a lot of them ask for
it?'

'What, ask to be raped?' Jane shook her head and her
voice grew loud, 'How can anyone ask to be raped?'

She jumped to her feet, swaying slightly and glaring as
if interrogating Lisa, who shrank back in her seat. 'Where
do you walk your dog?'

'Well, on Barnes Common . . .'

'Barnes Common is notorious, women have been
attacked on Barnes Common!'

Lisa rallied a little. 'Yes, I know, but I wouldn't go there
late at night!'

'There are bushes, gullies, hidden areas. You could have
a knife at your throat, your knickers torn off you, and
bang! You're dead. But you weren't asking for it!'

'I . . . I was really talking about prostitutes . . .'

'What about them? Do you know any? Does Sue know

any?' She turned to the men, she had their attention now. 'How about you? Can you three tell me, hands on hearts, that you've never been with a tom?'

Lisa whispered to Sue, 'What's a tom?'

Tennison snapped, 'A tart!'

In the ensuing silence, the telephone rang. Peter said, 'It'll be for you, Jane.'

She weaved her way to the door, but turned back, blazing, when she heard Peter say, 'I'm sorry about that!'

'Don't you ever make apologies for me! We were just having a consev . . . a conservation!' She slammed the door.

'Keep her off the building site, Pete,' Frank said in a low voice.

'Actually, I'd like an answer to her question,' said Lisa.

'I think that went off all right, didn't it?' Jane, creaming her face, was talking to Peter.

'You asking me?'

'No, I was talking to the pot of cold cream! You're going to do the deal, aren't you?'

'Yeah . . . Did you have to bring up all that about tarts?'

'Put a bit of spark into the evening.'

'It wasn't your bloody evening!'

'Oh, thanks! I broke my bloody neck to get that dinner on the table!'

'It's always you, Jane! You, you, you! You don't give a sod about anyone else!'

'That's not true!'

'You care about the blokes on your team, your victims, your rapists, your "toms" as you call them, you give all your time to them.'

'That's my job!'

'Tonight was for my job, Jane. But no, you've got to put your ten cents' worth in!'

'OK, I'm sorry ... sorry if I spoilt the evening!'

The tiredness swept over her like a tidal wave. She had no energy to argue, and went for the easy way out, giving him a smile. 'OK? I apologize, but I think I had too much to drink, and they were so boring ...'

He stared at her, infuriated. Her comment really got to him. 'This is business, Jane, do you ever think how boring all your fucking talk is? Ever think about that, ever think how many conversations we've had about this guy George Marlow? You ever consider how fucking boring you get? Do you? I don't know him, I don't want to know about him, but Christ Almighty I hear his name ...'

'Pete, I've said I'm sorry, OK? Just let it drop.'

He was unwilling to let it go, but he shrugged. Jane put her head in her hands and sighed. 'Pete, I'm tired out. I'm sorry tonight didn't go as well as you'd planned, but you've got the contract, so why don't we just go to bed?'

The memories of the day swamped her: the smell of the factory, the smell of the two tarts' flat, her feelings, the smells, all muddled and out of control ... She couldn't stop the tears, she just sat hunched in front of the mirror, crying, crying for the waste, the little tart who had been raped by her stepfather when she was seven, little Jeannie with no one to bury her, who Jane didn't even know, yet she was crying for her and all the other Jeannies who lived and died like that and nobody gave a shit for . . .

Peter squatted down and brushed her hair from her face. 'It's all right, love. Like you said, I got the contract. Maybe *I* had a few too many . . . Come on, let's get you to bed.'

Jane went to bed, but she didn't sleep for a long time. When she woke she found the kitchen full of the debris of dinner; not a single dish had been washed. She put her coat on, ready to leave for work, and took two aspirin with her coffee.

Peter, his hair standing on end, joined her.

'Pete, I've been thinking over everything. Last night . . .'

With a grin he reached for her, tried to kiss her. She stepped back. 'I love you, Pete, I really do, but you're right. It doesn't work, does it? I do put my work first. I don't think I can change, because I'm doing what I always wanted, and to succeed I have to put everything into it. I have to prove myself every day, to every man on that force – and to myself . . .'

She was telling him that they could never lead the sort of life he wanted. It hurt a lot, and he wanted to gather her in his arms, make it all right. But the doorbell rang.

They just looked at each other, with so much more to say and no time to say it in.

Peter said quickly, 'Don't say anything more now, let's talk it over tonight. Maybe I haven't been easy to live with, maybe if I was more secure . . .'

The doorbell rang again. 'You'd better go, Jane.'

'I don't know what time I'll be back.'

Peter stood for a moment after she'd left, surveying the kitchen, then he lashed out at the stack of dishes on the draining-board, sending them crashing into the sink.

Tennison sat silently beside Jones as he drove. It unnerved him. Eventually he said, just to break the silence, 'Still no trace of Marlow's car.' She didn't react. 'Are you OK?' he asked.

'I want that bloody car found!' she snapped.

'Trouble at home? I got all your shopping OK, didn't I?'

'Yeah!'

'I got an earful when I got home. My dinner had set like cement.'

'The difference is that you get your dinner cooked for you. At my place, I'm the one who's supposed to cook it.' She thought a moment. 'Shit's gonna hit the fan this morning, though. You got an aspirin?'

Chief Superintendent Kernan had come in early to review the Marlow case, and for once Tennison had got her oar in first. Now he listened in growing anger as Tennison and Otley raged at each other, but he let them get on with it. 'George Marlow was questioned in nineteen eighty-four about the murder of a prostitute, Jeannie Sharpe. John Shefford, then a DI, was on the investigating team. He was transferred to London because it was discovered that he'd been having a relationship with the murdered girl!' Tennison stormed. 'None of this is in the records. We now know that he was having a sexual relationship with Della Mornay; he must have known he'd identified the wrong girl, but he was prepared to cover that up as well!'

Otley was seething. 'Everything you're saying is a pack of lies, and if John Shefford was alive . . .'

'But he's not, he's dead, and you're still covering up for him. *You* requested the Oldham case, *you* wanted to go up there because you knew Shefford was involved . . .'

'That's not true! Della Mornay was a police informer . . . '

'She was also a prostitute, picked up and charged by John Shefford when he was attached to Vice – and what a perfect job for him!'

Tennison's last remark brought Kernan to his feet. 'That's enough! Just calm down!'

'Sir, I have been working against time ever since I took over this investigation, at first because of George Marlow's release, now because I'm going to be pulled off it. George

Marlow is my only suspect, still my suspect for both murders, and now very possibly a third: Jeannie Sharpe.'

'I don't know anything about any previous case up north,' Otley insisted. 'I know some of the men fraternize with the girls on our patch . . .'

'Fraternize! Christ!'

Kernan thumped his desk, really pissed off. He pointed to Otley.

'Come on now, did Shefford think there was a connection between the first murder and the one in, er . . . Oldham?'

'I dunno, but I wanted to check it out. There was no ulterior motive.'

'So you knew John Shefford had worked in Oldham? Knew he'd been on this—' Kernan thumbed through the file '—this Jeannie Sharpe case?'

Otley was falling apart. He shook his head. 'No! I didn't know anything, but when I read the report and saw John's name down . . . Look, I know you knew, we all knew, he was a bit of a lad, so I just reckoned maybe I should check it out. That's all there was to it, nothin' more. If, as ma'am says, he was having a relationship with this tart, I knew nothin' about it.'

Tennison couldn't keep quiet. 'Just as you knew nothing about his relationship with Della Mornay? Bullshit! You knew, and you've been covering up for him . . .'

Kernan gave her the eye to shut up and keep it shut. 'Did you get anything from your trip to Southport, Bill?'

Otley shook his head. 'We're still checking, but no.'

Kernan nodded, then gave him a hard look. 'Well, keep at it. You can go.'

Otley hesitated. It was obvious that Kernan wanted him out of the office and wanted Tennison to stay. With an embarrassed cough, he turned to her.

'Maybe we got off to a bad start,' he said quietly. 'Should have taken a few weeks off after John . . .'

She gave him a rueful nod. 'I'll be in the Incident Room,' he said, and opened the door.

They waited until he had gone, then Kernan turned to Tennison and asked, 'What do you want to do?'

She looked him straight in the eye. 'I worked with a good bloke, in Hornchurch. Detective Sergeant Amson.'

Finally Kernan nodded. 'That's the deal, is it?'

'He's available, could be here in an hour or so. I'm going to drive up to Rochdale to see the woman Marlow attacked there. It would be a good opportunity to fill him in on the investigation.'

Kernan nodded again. Knowing she had won, Tennison went on, 'Marlow served eighteen months. All the cases were either before or after he was in jail. I want the surveillance put back on him.'

'OK. I'll do my best to hold Hicock off.'

'Thank you, sir. Detective Sergeant Amson.'

'I got it the first time.'

At ten Tennison was in the car park, getting some things from her boot, when Otley came up beside her.

'I reckon we got off on the wrong foot. I was just going back to the pub, wondered if you wanted a drink?'

'Has the Super not spoken to you?'

'No, I went and put a couple under my belt. I didn't know about John's spot of trouble in Oldham . . .'

Tennison said quietly, 'Yes, you did. You're off the case, Bill. I'm sorry, you've already been replaced.'

Otley seemed to shrink before her eyes. He turned to go and she said to his back, 'I want the names of every officer on my team who's taking sexual favours from prostitutes.'

He faced her again, but he had no anger left in him. She gave him a small nod and walked towards a car that had just drawn in to the car park. It was driven by the burly new sergeant, Terry Amson. He got out and opened the passenger door for her.

'I owe you a big one. My arse was dropping off in Hornchurch, I was sitting on it so much. How are you doing?'

She beamed and punched his arm as she climbed in. 'I think I'm doing OK.'

As he returned to the driving seat he gave Otley a small wave of acknowledgement. It wasn't returned. Otley's dejected figure was still standing there when they drove away.

Chapter Nine

Terry Amson drove fast and well up the motorway while Tennison put him in the picture on the murders.

'So we have three girls, Della Mornay, Karen Howard and Jeannie Sharpe, who were all strung up, with these clamp marks on their arms. The first two are different, but it's quite a coincidence.'

'Maybe he just perfected his technique! Have you tried talking to any of the guys he was banged up with? He's talkative, isn't he?'

'You could dig around while I'm with Miss Gilling, see if you can set something up for when we get back. And have a look at Marlow's statements, you never know what a fresh eye will come up with.'

The little terraced cottage that Pauline Gilling shared with her father had a neat, well-cared for garden. The inside was daintily decorated with Laura Ashley paper and a large collection of little glass animals, giving it a fragile feel which was echoed in Miss Gilling herself.

In her late thirties, she appeared older, with a pleasant but worried face. It took a while for her to unlock the front door, which was festooned with chains and bolts.

She sat on the edge of her chair and recounted the events of that day in a soft voice. It was as though she had learned it by heart; her eyes glazed slightly and she focused somewhere beyond the wall.

'It was the seventh of November, nineteen eighty-eight. At four-thirty in the afternoon ...'

Tennison prepared herself to work this lady over. Without taking her eyes from Gilling, she settled herself on the sofa and took out a cigarette, nodding encouragingly.

'I was working in a florist's, and it was half-day closing. I don't work there any more.' She was wringing her hands unconsciously. 'The shop is called Delphinia's, and the owner's name is Florence Herriot. November the seventh is her birthday. She asked if I would go to the pub with her at lunchtime, for a sherry. I had an appointment at the hairdresser's, so I did not arrive until ...' She gave a strangled little cough, as if her throat was too tight, and continued, 'I arrived at two-thirty-five. I had a glass of sherry and stayed for approximately half an hour. I always come home to get father's lunch, but on early closing day I have my hair set, so I leave a tray for him.'

There was that strange little cough again. She was really tense now; her hands continually smoothed her skirt over her knees, which were pressed tightly together. Tennison said nothing, just waited for her to go on.

Her body went totally rigid and she had to force herself to speak. 'I . . . I went up the path, I had my key out. I'd opened the door a few inches when . . . he called my name. "Pauline! Hallo, Pauline!" I turned round, but I didn't recognize him. He was smiling, and . . . he walked up the path towards me, and he said, "Aren't you going to invite me in for a cup of tea, Pauline?"'

She froze, like a rabbit caught in car headlights. Her mouth was open, but she made no sound. Deliberately, Tennison coughed, and she shook her head as if awakening, then started gabbling. 'I said I was sorry, I thought there was some mistake, I didn't know him. He came very close, pushed me into the hallway, got me by the throat, kept pushing me backwards . . . I was so terrified I couldn't scream, I was afraid for my father. I tried to defend myself with my handbag, but he grabbed it and hit me with it. The clasp cut my cheek open and broke my front teeth . . .'

After a decent interval, Tennison prompted gently, 'And then your father came in?'

'Yes. He was upstairs, I was lying on the floor, and he

kept kicking me, then Daddy called out and he ran away. My father is blind, he couldn't see him, couldn't be called to identify him . . .' She was going to cry.

'But you were able to pick George Marlow out of the line-up?'

Gilling swallowed, held back her tears. 'Oh, yes. He was clever, though; he had a beard when he attacked me, but he shaved it off before the identity parade. I still recognized him. It was his eyes, I will never forget his eyes . . . I know, if it hadn't been for my father, George Marlow would have killed me.'

Tennison crossed the room and squatted beside Gilling's chair. 'Thank you, you did very well, and I'm sorry to have made you go through it all again.'

Gilling shrank from her, fearing to be touched, and stood up. Her nervousness was beginning to grate on Tennison.

'I go through it all the time, every time the doorbell rings, every strange sound at night . . . I see his face, keep expecting him to come back, to finish . . . I had to leave my job, I can't sleep. He should have been put away for years, but they let him go after eighteen months. I live in terror of him coming back, because he said he would, he said he'd come back!'

Tennison climbed into the patrol car and breathed a sigh of relief. Beside her, Amson was immersed in a file.

'Marlow had a beard at the time of the rape, shaved it off for the line-up! That matches with what the toms said in Oldham, they thought the guy had a beard.'

He looked up. 'D'you think there's any truth in the story that she gave Marlow the come-on? She's, what, thirty-eight now, and a spinster . . .'

Tennison bridled. 'So am I, it doesn't mean I want myself raped, and my front teeth kicked in!'

'Take it easy, it's just that from the description she's a bit of a dog. Marlow, on the other hand, is a good-looking bloke, like myself.'

She replied with a laugh, 'Be very careful, Sergeant, or you'll be back rotting in Hornchurch!'

Two men were painting the row of garages on Marlow's council estate. They were making quite a good job of it, considering neither of them had done much in that line before. A few yards away George Marlow was standing, hands in pockets, watching them.

One of the men went to his nearby van for a new tin of paint. He opened it and stirred it with a screwdriver, then wiped the blade on his already paint-covered overalls.

'Excuse me, are you going to be painting the whole block, or just the garages?' Marlow asked.

'Just this lot, far as we know, mate,' DC Lillie replied.

'They aren't for residents, you know. Council rents them out to anyone who can afford them. The tenants have to park in the bay over there, known as Radio One . . .' He flashed a grin at Lillie. 'Means you had one when you parked it!'

He waited for a response, which didn't come, so he went on, 'I had one, but it was nicked.'

'What, a radio?'

'My car. Rover Mark III, three-litre automatic. More'n twenty years old, collector's item, you know.' He stared down into the tin of paint, then up at the garages.

Rosper joined in. 'You leave it out? Bodywork must 'ave rusted up?'

Marlow touched the paint on the nearest garage door, then peered closer. 'Had a bit of filler here and there. Suppose some kids nicked it for a joyride, be stripped down by now. Had all my emblems and badges on the front, RAC and AA, owner's club . . . all on a chrome bar at the front.' He examined the paint again. 'I'm in the paint business, typical of the council . . .' He put a hand out towards Rosper. 'Can I just borrow your brush? Like to see how this goes on . . .'

He dipped the brush in the paint and applied a stroke as Rosper and Lillie exchanged glances behind his back. Totally unaware, he said, 'You work out, do you?' He glanced round at Rosper. 'You look as if you do. What gym do you use?'

He chatted on, painting the door, while they stood and watched.

Late in the afternoon, Tennison and Amson arrived at Brixton Prison to interview convict 56774, Reginald McKinney. While they waited for him to be brought to them, Amson explained that McKinney had shared a cell with Marlow in Durham and had been picked up again a few weeks ago for breaking and entering.

The warder who brought McKinney told them there was a call from the station for them. Tennison asked Amson to take it, then offered the tall, skeletal prisoner a seat.

He was suffering from a migraine, and had come from the hospital ward. One of his eyes watered and his face was twisted in pain. 'We'll try and keep this short, Reg. Now, you shared a cell with George Marlow in Durham, that right?'

'That is correct.'

His eyes were crossing, it was like putting questions to a demented squirrel. 'You told your probation officer that you had met Marlow after your release.'

'That is correct.'

'And you were living in a half-way hostel in Camberwell then, yes? So where did you meet?'

McKinney looked up as Amson returned. He kept his back to McKinney and leaned over to whisper to Tennison.

'There's a buzz on, looks like another one in Warrington. They'll get back to me when they've finished checking.'

Feeling a bit perkier, Tennison turned back to Reg. He said, 'I've forgotten what you asked me ... I've got a migraine.'

'Where did you and Marlow meet?'

'Oh, yeah ... Kilburn. We went for a curry, then he drove me back to my place. Bit of a schlepp, an' I offered to get the tube, but he said it was OK. He wanted to do some work on his motor, in his lock-up.'

Tennison was careful not to show the excitement she was feeling. 'Lock-up – you mean a garage?'

'I dunno ...' He stopped a moment and rubbed his head, in obvious agony. 'The car was, like, an obsession with 'im.'

'He never mentioned where this lock-up was?'

'No ... I got a terrible headache.'

A prison warder put his head round the door. 'Urgent call for DCI Tennison.'

Tennison took the call. The team were doing a good job; the Warrington murder had checked out, plus another one, in Southport. Both victims had identical marks on their arms.

George Marlow hung around the garages chatting and joking with Rosper and Lillie until dark. They got on well together, and had done a fair bit of painting, but the two DCs were beginning to wonder when he was going to go home – they couldn't paint all night. The flood-lights had come on around the estate and were just enough to work by, but it wasn't easy.

'Bit late to be painting, isn't it?' Marlow enquired.

'We're on bonus, mate,' Rosper told him. 'Never know what's gonna happen with all this council privatization, so we gotta make the cash while we can.'

Marlow sympathized with them, then launched into a story about a bet he'd had with someone at the gym where he worked out when they heard sirens coming close.

All three turned to watch the cars drive onto the estate. In the first one were DI Muddyman with DC Jones, behind them Tennison and Amson. They had barely come to a halt when Tennison leaped out and ran to catch up with Muddyman.

As they hurried towards Marlow's flat she gasped, 'He's got a lock-up, some kind of garage where he stashes his car. Look for a set of keys, anything that might fit that kind of place. Get the bloody floorboards up if necessary.'

'I don't believe this,' Marlow was saying with exasperation to Lillie and Rosper as he wiped his hands on a rag. He stood and watched Tennison, Amson and Jones leg-ging it up towards his flat.

'What are they after?' Lillie asked, watching him care-fully.

'Me! I'd better get up there, the old lady next door'll have heart failure . . .' He laughed. 'Not because of them, but because she's out playing bingo. Means she'll miss all the drama. Ta-ra!'

Moyra was at the door, looking at the search warrant. From the bottom of the steps Marlow called, 'Hi, you want me?'

Moyra was very near to tears as she stood in the hall and surveyed the wreckage of her home. The carpets had been rolled back, all loose floorboards had been prised up, the hardboarding around the bath had been removed, the toilet had been taken apart, even the U-bends of the handbasin and the kitchen sink had been disconnected. Every video had been taken out of its jacket, every book taken down from the shelves and shaken, every crevice in every piece of furniture delved into. Tennison and Amson had every key in the place laid out in the lounge and were examining them minutely.

Moyra's self-pity turned to rage, and she screamed, 'I don't believe this! I want everything put back as it was, and what you've done to the plumbing I want repaired professionally! You've had all our bloody keys down the nick before, why don't you tell me what you're looking for?'

Tennison gestured to Amson to close the door on Moyra, then turned to Marlow, who was standing in front of the fireplace, hands on his hips. 'Why don't you tell us, George? You know what we're looking for.'

'I know you've been asking the neighbours. I park my car outside, I don't have a garage.'

'But your car isn't always parked outside, George. We know you've got a lock-up.'

'When it's not parked here it's because I'm away on business. I drive — correction, I drove — for a living. Instead of all this, why don't you just try and find my car?'

There were thuds and hammering noises from the kitchen, and the sound of crockery being moved. Moyra's screaming voice could be heard telling Muddyman and Jones that the bottom of the percolator didn't come off. She started yelling for George.

Tennison turned to Amson. 'Tell them to keep it down out there. George, you've got a lock-up, we know it.'

'A lock-up? How many more times do I have to tell you? I park my car at the back of the flats!'

'We have a witness . . .'

'Not that old bat from next door!'

'No, a friend of yours.'

'What friend? I don't have one left because of your crowd. Mates I worked with for years turned their backs on me! You got a friend? Great, introduce me!'

'We have a witness who stated that you told him you had a . . .'

'Him? Was it someone I was inside with? Yes? Don't tell me, let me guess. It was Reg McKinney, wasn't it?' He shook his head, laughing. 'You must be desperate. Reg McKinney? He's no friend of mine. Stung me for fifty quid when we got out. He's a known nutter. Look at his record, in and out of institutions since he was a kid. He's no friend of mine, I told him to take a hike.'

There was a tap on the door and Amson opened up.

'Nothin',' said Muddyman with a shrug, 'but we need a plumber.'

In a low voice, Marlow told Tennison earnestly, 'I don't have a lock-up, I don't have a garage. If I had, maybe my motor wouldn't have been nicked. It's the truth!'

Suddenly anxious to get home to Peter, Tennison decided not to go back to the station to pick up her car, so Terry Amson gave her a lift home. She was very aware of the difference having a genuinely friendly face on her team made to her job. She knew she could talk to Terry and it wouldn't go any further.

Amson was saying, 'If he's got his car stashed somewhere between Camberwell and Kilburn, we'll find it.'

'If!' She looked at him sideways. 'Terry, now you've met him, what do you think?'

'For real? If he's lying, he's one of the best I've ever come across.'

'Yeah,' she said with a sigh. 'Tonight, for the first time,

I had doubts.' She pointed ahead. 'It's the second house along.'

When he had stopped the car she turned to him. 'What do you think about John Shefford?'

'As a suspect? He was a crack officer, you know.'

She said sadly, 'He was also in the vicinity when Karen, Della and Jeannie Sharpe were killed. We're going to have to check him out on the two that just came in.'

'You know I'm with you on this, Jane, but there's only so far I'm prepared to go. I've got a wife and four kids to support, remember.'

'I don't like it any more than you.' She put her hand out to open the door. 'Just keep it under your hat, but we've got to check it out. So you pull Shefford's record sheets, first thing in the morning, OK? You want to come in for a drink?'

Amson shook his head and Tennison climbed out. 'G'night!' she said, as he started the engine.

Jane felt for the hall light switch, pressed it down. The flat was quiet; she dumped her briefcase and took off her coat, shouting, 'Pete! Pete?'

There was no answer. She opened the kitchen door to find it clean and tidy, nothing out of place. She tried the bedroom; it was just the same.

Sighing, she unbuttoned her shirt and opened the wardrobe. One half of it was empty. She checked the chest-of-drawers – all Peter's were empty! Turning away, she unzipped her skirt and let it slide to the floor, stepped out of it and walked towards the bathroom.

As she opened the door the phone rang. She let it ring, looking around to see only one toothbrush, one set of towels. The answering machine clicked into action and she waited, listening.

'Jane, it's your mother . . .' Jane saw the white envelope propped against the phone and reached for it. 'Didn't you get my message this morning about Pam? Well, in case you didn't, she's had a girl, eight pounds seven ounces, and she's beautiful! She was rushed into St Stephen's Hospital last night, I'm calling from her room . . .'

Jane picked up the phone as she ripped the envelope open. 'Hallo, Mum! I just got home.'

Jane drove to the hospital and parked, with the unopened letter from Peter on the seat beside her. She turned the lights off and reached for the white manila envelope with her name hastily scrawled on it.

It contained one sheet of her own notepaper. *Sweetheart,* she read, *I took on board everything you said this morning. I can't quite deal with you, or the pressures of your work, and at the same time get myself sorted out. I am sorry to do it this way, but I think in the long run it will be for the best, for both of us. I still care for you, but I can't see any future in our relationship. Maybe when we've had a few weeks apart we can meet and have a talk. Until then, take care of yourself.*

It was signed simply, *Peter.* She laid it face down on the seat and sighed, then realized that there was a postscript on the back.

I'm staying with one of my builders. When I get an address I'll let you know where I am, but if you need me you can reach me at the yard. Then he had put in brackets: *(Not Scotland Yard!).*

Jane opened the door slowly, but remained sitting. Was it always going to be like this? Peter wasn't the first, she'd never been able to keep a relationship going for more than a few months. She flicked her compact open and delved into her bag for a comb, stared at her reflection in the oval mirror for a long time. She looked a wreck, her hair needed washing and the make-up she had dashed on in a hurry that morning had long since disappeared. She studied the lines around her eyes and from her nose to her lips, the deep frown lines between her brows. She fished in her bag and brought out her lipstick, closed the mirror and ran the lipstick around her mouth without looking at it. She was so used to freshening up in a hurry that she didn't need a mirror.

Locking the car, she walked briskly towards the bright hospital entrance. An anxious-looking woman in a wheel-chair was holding an unlit cigarette. Jane smiled at her and she gave a conspiratorial grin.

'I don't suppose you've got a match, have you?'

'Yes, love.' Jane took a half-used book of matches from her pocket. 'You keep them, and mind you don't get cold. It's freezing out.'

As Jane headed for the night nurse at reception, she thought to herself, 'So what if you're going home to an empty flat? You've done that most of your adult life.' By the time she reached the desk she had persuaded herself that she preferred it that way.

She gave the nurse a cheerful smile. 'I've come to see my sister. I know it's late . . .'

After signing the visitors' book she headed towards the lifts, as directed. The woman in the wheelchair called out, 'Thanks for the matches!'

'That's all right, love. Good night, now!'

The corridor was deserted. Jane checked each room, peering through the little windows, until she found the right one. She could see Pam through the glass, holding the new baby, Tony's arm resting lightly around her shoulders. Although it was way past their bedtime her two little boys were there too, spick and span, swarming over the bed and admiring their new little sister.

Watching them, Jane's hand tightened on the door handle, but she found she couldn't turn it. They formed a picture of a family in which she had no place. She turned away and walked slowly back down the corridor.

*

She headed automatically towards the river, needing quiet, space to think. It was an ordeal to cross the King's Road; she found herself shrinking from the traffic, from the faces passing her in their shiny cars; happy faces, drunken faces, all going somewhere, all with a purpose, with some-one ... She found herself in Cheyne Walk, beside the water. Tonight the Thames looked like a river of oil, slug-gish and smooth, and she could not shake off the feeling that dead and rotting bodies floated just beneath the sur-face. She had come here to celebrate a new life, but all she could see was death, and pain.

By the time she returned to the hospital, visiting hours were officially over, but she slipped along to the private section without being stopped.

The room was decked with flowers and bowls of fruit, and the baby lay asleep in her cot, but Pam's bed was empty. This time she didn't hesitate, she walked into the room and gazed down at the baby girl, moved the blan-ket gently away from her face.

Soft footsteps behind her announced Pam's return. Jane looked up, smiling, back in control.

'Hi! Just checking she has all her fingers and toes! She's OK? Bit of a dent in her head, though ...'

Pam climbed cautiously into bed. 'Her skull is still soft, it'll go. If you'd been here earlier you'd have seen Tony and the boys. Mum's staying until I go home.'

'I feel a bit cheap – no flowers, no fruit. But I'd just got in from work.'

Pam was still in pain. She shifted uncomfortably in the bed.

'Could you just plump up my pillows?' she lowered her voice. 'You know we got this on Tony's firm? It's a new scheme, a private patients' plan. We can all get private medical attention now ...'

Jane rearranged her sister's pillows and straightened the sheets, then kissed her sister's cheek. 'Well, congratulations! What are you going to call her, Fergie? Eugenie? Beatrice? I mean, now it's all private ...'

Pam pulled a face. 'Well, Mum's actually hinted ...'

'What? No, you *can't* call her *Edna!*'

They were interrupted by a nurse, who gave Jane a pleasant smile that none the less indicated that she shouldn't be there. 'It's time for her feed, I'm afraid. Beautiful, isn't she?'

She disappeared with the baby, and Jane prepared herself to leave.

'You can tell this is private: no bells and everybody out!' She kissed Pam's cheek and smiled. 'I gotta go, anyway.'

'Thanks for coming. Give my love to Peter.'

'If I see him I will ...' She hesitated at the door. 'It's all off.'

Pam was instantly concerned. 'Oh, no! Why?'

Jane shrugged. 'You know me.'

'Is there someone else? I mean, are you OK?'

'No, there's no one else. I'm . . . It was a mutual decision.'

'Well, you know what you're doing. Is the case we saw on television over?'

Jane paused before she answered. Her family's total lack of understanding when it came to her work, to herself, on top of Peter leaving, swamped her, but she managed to keep her smile in place.

'No, I haven't got him – yet!' She gave her sister a little wave. 'G'night, God bless the baby.'

As she closed the door behind her, only the expression in her eyes betrayed Jane's loneliness. She had made a tremendous effort, forcing herself to come here. Having done her duty, at last she could go home and cry.

Chapter Ten

'What in Christ's name do you think you're playing at?' Kernan demanded.

'We had good reason to search Marlow's flat,' she protested. 'Bloke he was in jail with said he had a lockup . . .'

'I'm not talking about Marlow! You've had Sergeant Amson going over Shefford's record sheets.'

How the hell had he found out so quickly? She opened her mouth to speak, but Kernan ploughed on, 'If you want information regarding one of my ex-officers, then you know bloody well you should have come to me!'

'I think we've got our wires crossed here.'

'Don't bullshit me, Jane! Are you so desperate? It's pretty low, just because you can't prove your case, to try shifting the blame to John Shefford!'

'I first mentioned my suspicions to Sergeant Amson last night, and until I have more evidence . . .'

'I'm telling you, back off! If there was one viable piece of evidence against DCI Shefford, you should have brought it to me. And don't harp back to the diary, that's sorted, and Otley's paid for it. Don't try to do my job, Inspector.'

She tried again. 'We've got two unsolved cases, one in Warrington and one in Southport, both with similar bruising to their upper arms, hands tied with the same sort of knots. George Marlow was in the vicinity when both . . .'

'Are you telling me Shefford was also in the vicinity? Have you got the evidence to start an internal investigation?'

'I don't know if Shefford was ever attached to . . .'

He wouldn't let her finish. 'I'm telling you he wasn't, because I've checked!'

'I apologize, but under the circumstances . . .'

'Under the circumstances I am bringing in DCI Hicock! Don't you know what you've done, Jane? You've been running around the country trying to rake up dirt on one of the best officers I ever had! It stinks, and I won't take any more of it.'

'Shefford falsified evidence, and is known to have been on close terms with two murdered girls, both prostitutes – Della Mornay and Jeannie Sharpe. Of the two other cases we have uncovered, one was a prostitute . . .'

Kernan strode to the door. 'The man is in the graveyard.'

'So are they, sir. Re-opening cases as far back as nine-teen eighty-four is a slow procedure.'

'I've nothing more to say, I'm bringing Hicock in as soon as he can get here. You concentrate on the investi-gation you were assigned to for as long as you remain on it, is that clear? And if you want some advice, put in for a transfer. I want you off the Marlow case, and I want your report on everything that went down yesterday on my desk by lunchtime, is that clear?'

'Yes, sir!' said Tennison.

Amson came racing up the corridor as she left Kernan's office, waving a sheet of paper.

'We've got another one! Blackburn, 'eighty-seven!'

Tennison hurried to meet him and grabbed the paper, but Amson wouldn't let it go until he'd finished. 'It's about one a year, apart from the time Marlow was in jail! Caplan and Haskons are still watching him, and everyone else is mustered in the Incident Room – apart from these three.'

Tennison looked puzzled, and he finally handed over the note. 'Otley coughed up the names of the blokes who were fooling around with the toms! They're waiting for the Super to call them in now.'

'What about Shefford?' she asked urgently.

'He's in the clear, on all the new cases. He may have done a surface job on the Jeannie Sharpe murder, but then he wasn't the DCI on the case, so you can't put it all down to him. And he wasn't around when the others were killed.'

'I'm glad,' Tennison said. He gave her a disbelieving look and she protested, 'I am! Even if it dropped me right in the shit!'

Amson looked around and lowered his voice. 'As a matter of interest, did you know that the Chief and Shefford were' – he crossed his fingers – 'like that? They played golf every weekend – not at Sunningdale! Chief was Shefford's guv'nor when he was on Vice.'

Tennison shook her head and raised her eyes to heaven. 'I think I'll leave that one well and truly alone!' she said.

At least thirty people were crammed into the Incident Room. The air was thick with smoke. Every chair was taken, and the latecomers were sitting on desks or propped against the walls. While they waited some drank coffee and ate sandwiches, but most of them just talked. The din was deafening.

Sergeant Terry Amson was setting up a projector in the centre of the room. Tennison was thumbing through her notes while she waited.

She looked up when the door opened. It was DI Burkin and two others, returning from the Super's office. They all looked rather sheepish.

'Sorry, guv, we've been upstairs.'

Tennison nodded, well aware that these were the men who had been a bit too familiar with the local prostitutes. She gave them a moment to disperse amongst the others.

Burkin had found a place next to Muddyman, who asked him what was going on.

'Got our knuckles rapped for off-duty leg-overs. She's got eyes in the back of her head, that one! Just a warning this time, so maybe she's not all bad, but rumour has it that Hicock's definitely taking over, no kidding. He's in, she's out.'

Tennison stood up. 'OK, can I have a bit of hush?'

She waited for the room to grow quiet. Slowly they sorted themselves out, and she was able to start the meeting. She played it to the gallery.

'Right. I've been told that unless we get results very quickly indeed, I'm on traffic . . . Joke! I don't think it's quite that bad, but there will be some changes around here if we don't pull something out of the hat. In case I don't get another opportunity, I'll say now that I appreciate your back-up, and all the hard work . . .'

There were moans and unprintable comments as the word went round. Tennison yelled, 'Come on, settle down! Maybe there's something we've missed, something that, if we all think about it, will whack us right between the eyes. OK, Sergeant . . .'

The lights went off, the blinds went down, and Amson ran the mock-up of Karen Howard's last night. They watched her stand-in talking to the builder who had tried to help her, then crossing the road and walking up Ladbroke Grove.

'Oh, boy, we gonna watch you again, guv?' Tennison recognized the voice from the darkness as Rosper's.

Amson summarized all the evidence as they watched. 'Karen Howard, our first victim. Her body discovered in Della Mornay's bedsit and mistaken for her.'

The film ended, followed by close-up stills of Karen's badly beaten body, then her various appalling injuries. The last frame was of the bruising on her arms.

'OK, take a good look at these marks. Now we have the other victim, Della Mornay, who was killed approximately six weeks before Karen . . .'

The shot of the decomposed body was sickening. The close-ups showed her upper arms and what appeared to be bite marks.

'The foxes had a go at her, and the dog belonging to the man who found her. But look at the arms again: the same marks, almost identical to those found on Karen.'

Another body was flashed up on the screen. 'Jeannie Sharpe, killed in Oldham in nineteen eighty-four. Again, note the bruising and welts on the upper arms. Fourth victim . . .'

Amson pointed to DI Muddyman and whispered, 'You ready?' Muddyman climbed to his feet.

'Another video now, this time of Angela Simpson,

whose family sent it to us. She was knifed to death in a public park in nineteen eighty-five. She was a hairdresser, well-liked kid, about to get married. This is her engagement party.'

The sweet face of Angela Simpson smiled into camera, showing off her engagement ring, then self-consciously kissing the young man beside her. Her smiling fiancé gave a thumbs-up sign, and Angela turned to the camera, laughing, and put her hands over the lens. Then she loomed very close and kissed the camera.

'During the house-to-house enquiries, George Marlow was interviewed. He had been staying in a bed and breakfast only fifty yards from the gates of the park where she was found. There were no marks on her upper arms, but look at this . . .'

There was a shot of Angela, lying face down, legs apart. Her hands were tied behind her back.

'The rope, the way the hands were tied, were just the same as in victims one and two.'

There was a slight commotion as a WPC entered and tried to find Tennison in the dark. She delivered a brief message and departed, clocked by the men. Frank Burkin stood up to take DI Muddyman's place.

'The fifth girl' – Burkin waited for the shot to appear on screen – 'was Sharon Reid. She was sixteen, still at school, and worked part-time in a local beauty salon . . .'

When he had finished they broke for lunch, and the

discussion was continued less formally in the canteen. Reading the menu, DC Lillie was reminded about the old woman, the one found in the chicken run. She had had similar marks on her arms to the others. He asked Sergeant Amson, who was in the queue behind him.

'Marlow was in the vicinity, that's good enough for me to try and pin it on him.' He looked around Lillie to see what the hold-up was. 'Come on, Burkin!' he yelled.

Lillie persisted. 'But they didn't all have clamp marks ... Oh, not ruddy Chicken Kiev again! The garlic's a killer!'

Burkin, his plate full, moved away from the counter, and joined Muddyman, who was holding forth about Marlow.

'I've been watching him for weeks now, he's a real friendly bloke, right? He chats to the lads every day. Just because he was in the area, it doesn't mean he's guilty.'

Burkin picked up the lurid plastic tomato from the table and squeezed ketchup all over his plate, then stuffed a huge forkful of chips in his mouth. Bits of potato flew everywhere while he talked.

'There must be hundreds of salesmen workin' that area, you could take your pick. You ask me, all that film was about this morning was that we've got more bloody tarts being bumped off' – he paused to burp – 'an' no bloody suspects.'

The 'bing-bong' sounded and a voice requested the

presence of DCI Tennison in Administration. The men ignored it and carried on talking about Marlow; everyone who had had contact with him seemed to be convinced that he was a good bloke and therefore not a murderer. Terry Amson arrived and picked up on the conversation.

'He lied about the lock-up, we know that.'

'We've only got the word of an old lag on that, it's not proof,' Burkin retorted. There was another call over the PA system for Tennison. 'Looks like the boss is gonna get the big boys pullin' the rug on her . . . Coffee all round?' He looked at Lillie. 'Your turn.'

Maureen Havers found Tennison hiding in the locker room, eating a large hamburger.

'Is DCI Hicock a big, red-haired bloke? He's in with the Commander and the Super's there too. You're being paged all over the station.'

'Am I?' Tennison asked innocently. 'Well, they'll just have to find me.'

Having successfully evaded her bosses, Tennison returned to the Incident Room to continue the briefing. She pinned photographs of all six of the victims on the notice-board while she waited for everyone to settle down.

'Right! Six victims, no set pattern. They did not, as far as we can ascertain, know each other. They didn't look alike, they belonged to different age groups, different professions. Apart from certain minor similarities they were not all killed in the same manner. The only link between them all is that Marlow was in the area when they were murdered. Did he kill all six? Is there something we've overlooked, another link?'

Muddyman was slumped right down in his chair, totally relaxed. He waved a hand to attract Tennison's attention.

'In the case of Karen, a witness stated that she heard a man call out her name. It was the same with Jeannie. But what about Angela, the little blonde one? She was killed in the shrubbery in broad daylight, a good distance from the path, which was her usual route home. So how did she get there? If someone had called out to her ... And the one who was raped, Gilling, she said he called her name ...'

'Point taken,' said Amson, 'but you've got two toms, one hairdresser, a schoolgirl ... How did he get to know their names, if he knew them?'

Havers had made her way to the front, using her elbows, and was standing by the photographs. She raised her hand, about to say something, but lowered it, not sure of her ground. She moved closer to Tennison and touched her arm.

'Boss, I think ... It may be off the wall ...'

'Anything, my love, I'm right up against it. What you got?'

'I did a bit of checking, but it all falls down with Gilling. She was a florist, but there's one link with the others. It was mentioned once . . .'

'To Marlow?'

'No, not him – Moyra Henson.'

Tennison could barely hear her against the growing racket in the room. 'Come on, lads, keep it down a bit!' she yelled, then turned back to Havers.

'Go on.'

'When she was brought in for questioning I typed her statement. She put herself down as unemployed . . .'

'Yeah . . . Quiet! Quieten down!'

The noise slowly subsided. Some of the men closed in on Tennison and Havers, realizing something was going on.

Havers coughed nervously. 'She was picked up for prostitution, fifteen years ago, according to her record. But on that charge-sheet she's down as a freelance beautician. If she worked when she was travelling around with Marlow, he could have met the girls that way. But Gilling doesn't fit in . . .'

'Good on ya, Maureen!' Tennison gave her a quick hug. 'We'll check it out.'

Unaware of the tension, Jones walked in carrying an MSS internal fax sheet. 'This might be useful, ma'am,' he said to Tennison. 'I've checked back on Marlow's past addresses. They've been in Maida Vale for three years, and before that they were in Somerstown, not far from St Pancras. He's had the Rover for twelve years, so what if he had a lock-up close to his previous flat?'

Rosper had a sudden thought. 'Yeah! Those garages we've been painting, Marlow told us he tried to rent one, but the council leases 'em out to the highest bidder. Maybe he kept his old garage because he couldn't get one near by . . .'

The phone rang and DI Muddyman answered it, then covered the mouthpiece. 'Guv? You're wanted upstairs, you here or not?'

'No, I'm not! Go and bring that hard-nosed cow in!'

Moyra wasn't happy at being taken down to the station, and she made sure the whole estate knew about it.

'Had a good eyeful?' she screeched at her next-door neighbour as she was led out to the car. 'I tell you, they get more mileage out of you lot than a ruddy video . . . *Don't push me!*'

Marlow trailed behind them. 'I don't understand, do you want me as well?'

Tennison emerged from the car and held the back door open for Moyra. 'Not this time, George.'

They left him standing there, still trying to work out what was going on.

*

Tennison had a quick wash and checked that the Super had left for the day before she emerged with Maureen Havers from the locker room, ready to interview Moyra.

Amson was pacing up and down the corridor outside. 'Mrs Howard is sending some of Karen's latest model photos by courier, shouldn't be long. You all set? Got plenty of cigarettes?'

She took a deep breath and nodded, then followed Amson and Havers along the corridor to room 4-C.

Havers went in first, followed by Amson, who held the door open for Tennison. After a beat, Tennison followed, like a prize-fighter.

'I am Detective Chief Inspector Jane Tennison, this is WPC Maureen Havers, and Detective Sergeant Amson. Thank you for agreeing to answer our questions . . .'

'I had an option, did I?' Moyra interrupted.

Amson placed a thick file on the bare table in front of Tennison. She opened it and extracted a statement.

'You were brought into the station on the sixteenth of January this year, is that correct?'

'If you say so!'

'Is this the statement you made on that occasion?' Tennison laid it in front of her.

Moyra glared at it. 'Yesss . . .'

'And is this your signature?'

'Of course it bloody is!'

Thank you. I would like to draw your attention to the

front page – here. It states that you are unemployed, is that correct?'

'It says so, doesn't it?'

'So you are unemployed.'

'Yes, I'm on the bloody dole. What's that got to do with anything?'

Tennison extracted another document from the file and put it in front of her. 'We have this previous statement from you, dating back to nineteen seventy-five. You were charged with soliciting, and stated your profession as beautician.'

'Is there a law against it?'

'Did your training include a hairdressing course?'

Moyra was getting rattled. She answered abruptly, 'No!'

'So you are not a hairdresser?'

'No, but I once had a Siamese cat.'

'So you are a freelance beautician?'

'Yeah, you know, manicures, hands, facials.' She peered at Tennison across the table. 'You could do with a facial, smoking's very bad for your skin.'

'Do you work as a beautician?'

'What do you want to know all this for? You think George is a transvestite now, do you?'

'George Marlow, your common-law husband, is still under suspicion of murder. I need the answers to my questions to help us eliminate him from our enquiries.'

'Pull the other one, you're just interested in incriminating him.'

'I'd like you to tell me where you were on these dates: March the fifteenth, nineteen eighty-four ...'

'No ruddy idea, darlin'. Ask me another.'

'The second of November nineteen eighty-five. Twenty-third of July, nineteen eighty-six. Ninth of April nineteen eighty-seven.'

'I dunno, I'd have to look in me diaries, not that I've got them that far back.' She bent down and started fiddling with her shoe.

'They were dates when your common-law husband was travelling in Warrington, Oldham, Burnley, Rochdale ...'

Moyra looked up. 'Oh, in that case I was with him. I always travel with him.'

'So on the dates that I have mentioned, you are pretty sure that you were with George, yes?'

'I travel with him, I stay with him.'

'Doing freelance work as a beautician?'

'Well, yeah. I do a bit.'

'In salons?'

'Yeah, no law against that.'

'There is if you've been claiming unemployment benefit and not declaring income, or paying tax on it. There's a law against that.'

Moyra actually shrank back in her chair, though her

answer was bold enough. 'It's nothing, just a bit of cash, you know, pin money.'

'How long do you think it would take for me to check out just how much you've been earning?'

'You bastards never give anyone a break.'

'I'll give you a break, Moyra. No charges if – *if* – you give us a detailed list of the salons you've worked in, the names of your clients . . .'

As Tennison placed a pen and a sheet of paper in front of Moyra, Amson leaned over and whispered to her. With a nod to Havers, she followed him from the room.

'If this pins any of those cases on Marlow, she's virtually making herself an accessory!'

'What are you suggesting?' Tennison snapped. 'Get her lawyer in just when she's co-operating?'

'You're jumping the gun. What we need is a lever, something to push Marlow with. She's his alibi, and so far she's not backed down on that.'

Tennison banged the coffee machine with the flat of her hand. 'Christ, you're right! An' we need a fucking lever to make this machine work . . .' She looked at her watch. 'OK, leave it with me. I'll have one more go.' She smiled. 'But gently does it!'

Moyra was beginning to look tired. She leaned her head in her hand.

'I've listed the salons, but that doesn't mean to say that

I work there regular. Sometimes they don't have any customers for me, and it's mostly manicures.'

'What's this Noo-Nail?' Tennison asked, looking over the paper.

'It's American, paint-on nails; your own grow underneath.' She held out a hand for Tennison to inspect. 'See, they look real, don't they? But that part's false.'

Havers, trying to look interested, stifled a yawn. Amson was half-asleep.

'Aah, I see!' Tennison nodded, then asked nonchalantly, 'Did you do Miss Pauline Gilling's nails?'

Without a flicker, Moyra replied, 'Look, love, I do so many, I don't know all their names.'

'Surely you'd remember Pauline Gilling? George was sent down for attacking her . . .' She pushed a photograph across the table.

Moyra refused to look at the photo and snapped, 'No, no! An' she lied, she came on to George! She'd been in the pub, she lied . . .'

'What about Della Mornay? Did you do her nails?' She put another photograph on the table.

'No!'

'Take a look, Moyra. Della Mornay.'

'I don't know her!'

'No? You stated that George returned home on the night of the thirteenth of January this year at ten-thirty . . .'

Under pressure again, Moyra fought back. 'Yes! Look,

I know my rights, this isn't on! I've been here for hours, I've answered your questions, now I want a lawyer.'

'George's car, the brown Rover, where is it? We know he has a lock-up, Moyra, and we'll find it, it's just a question of time. I'll need to talk to you again.' She stood up. 'OK, you can go, thank you.'

'Is that it? I can go home?'

Tennison nodded and walked to the door, leaving Moyra nonplussed.

It was light before Moyra got home. George made her a cup of coffee and brought it to her in the lounge.

'Bastards are going to get me for fiddling the dole and tax evasion. They know I've been working.'

'They kept you all night just for that?'

'There were a few other things.'

'What? What did she want to know? Ask about me, did she?'

Moyra stood up and started unbuttoning her blouse. 'What do you think?'

She walked out of the room and, after a moment's hesitation, Marlow followed her to the bedroom. She tossed her blouse aside and unzipped her skirt, leaving it where it fell. He picked them up and folded them while she went into the adjoining bathroom and turned on the bath taps.

'What are you following me around for?'

'I just want to know what went on!'

She turned on him, snapping. 'They wanted to know about the bloody florist! Kept asking me about her. I've stood by you, George, but so help me if I find you've been lying to me I'll . . .'

She turned and walked out. 'Put some Badedas in for me . . .'

He picked up the big yellow bottle and squirted some of the contents into the water, then stood in the doorway, watching her cream her face.

'I've never lied to you, Moyra, you know that.' He reached out to touch her but she slapped his hand away, finished wiping her face with a tissue.

'Where's the car, George?'

'It was stolen, I don't know where it is.'

She picked up her hairbrush. 'It wasn't here, George. You came home that night without it. I remember because your hair was wet, you said it was raining.' She turned to him while she brushed her hair, slowly. 'Is it in the lock-up? They're going to get you because of that bloody car . . . They can plant evidence, you know, and they're out to get you.'

'What did they say?'

'The bath'll run over.'

'What did they say?'

'Maybe they've already found it, I dunno. I've got my own problems. They'll get me just for doing a few manicures.' She threw the brush down on the dressing-table and stormed into the bathroom. Marlow picked up the brush and began to run it through his hair.

Peter looked around the bedsit. It was clean and close to the building yard. The best thing was the rent, a hundred a week. He had paid the landlady up front for a month. Dumping his suitcase without bothering to unpack, he went straight out again, arriving outside Marianne's just after breakfast. He watched from a distance until Marianne's husband had taken Joey to school, then rang the bell.

Marianne offered her cheek, which he kissed, and coffee, which he accepted. She tidied the breakfast dishes into the dishwasher and sat opposite him at the kitchen table.

'I've moved, so if you need me, here's my new address,' he told her.

'Oh, so it didn't work out with the policewoman?'

'No, it didn't.'

'I'm sorry.'

'Really? Because I won't be able to have Joey to stay? Well, wrong, because he can stay with me for as long as need be.'

Marianne unfolded the small note of his address and got up to pin it on the notice-board. He sipped his luke-warm coffee and asked, 'How are you?'

'I'm fine. Do you want toast?'

'No. I want to know if this new baby's mine. Is it?'

'What?'

'Come on, don't mess me around. I got the sort of nudge, nudge when you came round, so tell me the truth. Is it mine?'

'Well, of course not, don't be ridiculous!'

'That afternoon, it could have been mine, couldn't it?'

'No, I'm too far gone. I must have been pregnant, or just . . . Look, Pete, that was a stupid mistake, and I don't know why I let it happen. I'm sorry if by going to bed with you that one time I let you think . . .'

'Wait, wait! I don't think anything, I just wanted to know for sure, and now I do, I'll go.'

She caught his arm. 'I'm sorry, Pete, I know how much I've hurt you, and I'm truly sorry. But it was just something that happened.'

'Just something?'

Peter walked to the front door. He felt helpless, inadequate, there was so much more to say but he didn't know how to begin. The sweet smell of her in her dressing-gown, her softness, got in the way of his anger. It always had.

His hand was on the door, about to open it, when he turned back. 'I want Joey, every other weekend. I'll start paying maintenance as soon as my business is on its feet.'

Marianne nodded, but before she could say anything he had the door open. 'Goodbye, then,' she said at last.

Peter didn't reply. All the way down the neat gravel path, across the street to his truck, he couldn't even think straight. How had it happened? One day, a wife he adored, a son he doted on, a secure business, a house – albeit with a mortgage ... He had had so much, and now it was gone. Marianne had a bigger house, a new husband, another baby on the way, and all Peter had was a rented bedsit and a suitcase. Even his business was in bad shape. In fact, no matter how he viewed his life, he was on a downward spiral. He just couldn't understand how it had happened that his best friend, a man he had been at school with, trusted and liked, had taken everything from him.

As he drove off, Marianne watched from an upstairs window. She felt wretched, part morning sickness and part guilt. She was genuinely sorry for him, sorry for leaving him, sorry for everything that had happened. He was such a kind, gentle man. She had never set out to fall in love with someone else, it was just one of those things. It upset her that he had believed the new baby was his, but she hadn't lied.

She patted the curtains back into place and ran herself a bath. While she waited she started making out a list of groceries and Peter was forgotten.

*

Peter unpacked his belongings and went to a café for a bacon sandwich and a cup of tea. He arrived at work much later than usual and one of his chippies asked if everything was OK.

'Yeah, everything's fine.'

'How's the Inspector?'

'That's all in the past.'

'Can't say I blame you. That one looked as if she'd nick you if you laid a finger on her!'

Peter laughed loudly, and the chippie pushed the day's mail across the untidy desk. 'Looks like a lot of bills to me, guv'nor. Be out back if you need me.'

Peter had hardly given Jane a thought since he left. She had been important to him for the time he had been with her, but he knew he wouldn't see her again. There really wasn't any point. If the truth was on the line, there was a side to her that he hated, that masculine, pushy side. She had never been his kind of woman, and he doubted if any man could cope with a woman who loved her career more than anything else. At least he wouldn't have to listen to all the ramifications of who had done what, how and to whom, and what she was going to do about it. He wouldn't have to hear about her 'toms', her 'lads', or that bloody George Marlow. The next girl would be young, pretty and without prospects, and he'd make sure she could cook, didn't mind ironing shirts and liked kids.

*

'Boss! Karen's photographs have arrived.'

Tennison turned from the washbasin where she was brushing her hair. 'Be right with you.'

'Everybody's waiting in the Incident Room, and . . . the Super's in there.'

Tennison was suddenly not so cheerful. 'Shit! OK, I'll be there.'

A few moments later she found Superintendent Kernan standing in the middle of the Incident Room among a general hubbub. The moment she entered the room, silence fell.

'Sorry, guv, you wanted to see me?' She felt a flush creeping up her face.

'Just a few moments.' He gestured to the door, then said to Amson, 'Carry on.'

Tennison waited for him at the door and followed him out, hearing Terry Amson saying, 'Right, I want everybody to have a look at these new photographs of Karen Howard . . .' She closed the door behind her and faced Kernan.

'This was on my desk when I came in.' He handed her a sheet of paper. 'They backed you one hundred per cent, refused to have Hicock take over. Did you know about it?'

Every single man had signed the petition. Tennison's eyes brimmed with tears. 'No . . . No, I didn't.'

'Things have taken a big turn, eh? You're lucky.'

'Luck had nothing to do with it, sir. We've worked our butts off.'

'Let me have all the new information as soon as possible, and' – he smiled – 'good luck!'

He strode away and she opened the door. All the men in the room had their backs to her; they were watching Maureen Havers.

'These shots were taken on the day Karen died,' said Havers, pointing to a group of photos on the notice-board. 'You can see quite clearly that her nails were short. But these' – she pointed to another group – 'these were taken a week before. Look at her hands.'

In the second batch Karen's nails were long and red. Sergeant Amson turned to Jones. 'Get on it, check with her flatmates, see where she got them done!'

While Jones looked up the number, the others crowded around the photos. Still not one man had turned towards Tennison. Jones picked up the phone and started dialling.

Highly embarrassed, Tennison walked to the centre of the room. 'I won't harp on, but I want all of you to know that I appreciate you backing me up . . .'

Muddyman hurtled in, shouting, 'Suspect's on the move, guv'nor, with his girlfriend! The lads reckon something's going down!'

Jones was through to the flat. 'Lady Antonia? This is

DC Jones from Southampton Row police station. We need to know if Karen used a beauty parlour or hair salon, and if so do you know if she had ... excuse me ...' He beckoned frantically to Havers. 'What do you call them?'

'Nail extensions.'

Excited, Tennison was getting into top gear. 'Right, I reckon this is it, we've got him on the run ...'

Jones slammed the phone down. 'Yes! She went to a place in Floral Street, Covent Garden; had an account there!'

Amson, already on the move, pointed at Jones. 'Check it out, Daffy! Take Rosper with you, and keep in radio contact!'

Tennison was champing at the bit. 'Let's go! Terry, you're with me!'

She ran out, Amson on her heels. DC Jones grabbed his jacket, a rather smart double-breasted job, and bellowed to Rosper, 'Let's go!' But he paused a moment beside Maureen Havers and winked. 'Good on ya, Maureen! See ya in the bar tonight.'

She watched him leave. 'What a bloody prat! Since he got those suede shoes he thinks he's Don Johnson ...'

It was suddenly quiet, as it always was before the scream went up. Havers looked at the photographs Karen Howard's mother had sent, glossy six-by-ten modelling shots. They had only been interested in her nails, but now she looked at the girl's lovely face. Karen had been a beautiful girl with a freshness to her skin that shone out from the photographs. Her hair was silky, her eyes bright. It was obvious that she had still been an amateur, the poses weren't quite right, but maybe that was what gave her an air of innocence, of childlike vulnerability.

Havers was not the only police officer, male or female, who felt protective towards such victims, as if it was their responsibility to ensure that they could rest in peace. She brushed her hand across the photograph.

'I think we've got him, Karen, love,' she whispered. The dead girls stared sightlessly into the empty room: Karen, Della, Jeannie, Angela, Sharon, Ellen, as if they too were waiting to rest.

Chapter Eleven

As her patrol car raced through the heavy traffic, Tennison sat next to the driver, listening in on the open channel. Amson was sitting on the edge of the back seat, trying to see where they were going.

DC Oakhill was reporting George Marlow and Moyra Henson's every move direct to them.

'Suspect leaving taxi now, with Henson. Entering Great Portland Street station. They've split up, she's gone down to the trains and he's coming out on the north side, over.'

DI Haskons cut in. 'I got him! I'm on foot, heading down the Euston Road, outside Capital Radio, repeat, I'm on foot. He's hailed another bloody taxi, over.'

'I'll take the woman . . .' Oakhill's voice faded out.

'We'll go straight to Euston, see if we can head him off at the pass,' said Tennison.

*

George Marlow leaned in at the taxi window to speak to the driver, and pointed towards Euston. Then he hopped in the back, but the taxi made a left turn towards Camden Town.

A plain car, driven by DC Caplan, slotted into the traffic behind the cab. His passenger, DI Muddyman, reported, 'OK, we're there. Suspect in black cab, heading for Camden Town. No, right, he's turned right, towards Euston again. We've got him, we've got him now, turning right again, back towards the Euston Road, over.'

DC Jones rushed out of the Floral Street beauty salon and stuck his head through the car window to talk to DI Burkin.

'They had her down for a full day on the second of January, the day before that modelling job where she had the long nails. But she didn't book a manicure, and they don't do these nails, whatever they're called. One of the assistants, a Dutch chick, says she recommended a woman in the market.'

'Shit,' Burkin said. 'We can't get the car in there. You leg it, and I'll meet you in Southampton Street.'

The black taxi weaved its way down a side street and reached the corner of Euston Road. There were two vehicles now between it and Muddyman's unmarked car.

The cab edged into the solid traffic on the Euston Road. Marlow was out of the door on the far side and had disappeared into a junk furniture store before any of them could blink.

'Shit! This is Muddyman. Marlow's out of the cab, taxi is empty, repeat, Marlow again on foot. Biker, come in, biker . . .'

Outside the junk shop the cyclist in the skin-tight Lycra pedal-pushers slowed down and bent to fiddle with his toe-clips. He spoke softly into his radio.

'He's out, heading along the Euston Road again, on foot, over.'

On the opposite corner, Muddyman was out of the car and following, keeping a good distance from Marlow.

Oakhill came close to losing Moyra Henson in the crowded complex of tunnels and staircases at Baker Street, and had to force the doors open to board the south-bound Jubilee line train. He threaded his way through the carriage to stand by the next set of doors. Henson was staring into space; then she turned and studied her reflection in the dark window, and fished in her handbag for a square, double-sided mirror. She licked her lips and threaded her fingers through the front of her hair and shook it out, then folded the mirror and zipped it back into her bag.

She was totally unaware of Oakhill watching her, strap-hanging only a few feet away.

*

Amson was leaning between the front seats with a map in his hand. 'He's here, could be heading for Euston or King's Cross, but he's ducking and diving . . .'

'Hold it, Control's coming through.' She raised a hand to the earpiece on which she was picking up relayed messages. 'He's jumped on a number seventy-three bus. No, he's off it, he's turned in the direction of Battle Bridge Road, behind King's Cross station . . .'

Amson pointed it out on the map. 'That's here. Doesn't look like he's going for a train, but there are lock-ups in the railway arches all along here . . .'

'Come on, you bugger, go for the car, get your bloody car!'

A voice said in her ear, 'You're out of luck, car five-four-seven. Your man's just gone into a café, he's sitting talking to the owner. It's the taxi stopover . . .'

Tennison pursed her lips and tapped her foot regularly against the transmission tunnel of the car. Her ear was aching because she was so uptight at the possibility of missing a radio call that she kept pressing the earpiece harder into her ear.

'What the fuck d'you think he's doing?'

Amson shrugged. 'Could do with a cup of coffee myself.' His fingers drummed against the back of her seat. He was shrugging it off, but like everyone else he was right on the edge, waiting, waiting . . .

*

Among the crowded little stalls selling jeans and T-shirts, DC Jones found a tiny booth containing only a small, white-covered table and two chairs. A sign nailed to the top of the wooden frame announced: 'Noo-Nails by Experienced and Qualified Beautician'.

Annette Frisby, the proprietress, was bending over a client's hand, carefully painting her new nails a violent pink. Jones squashed himself in beside them and showed Annette his identification and a photograph of Karen Howard.

'Have you ever done this girl's nails?'

She squinted at the photo. 'I couldn't tell you, I do as many as eight a day . . .'

'Look at her again.' He tried to squat down to her level and pointed at the beautiful young face. 'She was found murdered, on the fourteenth of January last. Look again, did she ever come to this stall?'

'January? I wouldn't have been here anyway. My friend takes over when I can't do it.'

Jones ground his teeth in frustration. 'Have you got her name and address?'

The café was too small to contain more than a long bar and a few stools. George Marlow was sitting at the far end, drinking cappuccino.

The only other customer got up and left. Marlow approached the man behind the bar.

'Can I have the keys, Stav?'

Stavros pulled a cardboard box from beneath the bar. 'Been away, have you, John? Haven't seen you for a long time.'

'Yeah. Mum was taken bad.' Marlow held his hand out for the keys. 'What's the damage?'

From across the street it wasn't possible to see the object that had been passed to George Marlow, but when he opened his wallet Muddyman could see him counting out ten-pound notes.

Moyra Henson had changed tubes twice, doubling back on herself, then she hurried onto a Central line train. Oakhill was certain that she had no idea he was tailing her.

He was four or five bodies behind her as she went up the escalator and emerged at Oxford Circus. Keeping well back, he radioed in for back-up, fast; Oxford Street was packed with shoppers and Moyra was moving like the clappers. He stayed on her tail in and out of Richard Shops, then across the road to Saxone, back again to another shoe shop, then on up the street to Next.

His back-up arrived; a plain-clothes WPC to take over the close tail, plus a patrol car. The WPC followed Moyra in and out of shops as far as Wardour Street, where she entered a shopping mall. The driver of the patrol car and the uniformed officer took up their positions near the exits. Oakhill kept about fifty yards back from Henson, while the WPC peered into windows and watched Moyra try on shoes from a few feet away.

The patrol car was parked a good distance from the café and Muddyman, directly across the road, kept the radio contact going, informing Tennison that it looked as though the suspect was on the move again.

'Yeah, he's buttoning up his raincoat. Shit! He's sat down again. He's having another bloody coffee!'

Tennison's foot was still tapping and she was chain-smoking, building up a real fug in the car.

A message started coming through from Jones. 'Would you believe Moyra Henson sometimes works from this booth in Covent Garden, and she was working here in January. An assistant at the Floral Street Health Club told me she directed Karen here. The woman who runs it can't say if Karen had had her nails done here or not, but she says that when Henson was working here Marlow used to pick her up! Moyra could have done Karen's nails, and if he saw her, knew her name . . .'

DC Jones was standing in the middle of a breakdancing troupe, battling to make himself heard. The steel girders above the stalls distorted the radio waves.

'How long does this Noo-Nail treatment take?' Tennison's voice asked.

'The woman said she can do eight a day, so it must take a while.'

'You hear all that?' Tennison asked Amson. He nodded. 'That's how he could have known their names! If the treatment takes a while and he was hanging around . . .'

Tennison stubbed out her cigarette. They were both beginning to sweat; it was coming down, they could feel it.

'It's the two of them, then!'

'Looks like it,' Tennison replied. 'Let's pick Moyra up now, and see if the lads back at base have come up with anything from the cross-check. Della and Moyra both came from Manchester originally, it's just their ages, Della was a lot younger. Car five-four-seven to base . . .'

'Looks like she's been lying from day one!'

While Tennison gave the go-ahead for Moyra Henson to be picked up, Muddyman radioed in that Marlow was on the move. Then there was silence, but the crackle of the open channel added to the tension. Everyone was waiting . . .

'He's moving fast now, turning left out of the café, crossing the road. He's stopped, he's on to me, looking over . . .'

Another voice cut in. 'I've got him! He's just passed me, walking briskly, crossing the road again. He's heading for the lock-ups, he's walking right along Battle Bridge Road to the lock-ups . . .'

The radio controllers nearly deafened Tennison with their cheering, as if Arsenal had scored a winning goal in the Cup Final. Like the men in the street, they were feeding Marlow's every move to the cars and to the rapidly closing ring of officers in the area. Now they passed on the instructions for the lads to take up their positions . . .

'Yes!' Tennison yelled, and punched Amson's arm. 'He's going for the goddamned lock-ups, I knew it, I knew it!'

Amson tapped the driver on the shoulder to warn him to be ready. He started the engine.

Tennison was gabbling. 'Everyone keep back, just hold your positions, don't frighten him off . . . Stay put until we get the go . . . Over . . .'

They could only listen, they couldn't move out, couldn't see, in case they tipped Marlow off, as the team moved in. Some were dressed as mechanics, bending over broken-down cars, another pedalled past with a ladder, someone else drove a grocery van, but they were moving in, surrounding Marlow. The tension was explosive . . .

George Marlow strolled casually along the street. He passed two open lock-ups where mechanics were at work. Cars in various stages of repair littered the street.

He reached the corner where a road ran at right angles under the railway lines. He paused, looked around, checking carefully to see if he was being followed.

'Hold your positions, no one move,' Tennison

instructed. 'Let him open up and get inside before you grab him.'

Apparently satisfied that he was in the clear, Marlow walked unhurriedly, swinging the keys around his finger as he went. He approached a lock-up that looked as though it hadn't been occupied in years. A small access door was set into one of the huge main doors.

Tennison's tense voice broadcast softly, 'I want him to use the keys, everybody wait . . . wait . . .'

After another long look around, Marlow stepped up to the small door and selected a key from the ring.

Muddyman's voice was low, breathy. 'Shit, I think this is it, he's going for it. Stand by, suspect has his key in the lock. He's opening up! He's opening up!'

The small door swung open and Marlow raised one leg to step over the high sill as Tennison shrieked, 'Go! Go! Go!'

The cars converged into the street, sirens wailing, but before they could get to Marlow the lads emerged from their positions like greyhounds after a hare: Rosper, Caplan, Lillie and Muddyman. They charged across the street and before Marlow could step right inside they had him. Rosper, the first there, grabbed Marlow by the scruff of his neck, almost tearing the raincoat off him as he dragged him from the doorway. Marlow stumbled as his foot caught on the sill, and the next moment his head was cracked back on the edge of the door. They all wanted a go at him – it was part tension, part adrenalin – and they handled him roughly, pinching the skin on his wrists as they handcuffed him.

Muddyman was shouting the caution as Tennison's car screamed up. She was about to get out when she hesitated, to give the boys a chance to spot her and ease up on Marlow. It was in that moment, no more than a few seconds, that she saw another side to her suspect.

He seemed completely unconcerned at being knocked around, arrested. In fact he was unnaturally calm. He looked up with a puzzled frown, first at Rosper, then Lillie. Tennison did not hear what he said, but she could see the expression on his face as if he was angry with himself.

But the lads heard him: 'Ahhh . . . the painters.' He seemed satisfied that he had recognized them, but there was still a look of irritation on his face. He hadn't suspected them, in fact he had trusted them. He had been foolish, made a mistake. They were not painters.

Moyra Henson emerged from a boutique with a large carrier bag and strolled along the mall, stopping beside the plain-clothes WPC, who was loaded with bags, to look in the next window. Their elbows nearly touched.

She was so intent on the goods in the shop that for a moment she didn't clock the reflection of the uniformed officer speaking into his radio a few feet away. Oakhill moved in and the WPC right next to Moyra dropped her bags and held out her ID.

'Moyra Henson, I am WPC Southill. We would like you to accompany us to the Southampton Row—'

Moyra swung her boutique bag to slap Southill in the face, then went for her, kicking and spitting, screaming that she wanted to be left alone. Her screeching drew everyone's attention: shop assistants rushed out to see what was going on, customers rammed into each other on the escalators, as Moyra's screams echoed throughout the mall. Her face was puce with hysteria.

She seemed to cave in suddenly, her back pressed against the window, hands up.

'I just want to be left alone, ahhhh, please, please leave me alone! Don't touch me! I'll come with you, just don't touch me!'

She started to retrieve her fallen purchases and stuff them into the torn boutique bag. She had hurled her handbag to the floor, spilling cosmetics, wallet, mirror all over the marble floor, and she insisted on picking everything up herself. She was crying now, her mascara running down her face, her hysteria over.

She allowed herself to be led to the waiting patrol car where she sat, sniffing noisily, her nose all red, and stared out of the window. As the car moved off and the siren started up, she seemed to gather her senses, taking a hankie from her bag and blowing her nose. WPC Southill watched closely as she pulled out a perfume atomizer and gave Oakhill the nod to check it.

'It's perfume, Chanel, and it's very expensive. Cost over thirty quid, and I only use it sparingly – I mean, too much and you overdo it. So if you don't mind giving it back? What'd you think I was gonna do, spray it in the driver's eyes and make my escape? Screw you, screw the lot of you, you're all wankers!'

She spent the rest of the journey to the station checking her wallet, counting her money and repacking everything in orderly fashion. But she didn't say anything else; she felt there wasn't any point.

The lock-up was cavernous. Water dripped constantly, forming pools on the floor, and the shape of it amplified the eerie sounds of the trains overhead. The place stank of damp, ancient oil and many other things.

The far end was pitch dark. Near the centre of the empty space Tennison could just make out a large, shrouded shape in the gloom. She chose to ignore the little scuttling, splashing noises of the rats.

'Everybody watch where you stand,' Tennison ordered, her voice echoing. 'Lights, are there any lights?'

Fluorescent lights blinked on slowly, casting a cold, blueish light which reflected in the puddles. Tennison advanced, picking her way slowly and carefully until she reached the middle. She lifted the old tarpaulin by one corner, exposing gleaming chrome and gold-brown paint-work.

'Well, we've got the car!' she called briskly, peering inside it. There was no radio between the seats. 'I want the Forensic crowd down here ASAP. The less we move or touch, the better.'

DS Amson was tiptoeing through the pools of water towards her. She stepped back, knocking into him, and turned to give him an earful when she saw his smile freeze. He was looking past her to the far end of the lock-up. Tennison followed his eyes.

'Oh, my God,' she whispered, and pointed. 'This is where he did it.'

Arrayed on the wall like an exhibit in a black museum were chains, shackles and a hideous collection of sharp-ened tools.

'How are you going to play it?' Kernan asked Tennison.

She was tense, champing anxiously at the bit. 'Henson first, break the alibi. Marlow's brief's on his way in.'

'Right, Jane, and . . . well done!'

'Not done yet,' she replied, flexing her fingers. 'Not yet.'

Flanked by Amson and Muddyman, with Havers in her wake, Tennison swept along the corridor to the interview room. Muddyman and Amson entered first, going to opposite sides of the room. Tennison walked straight to the table where Moyra Henson sat smoking, her solicitor beside her. Tennison could feel the change in her; she was afraid.

She addressed the solicitor. 'Mr Shrapnel? This is Detective Inspector Muddyman, Sergeant Amson and WPC Havers.' With a nod to Havers to close the door, she sat down and placed some files on the table. 'You have been made aware that your client has not been arrested at this stage, but is here of her own free will to answer questions and assist in the investigation into the murders of Karen Howard and Della Mornay.'

'Yes, I am aware of the situation, and my client is prepared to assist in any way that will not incriminate her or instigate criminal proceedings against her,' the small, grey-suited man replied.

For the first time since entering the room, Tennison looked directly at Moyra.

'At twelve forty-five today we gained access to George Arthur Marlow's rented lock-up garage in King's Cross. A brown Rover car, registration number SLB 23L, was discovered on the premises, together with certain incriminating evidence. In your recent statement you claimed that you had no knowledge of the whereabouts of this car, is that true?'

There was no bravado left in her. 'I didn't know anything about it, I thought it had been stolen.'

'In the same statement you gave George Arthur Marlow an alibi, stating that he returned to the flat you share on the night of the thirteenth of January, nineteen-ninety, at ten-thirty. Is that correct?'

Moyra glanced at her solicitor, then back to Tennison and gave a nod.

'When I interviewed you on that occasion, you were shown pictures of murder victims, do you remember? You stated that you had never met any of the women in the photographs.'

Again Moyra nodded and looked to Mr Shrapnel. Tennison opened one of her files and brought out two photographs.

'On the sixteenth of May, nineteen seventy-one, you and Deirdre Mornay were on trial at Manchester Juvenile court.' She laid the photograph of Della on the table. Moyra did not react. 'In early January of this year, Karen Howard was a customer at the booth in Covent Garden that you took over from Annette Frisby.' Karen's photo was put in front of Moyra. Again she did not react.

Two more photographs; this time of the bodies of the murdered girls.

'Moyra, you are not looking at the photographs. If you don't want to look at Della, then look at Karen. George called out to her, offered her a lift, then took her to King's Cross and tortured her, mutilated her. But first, he hung her on the wall in chains and raped her. Look at it, Moyra, see her hands tied behind her back, the marks on her body ... *Look at her, Moyra!*'

Shrapnel raised his hands as if to say, 'That's enough!'

'Your client, Mr Shrapnel, stands to be accused as an accessory to murder. Don't you think she should know what that crime involved?'

'My client has co-operated fully—'

Slowly, Moyra put out a hand and picked up the photos.

'Your client, Mr Shrapnel, has systematically lied to us. Now she has a chance to—' Tennison stopped and watched Moyra's reaction to the photographs; she stared at each one, then covered the one of Karen's body with her hands and closed her eyes.

Shrapnel was saying, 'Moyra is George Marlow's common-law wife . . .'

Tennison raised a hand to quieten him as Moyra started to speak to her.

'Would you get the men to leave, just the women stay . . . I won't talk in front of them.'

Amson gripped Shrapnel by the elbow and hurried out, followed by Muddyman. In the silence, Moyra sat with her hands over the picture of Karen, looking at Tennison with dead, unemotional eyes.

'I didn't know Della, I didn't even remember her. She was just a kid. But I did her nails, she used to bite them and . . . I didn't know her, it was just that she used to come and have the odd nail replaced, you know, if she'd broken one.'

Tennison nodded without speaking. Moyra didn't really want to talk about Della, this was not why she had wanted the men out of the room, there was something else. Moyra tugged at her skirt, darting glances at Tennison, her whole body twisting and turning, her hands picking at her own false nails. She looked at Havers, chewing at her lip, then back to Tennison. Then she leaned forward, her chin in her hand, as if she didn't want anyone else to hear.

'He . . . he did it to me once,' she whispered. Tennison leaned closer, but Moyra immediately sat back, coughed and stared at Havers. Tennison waited patiently while Moyra straightened her skirt yet again, twisted her hair. Then she released a deep sigh.

This time she didn't whisper. She faced the wall. 'He made this thing, with straps, for here.' She touched her arm. 'He said it made . . . it made the vagina tight, you know, stretched out, but it hurt me. I didn't like it, I wouldn't do it.'

She hung her head, as if the horror was slowly seeping into her brain. She still couldn't face Tennison; her head sank lower and lower until it was nearly resting on her knees.

'I didn't know, I didn't know . . . Oh, God forgive me, I didn't know . . .'

Moyra buried her face in her arms and began to sob.

*

Amson, Muddyman and Shrapnel were all leaning against the wall of the corridor when Tennison's face appeared in the glass panel. She opened the door.

'George Marlow *was* home by ten–thirty that night, but he went out again at a quarter to eleven. She doesn't know what time he returned.'

She stood very erect, head up, eyes glowing. 'We've got him,' she said quietly.

George Marlow lay in his cell, staring at the ceiling. A uniformed officer outside kept a constant watch through the spyhole. The key turned in the lock, and Marlow sat up, swinging his feet to the floor as his solicitor, Arnold Upcher, stepped in. With a glance at his watch, Upcher said, 'Five minutes!' to the officer, who remained in the open doorway. Upcher put his briefcase down on the bunk and faced Marlow. 'They are charging you on six counts of murder, George.' Marlow shook his head, sighed, and looked up. 'I don't know what's going on, Arnold. On my mother's life, I haven't done anything.'

Arc–lights had been brought into the King's Cross lockup to improve the illumination. White–suited Scenes of Crime men were moving in to start photographing and fingerprinting. The place was strangely quiet; only the constant rumble of the trains and the distant sound of a chained dog barking disturbed the silence.

The Rover had been surrounded by plastic sheeting. One man was kneeling on the plastic, leaning in through the open door, combing the fitted carpets with great care, passing anything he found to an assistant beside him.

DI Burkin and DC Jones were examining a row of old metal lockers.

'Oh, look at this!' exclaimed Burkin, holding up a hideous mask with cut-out eyeholes by his fingertips. He dropped it into a plastic bag.

In the next locker, Jones had found suits, shirts, ties, shoes, all covered in plastic dry-cleaner's bags.

'Even his sneakers, look . . . Neat bastard.'

Burkin sniffed. 'Jesus, this place smells like an abattoir.' He turned to stare at the wall where Marlow's chains and torture instruments hung, his nose wrinkling in disgust.

Two men were crouched near the wall, prodding at a small drain with sticks. Above the drain, where a single tap was fitted, a makeshift shower had been rigged up, with a plastic shampoo spray and a plastic curtain, spotted with black mould and streaked with blood. Beside it a dish contained soap, wire brushes and a plastic nail brush.

'This is caked in blood, we'll need swabs of it all,' one of the men was saying. 'Ugh, the drain's clogged with it, and this looks like skin . . .' He covered his face. 'Jesus, the stench!' he mumbled, retching.

Burkin had found a handbag. He handled it carefully,

wearing disposable plastic gloves. Inside was a wallet; he flipped it open.

'It's Karen Howard's!'

More arc-lights came on, bathing the Rover in a bright pool of light. The SOCO was holding a pair of tweezers up and peering at the tiny item they held.

'The carpet's been scrubbed, smells of cleaning fluid, and it's damp. What's this? Looks like a tiny gold screw.' He dropped it into the bag his assistant held open for him and something else caught his attention. 'Was your girl blonde?' he called over to Burkin and Jones as he carefully stashed a single blonde hair into a bag.

Burkin was examining a jacket, peering at it through the plastic bag. 'I got one of these jackets from his flat, he must have two sets of clothes ... See his shoes, did you take his shoes from the flat?'

DC Jones wasn't ready for it, couldn't understand how it happened, but one moment he was doing his job, sorting through the gear, and the next he burst into tears. He stood there, unable to control his sobs, almost in surprise.

Burkin put an arm around his shoulder. 'Go an' grab a coffee, a few of the others might feel like one, OK?'

'I'm sorry, I'm sorry, I dunno what made me get like this ...'

Peering into the cabinet again, Burkin replied, 'We all go through it, Dave. I think it's just natural, a release. ... Mine's black, no sugar.'

Jones threaded his way across the duckboards, mindful of the plastic sheeting. He had to turn back because he couldn't remember if it was four black and six white or the other way round.

The silent shadows of the men loomed on the walls where hideous splashes of blood, and worse, had dried. The greenish glow of the fluorescent lights and the brightness of the arc-lights did nothing to lift the dank darkness, the stench, the horror. This was where that sweet girl was brought; he could only imagine her terror, only imagine it.

DI Burkin had pulled out a thick black wardrobe bag, the kind used by the uppercrust type of dry cleaners. It was strong, would have fitted a full-length evening gown, and it had a zip from one end to the other. It was slightly open at one end and he could see a tangle of blonde hair jammed in the teeth. They knew Marlow was strong – this had to be how he had carried his victims undetected, zipped up in the wardrobe bag, hung over his arm . . .

It was not for Burkin to find out, that was down to Forensic, but he wondered. He placed it into a see-through evidence bag, tagged it, then bent to check over Marlow's shoes. They were all neatly wrapped in cling-film, ready to slip on and walk out, or walk into Della Mornay's bedsit. No wonder they had been unable to find a single item, a single fibre, in her room.

*

The tape recorder emitted a high-pitched bleep, and Tennison started talking.

'This is a recorded interview. I am Detective Chief Inspector Jane Tennison. Also present are Detective Sergeant Terence Amson and Mr Arnold Upcher. We are situated in room 5-C at Southampton Row Metropolitan Police Station. The date is Thursday the first of February, nineteen-ninety. The time is four forty-five pm.'

Tennison nodded to Marlow. 'Would you please state your full name, address and date of birth?'

He leaned forward and directed his voice towards the built-in microphone. 'George Arthur Marlow, twenty-one High Grove Estate, Maida Vale. Born in Warrington, eleventh September, nineteen fifty-one.'

'Do you understand why you have been arrested?'

He gave a half-shrug. 'I guess so.'

'It is my duty formally to caution you, and warn you that anything you say may be used in evidence. You have been arrested on suspicion of the murders of Karen Howard and Deirdre Mornay. Do you understand?'

'I am not guilty.' Marlow turned and looked at Upcher. 'Would you please describe to me the meeting that took place between yourself and Karen Howard on the night of January the thirteenth, nineteen-ninety.'

'I didn't know her name, I was told her name later,' Marlow began. 'She approached me. I asked how much she wanted. I drove her to some waste ground and had sex with her. I paid her for sex. I didn't know her, I had never seen or met her before. Then after I dropped her off at the tube station . . .'

'What about the cut on her hand? In a previous statement you said that she, Karen, cut her hand on the car radio which was between the seats.' Tennison held up the statement for Upcher to see.

'Yes, that's right.'

'The statement was taken on the fifteenth of January, nineteen-ninety. We have since discovered that there is no radio between the front seats of your car.'

He didn't seem to register what she had said. He began, 'I was at home at ten-thirty . . .'

'So, you arrived home at ten-thirty that night. Could you tell us what time you next left the flat?'

'I didn't, I watched television with my wife.'

'You are referring to your common-law wife, Miss Moyra Henson, is that correct?'

'Yes.'

'Miss Henson made a statement at three forty-five this afternoon. She states that you actually left the flat again at fifteen minutes to eleven. She cannot recall exactly when you returned, but you returned without your car. She says that your car was not stolen from outside your block of flats.'

'She's wrong! My car was nicked, I never went out again.'

'You have denied having any previous contact with Karen Howard.'

'Yeah, never met her before the night she picked me up ...'

'Miss Henson has, on occasion, worked at a booth in Covent Garden. She has admitted that she met Karen, and that she gave her a nail treatment. You were there at the time and you spoke to Karen. Is that true?'

'No.' Marlow shook his head.

'You have also denied knowing the other victim, Deirdre Mornay, also known as Della. Miss Henson agrees, however, that contrary to her first statement, in which she too denied knowing Miss Mornay, she was in fact lying. I suggest that you are also lying and that you did know Della Mornay.'

Marlow sat back in his chair, folded his arms. 'I don't believe you play these games. Moyra is scared to death that you are going to arrest her for tax evasion and claiming unemployment benefit. She's terrified of the police since she was picked up on a false charge of prostitution. Well, you don't scare me, I'm innocent.' He spoke to Upcher. 'I don't have to answer any more questions, do I?'

The team were kicking their heels in the Incident Room. Jones asked generally, 'How's the guv'nor? She must be knackered.'

Burkin shook his head. 'Taking a long time. After what we found in the lock-up, I don't think he'd admit to knowing his own mother right now.'

Slumped in chairs, perched on desks, propped against walls, they waited.

Marlow was looking tired. 'How many more times do I have to tell you?'

Tennison pressed on. 'This morning?' she prompted.

'I told you, I got an anonymous call, I dunno who it was. He says to me that he knows where my car is, he's seen it on the TV programme, right? It's been reported stolen, right?'

'What time was the call?'

'Oh, about ten ... Anyway, he says he knows where the car is, at King's Cross.'

'He told you that your car was in a lock-up at King's Cross, yes? Did he give you the keys?' Marlow shrugged, and she went on, 'Mr Marlow, you were seen unlocking the door.'

He answered angrily, 'Because he said I could get them from a Greek guy in a coffee bar. So I picked up the keys, but I didn't find my car because just as I opened the door the police jumped on me! I don't know why I have to keep repeating myself,' he said to Upcher. 'I've told them all this a dozen times ...'

Tennison showed no sign of fatigue or impatience as she asked, 'What was the Greek man's name?'

'I dunno, the tip-off just gave me the address of the café.' He sighed.

Arnold Upcher shifted his position, checked his watch and glanced at Tennison. He was getting fed up. He looked around; Amson had sat down in the corner.

'Stavros Hulanikis has sub-let the lock-up to a man he knows as John Smith for eight years. After you collected the keys from him this morning, an officer, Detective Inspector Burkin, took a statement from him. Your Greek friend also does certain items of dry-cleaning and laundry for you, doesn't he?'

Marlow shook his head in disbelief, not bothering to answer. Tennison continued, 'Come on, George, how did you get Karen into the bedsit? Where are Della's keys? You knew the place was empty, didn't you? You knew, because Della Mornay was already dead.'

Marlow leaned towards her. 'You are trying to put words into my mouth,' he said emphatically. 'Well that's it, I'm not saying another thing.' He appealed to Upcher: 'Tell her that's enough! I agreed to this interview, I've done nothing but assist them from the word go! I want to go home.'

Upcher replied quietly, 'That won't be possible, George,' then turned to Tennison. 'It's almost ten.'

Marlow was getting really uptight. He shouted, 'I wanna go to the toilet, I wanna have a piss, all right? I have to call my mother, I don't want her reading in the papers that you arrested me again! I want to be the one to tell her—'

'I agree to a fifteen-minute break,' Tennison told Upcher. To Marlow she said, 'You will not be allowed to see Miss Henson, or make any phone calls until this interview is terminated. I will arrange for Miss Henson to phone your mother . . .'

Marlow pushed his chair back as if to stand up. Amson moved towards him.

'No! They don't get on. I don't want Moyra calling my mother.' He sighed with irritation and stood up with his hands on his hips, facing Tennison. 'This is a mess, isn't it? Oh, all right, I did it.'

Upcher jumped to his feet. Tennison just sat and stared at Marlow, then managed to pull her wits together.

'Could you repeat that? You are still under caution.'

Marlow closed his eyes. She could see his long lashes, every line of his handsome face. He licked his top lip, then he opened his eyes. The colour seemed even more startling, the pupils were like pin-points. As if watching in slow motion, Tennison felt every tiny movement recorded in her mind.

He tilted his head to the right, then to the left, and smiled. No one in the room moved; they all focused on Marlow, on his strange, eerie smile.

'I said I did it.'

There seemed to be nothing else to say. Everyone in

the room except George Marlow held their breath, ready to explode, but he seemed totally relaxed. Eventually Tennison breathed out and said, 'Please sit down, George.'

He slumped into his seat. She watched him closely as she asked, 'What exactly did you do?'

He checked them off on his fingers. 'Karen, Della, Angela, Sharon, Ellen and . . .' He screwed up his eyes, trying to remember, then snapped his fingers. 'That's right, Jeannie . . .'

Only Tennison's eyes reflected the impact of his words. George Arthur Marlow had just casually admitted to killing all six victims.

Chapter Twelve

When George Marlow had been led back to his cell, DCI Tennison lit a cigarette and inhaled deeply. The welter of emotions inside her was under rigid control, and she showed none of it to the others in the room.

She had just caught the man she had devoted every ounce of her energy to catching, a man who had caused her the loss of the only lover she had ever really cared about, had deprived her of sleep for days on end, had nearly lost her her job and her self-respect. She sat quietly and smoked her cigarette down to the filter, then stubbed it out.

DC Jones, his face flushed, raced into the bar of the local pub. Pushing the other regulars aside, he stopped in the middle of the floor, raised his hands in triumph and yelled, 'He's bloody admitted it! All six of them, he's admitted doing the lot!'

The team rose to their feet as a man, although one of them was Maureen Havers. The cheer went up; Jones grabbed Havers and danced her around the floor as everyone congratulated everyone else.

A group of DIs from another team looked on the feverish celebration with interest. When Havers finally sat down again, one of them came over to her, carrying his pint.

'What gives?'

Beaming, Havers replied, 'Our guv'nor's just got a suspect to admit to six charges of murder! Biggest case this station's ever had . . .'

DI Caldicott returned to his own table and spoke to his mates. The racket in the bar was so great that no one else could hear what he was saying, but they all turned to stare at Tennison's team and raised their glasses in salute.

DCI Tennison was facing the Superintendent across his desk. He poured her a large whisky and said, as he handed it to her, 'Well, congratulations! The trial'll be a long process, but you go home now and get some sleep, you deserve it.'

'Yeah, I need it. It was a long night.' She looked and sounded exhausted. Downing the whisky in one, she stood up and made for the door.

The phone rang and the Super picked it up. 'Kernan . . . Yes, just a moment.' He covered the mouthpiece and spoke to Tennison. 'You were right to stick to your guns. Six counts of murder! And the beautician link . . . It was a woman's case, after all!'

He put the phone to his ear again, dismissively, and swivelled round in his chair; it's business as usual. 'I'm putting Caldicott on it,' he said into the phone. 'They're bringing the son in for questioning.'

Tennison rose to the bait. 'Fifty per cent of murder victims are women, so it looks as if I might have my hands full!' she retorted.

The door slammed behind her before Kernan could swivel round to reply.

'Woman's case, my arse!' Tennison muttered to herself, still seething about Kernan's comment. She spotted Maureen Havers peering at her from the double doors further down the corridor.

'Maureen, any of the lads about?'

Havers replied casually, 'Oh, I don't think so, we were all on two till ten. Oh, DCI Jenkins wants the Incident Room cleared, could you pop along before you leave?'

Pursing her lips, Tennison pushed through the other side of the doors and marched towards the Incident Room. Havers hung back and watched her go.

The Incident Room was crammed to bursting, but surprisingly quiet. Every single member of Tennison's team was there. Someone called, 'Here she is!' and they all watched expectantly as the door-handle turned.

Tennison walked in to cheers, whistles and the sound of popping corks. A huge bunch of flowers was pressed into her hand and Burkin started singing, the others quickly joining in: 'Why was she born so beautiful, why was she born at all? She's no bloody use to anyone, she's no bloody good at all!'

'Three cheers for our guv'nor, hip-hip . . .'

'*Hooray . . .!*'

Tennison nearly choked on her champagne, her back was slapped so hard. 'You bastards!' she spluttered. 'I thought you'd all pissed off! Cheers!'

She bit her lip, but the tears brimmed over. Then out came her great, bellowing laugh and she punched the air. 'We did it! We got him!'

Many months later, George Marlow stood in the dock to answer the charges against him. The Clerk of the Court read them out:

'George Arthur Marlow, you stand before this court accused of six indictments of murder. That on the four-teenth of January, nineteen ninety, you did murder Karen Howard, contrary to common law . . .'

Major and Mrs Howard were holding hands, staring straight ahead, unable to look at George Marlow, to turn their heads just a fraction to see him. He had taken their beloved daughter, he had raped her and mutilated her, and waiting for them to catch him had been the longest time they had ever lived through, a lifetime, Karen's lifetime. There would always be pain, that would never go away, and the confusion. Marlow had destroyed not just their daughter's life, but theirs.

'... That on the third of December, nineteen eighty-nine you unlawfully took the life of Deirdre Margaret Mornay ...'

Two prostitutes, friends of Della, leaned forward for a glimpse of her murderer. One of them sat back, afraid of her own feelings. Looking at him, with his handsome face, his fresh, immaculate white shirt, if he was to pick her up she wouldn't be likely to refuse him. They nudged each other and stared at DCI Tennison, who was sitting with the prosecution counsel. Her face was impassive. She gave them an almost imperceptible nod.

'You are also charged that on the fifteenth of March, nineteen eighty-four, you murdered Jeannie Avril Sharpe, that in January nineteen eighty-five you murdered Ellen Harding ...'

Carol and Linda had travelled down from Oldham. They were sitting in the gallery. Linda leaned forward on her elbows but could only just see the crown of his curly head. Jeannie had wanted to emigrate to Australia, she had wanted ... But she had never got anything, anyone to help her, love her. Now, maybe, she could rest in peace. Maybe.

Carol twisted a paper hankie in her hands. She could hear him as clear as anything, calling to Jeannie, calling her to come to his car.

In her wheelchair at the end of a row of spectators, Mrs Marlow sat, as well-groomed as ever. She held her head high, making no effort to wipe away the tears that trickled down her face. Her pale blue eye shadow, her carefully outlined lips and powdery cheeks framed in false, chestnut curls, seemed to crumble before George Marlow's eyes. He couldn't look at her, couldn't bear it; she was dying in front of him.

A young man sitting near her was leaning forward in his seat, staring intently at Marlow.

'. . . That in July nineteen eighty-six you murdered Angela Simpson . . .'

The young man's face crumpled when he heard Angela's name, and he cried. He tried hard to control himself, but the years between Angela's murder and the arrest of George Marlow had been a nightmare. Five years, five long years of his life under suspicion, always wondering if somehow he could have saved her. Five years of nightmares, but above all the loss of his childhood sweetheart, the only girl he had ever loved.

When George Marlow's eyes flickered towards him he had never known such hatred. He had never believed himself capable of killing, but he could have killed

Marlow with his bare hands; kill him, hurt him, make him feel the pain he had inflicted on Angela.

'. . . And in October, nineteen eighty-seven you murdered Sharon Felicity Read . . .'

Sharon's father sat stiffly at the back of the gallery in his best suit, starched shirt and bowling club tie. Sharon's mother had died, a year after they received the news; he had lost his wife and daughter because of the same man. Not a day passed without this quiet, respectable man remembering his daughter, his sweetheart, his own darlin' . . .

He wept because she had only just begun to grow into a woman, and he wept because he was haunted by his wife's face when he had told her that their daughter had been found. The arrogance of Marlow didn't anger him, didn't inspire him to revenge; it just left him with an overwhelming sadness, because nothing mended his heart.

Tennison kept her eyes averted from Marlow, her head bowed, but he seemed to draw her attention as if willing her to look at him. She stared suddenly as a door opened, throwing a wedge of light on to a dark figure, hunched at the back of the court. It was Moyra, and she had aged twenty years.

'George Arthur Marlow, having heard the charges against you, how do you plead?'

Tennison looked up at him. He was astonishingly handsome; his dark eyes, high cheekbones and glossy hair oozed vitality. She drew a sharp breath because he was looking at her. As their eyes met he seemed to smile, yet his lips did not move. It was just a lightness in his eyes . . . there was no anger, no malice.

'Not guilty, sir,' he replied.

**SIMON &
SCHUSTER**

This book and other **Lynda La Plante** titles are available
from your local bookshop or can be ordered direct
from the publisher.

978-0-85720-183-6	Backlash	£18.99
978-1-47110-021-5	Prime Suspect	£7.99
978-1-84739-647-1	Blind Fury	£7.99
978-1-84739-646-4	Silent Scream	£7.99
978-1-84983-436-0	Deadly Intent	£7.99
978-1-84983-435-3	Clean Cut	£7.99
978-1-84983-434-6	The Red Dahlia	£7.99
978-1-84983-433-9	Above Suspicion	£7.99

Free post and packing within the UK
Overseas customers please add £2 per paperback
Telephone Simon & Schuster Cash Sales at Bookpost
on 01624 677237 with your credit or debit card number
or send a cheque payable to Simon & Schuster Cash Sales to
PO Box 29, Douglas Isle of Man, IM99 1BQ
Fax: 01624 670923
Email: bookshop@enterprise.net
www.bookpost.co.uk
Please allow 14 days for delivery. Prices and availability
are subject to change without notice.